Requiem

Lauren E. Rico

Harmony

The Music of Requiem

The musical selections mentioned, both in passing and in detail throughout this book were carefully selected to complement the mood of each character and to reflect the tone of the story at that point in time. If you have the opportunity to listen to some of the selections as you read, I think you'll find the music adds an entirely new emotional depth and dimension. Happy reading and happy listening!

-Lauren

BARBER: ADAGIO FOR STRINGS
Dvořák: STRING QUARTET NO. 12 IN F, OP. 96
O'CONNOR: APPALACHIA WALTZ
MAURICE RAVEL: PAVANE FOR A DEAD PRINCESS
Dvořák: PIANO CONCERTO IN G MINOR, OP. 33
MAHLER: SYMPHONY NO. 1 IN D 'THE TITAN'
BACH / GOUNOD: AVE MARIA
BRAHMS: SERENADE NO. 1, OP. 11

For Stacey who told me to be patient.

Prologue: Jeremy

Watching my father die isn't nearly as entertaining as I'd hoped it would be. It's kind of cliché, actually. Even in the throes of death, the stupid son of a bitch is underwhelming. He's clutching at the collar of his shirt, trying to pull it free of the buttons that are causing it to strangle him. His face is a darkening red, and his frantic eyes are getting larger by the second. His breath is coming in labored wheezes.

The one thing I do find interesting is the fact that not once has he reached out to me, mouthed to me, or begged me with his eyes to help him. That's probably because he knows I'd laugh in his oxygen-deprived face. He won't give me the satisfaction. Oh, he did try to get to the phone on his own, but he just couldn't quite crawl across the floor. Gee, too bad. I could have reached it just by stretching out my arm.

I must admit I didn't come here looking to kill the guy. But when I realized he was headed toward a heart attack or stroke or whatever the fuck this is, I was only too happy to help him along. I have a way of getting under people's skin when I want to. And I *really* want to.

He's squirming now and his lips are starting to look blue. When I see that his eyes are starting to roll into the back of his head, I squat down beside him. I can tell there isn't much time left and I want to make sure the last words he hears on this earth come from my mouth.

He gasps in one last breath as best he can and tries to focus on me. I smile and put a hand on his shoulder, as if to comfort him.

"Don't you worry, dad. Mom won't be too far behind you. I promise you, I'll make sure of that."

And then he is gone.

Part One

Chapter 1

Brett

The car is silent, save for the gentle swish of the wipers on the windshield. It's raining just enough that I have to use them, and not quite enough so that they don't make that dragging rubber noise as they squeegee across. Next to me, my mother is staring out the passenger window, watching the world fly by in a blur.

"Trudy, why don't you let me cook for us tonight? I'd love to make a big pot of minestrone," Maggie offers from the backseat.

My mother turns toward her with a faint smile on her face. "You're so sweet, Maggie, and I would love that, but why don't we just heat up one of the casseroles that the neighbors have dropped by? I really don't have room for all of them in my freezer."

"Okay, maybe I'll just fix a salad to go with it then," Maggie suggests, determined to be helpful in some regard, no matter how minor.

"That would be lovely, dear," Mom agrees, turning back to the window.

Ralph Fourquet has been our family attorney since before I was born. So, when we walk into his dark mahogany and leather office, he's quick to pull my mother into his arms for a tight hug. He murmurs something into her ear that I can't hear. She nods and wipes the tears that have sprung to her eyes.

Ralph shakes my hand, and I introduce him to Maggie. He ushers us to a sitting area on the far end of his office so that we are on couches, facing one another. He opens up a leather-bound pouch and produces some official looking documents.

"Okay, well, Trudy, you and Danny were very good about keeping your affairs in order so, thankfully, there isn't much to be dealt with at this incredibly difficult time."

He skims through the pile of paperwork and produces what I recognize to be a last will and testament. "As we discussed last year, Trudy, you are the beneficiary of Danny's life insurance policy, and all joint savings and retirement funds will revert to your sole control. There is no mortgage on the house, and no outstanding debt to be paid, so this is all fairly cut and dried. As you know, Ray Page, Danny's friend from Chicago, has made an offer to buy the business."

"Wait, what?" I ask, leaning forward so fast that I nearly slip right off my tufted leather chair. "When did this happen?"

"A few days ago," my mother replies quietly. "Ray and Pam would like to get out of Chicago and move here, to Owl Bridge."

"And you agreed?"

I feel a little hurt not to have been consulted. She smiles at me sadly. "Sweetheart, if you had even the least bit of mechanical inclination, I would have given the business to you in a heartbeat. But you don't want it. And Ray has always been a good friend to your father. Honestly, I rather like the idea of him and Pam being close by."

I consider this for a second and realize she's right. Ray and my father go way back to their days together as mechanics in the Navy. That was even before my father met my mother. And now that she says it, I also like the idea of the Pages moving to town. They can be another source of support for Mom when I'm not here.

"I'm sorry. I didn't mean to be..."

She waves a hand at me. "No, Brett, I'm sorry I didn't mention it sooner. I didn't mean to exclude you from the decision, it just slipped my mind."

"Brett, you don't have to worry. The Pages are in fine financial shape, and have offered full value for the business. We'd be hard pressed to find a better buyer."

I nod. It's just so strange to hear them talking about my father's life's work this way.

"It's just a place. It's not *him*," Maggie offers quietly, as if reading my mind. She takes my hand in hers and squeezes hard.

"So," Ralph continues, looking at me, "your mother and father discussed what might happen in this event, and they made the decision —which your mother still holds to—that you should be the beneficiary of any funds collected from the sale of the garage."

I look at him, then my mother, and then back at him again.

"But, Mom, you need that money..." I start to protest, but that waving hand goes up again.

"I have more than enough with the life insurance and our retirement savings. And I plan to keep working, Brett. Once I decide to retire from the school system, I'll have a very generous pension and healthcare. I have more than I need."

"Mom..."

"No." She's shaking her head firmly. "You and Maggie are getting married soon. You're going to need that money to buy a house."

"Okay, first of all, we just moved into the SOHO brownstone, so nobody's going to be looking at houses anytime soon. And how much money are we talking about here, anyway?"

Ralph consults one of the papers in his stack. "Just shy of eight-hundred-thousand dollars."

My mouth falls open. I know it's not a good look, but there's nothing I can do about it. I can't even speak, but my mother is amused.

"Careful, Son, or you'll catch flies in there," she chides.

"I can't take it, Mom," I protest.

It's my mother who leans forward this time. "This is what your father wanted, Brett. And it's what I want, too. Please, I don't need to be worrying about you. This will put my mind at ease."

"Jesus, Mom, it's not like I'm a substitute music teacher. I play viola with one of the biggest string quartets in the world. I do just fine..." I stop abruptly when I see the look she's leveling upon me.

Trudy has decided. Period. End of discussion.

Ralph starts to go through the details of the sale when something occurs to me.

"Wait, wait, wait...what about Jeremy?" They both look at me as if I've started speaking Swahili. "You know, Jeremy? Your *other* son?" I remind her, which doesn't go over so well.

"I'm well aware of who he is, thank you very much, Brett," my mother snaps.

Shit.

Ralph steps in and tries to smooth things over. "Brett, your parents changed their will about a year ago to name you as sole beneficiary of the business. You're also your mother's sole beneficiary and will receive the balance of the estate after her passing."

"Mom, are you sure about this?" I ask with more than a little doubt. This is harsh. *Really* harsh for Danny and Trudy.

"I have never been more certain of anything in my life," she declares flatly.

Ralph seizes the moment to jump back in and redirect the conversation. Or, at least that's what he thinks he's doing. "Alright, then, with the autopsy results back, I assume you're ready to make the funeral arrangements?"

"Yes, please, Ralph. You have the prepaid plan that we purchased from the funeral parlor. Please just ask them to follow those instructions. The church will take care of the service itself."

"Whoa, hold on a sec..." I break in, shaking my head in confusion. "What are you talking about?"

"Your father and I preplanned our funerals..."

"Not that!" I cut her off. "Why was an autopsy done? I thought it was a heart attack. Since when do they do autopsies for natural causes?"

My mother meets my gaze squarely. "I requested the autopsy, Brett. It may have been natural causes that killed him, but I don't think there was anything natural about the way he died."

Now it all makes sense. The business, the will, the inheritance. She thinks Jeremy had something to do with my father's death, and I have no idea why, other than that my brother is a bastard. But I know my mother well enough to know that wouldn't be enough reason for her to make that assumption.

I'm missing something here. Something big. But, I won't be for long if I have anything to do with it. So I try to engage my mother repeatedly on the drive home, but she shuts me down every time. "Mom, it's just that..."

"Stop it. Right. Now," she cuts me off sharply, turning to face me from the passenger's seat. I almost pull off the side of the road.

"What?"

"How your father and I decided to divide our assets is up to us...*was* up to us," she corrects her use of the present tense, my father being dead and all. "I don't want to hear about this again. Do you understand me?"

She waits for an answer, and I feel as if I'm a naughty schoolboy again.

"Yes."

We spend the rest of the ride in an awkward silence. I sneak a glance back at Maggie. She's stunning, with her wild black curls pulled back into a severe bun at the back of her head. Even in the head-to-toe black that is the universal uniform of mourning. She catches me watching her and offers a sympathetic smile.

All I can think about is getting back to the house so I can spend some time alone with her, talking through all of this. She'll give me some perspective. I pull my mother's sedan into the driveway, and we all climb out into the crisp fall afternoon. I notice that the gutters need cleaning, and the leaves need raking and add them to my mental 'To Do' list. With my father gone, the 'man of the house' duties now fall to me.

Maggie and I trail behind her on the walk up to the porch, the three of us still silent. Mom gets the door unlocked and we follow her into the house.

"Honey, I need to lie down for a little while," my mother is saying even as she's crossing the living room. "I'm going to make a quick cup of tea and go to my room. Maggie, there are salad fixings in the fridge. I'll be up to make dinner at about—"

My mother stops cold. Stops speaking and stops walking, standing rooted and staring into the kitchen from its doorway.

"Mom?"

I'm so busy looking at her, that I don't immediately see *him*.

Chapter 2

Brett

"What are you doing here?" my mother asks Jeremy, who is seated at the kitchen table, chair leaned all the way back, propped against the wall. Add to that the faded jeans, Northwestern sweatshirt and Chuck Taylors and suddenly I'm seeing him as a fifteen-year-old again. There's an open beer bottle in front of him and a shit-eating grin on his face.

"Hi, Mom! Nice to see you, too!" he quips sarcastically.

"I locked the door when we left. How did you get in?" she demands.

"Oh, please, Mother. Like it was hard? You've kept your spare key under the same flowerpot for the last thirty years. You really should find another hiding spot for that, you know? Especially now that Dad is gone. No telling who might let themselves in."

My mother takes her jacket off, opens the door to the pantry and hangs it on a hook inside. When she closes it, she walks across the wide-plank wood floor to the old gas stove, which she lights under her copper kettle. She pulls a mug from the glass-front cupboard and starts to prepare her cup of tea, ignoring my brother as she goes. Jeremy and I look at one another for a long moment.

I don't think we've exchanged more than three words since I moved out of the apartment while he was out of town. After Maggie came into my life, I found I had precious little tolerance for my brother and his bullshit. And then, to catch him stalking Julia—threatening her and her unborn child—I knew I couldn't spend another night under the same roof as him. That seems like an eternity ago now, but I can tell he's having exactly the same recollections I am.

The kettle is boiling, and my mother pours the water into her mug. She looks at Maggie and I, who are still standing, gawking.

"I'm sorry, did either of you want a cup?" she offers over her shoulder. We both shake our heads no.

"I'd love a cup, Mom," Jeremy pipes up from the round oak table where we shared countless meals over the years. I can't help but notice he's sitting in my father's chair.

"You won't be staying long enough to have a cup, Jeremy," she replies without so much as a glance in his direction.

He laughs. "Subtle, Mom! What happened to your perfect manners?"

Now she's putting two sugar cubes in the tea and stirring. The spell finally broken, I move from the spot where I've been rooted, and pull the container of milk out of the fridge for her.

"Here," I say, setting it on the counter next to her.

"Thank you, Son."

"Yes, thank you, *Son*," Jeremy mimics her with extra emphasis on the last word.

"You know, I think I'm going to go upstairs for a bit..." Maggie starts to excuse herself, but I take her forearm gently before she can go.

"No, please. I want you here."

She nods and is the first one to join my brother at the kitchen table. I am in awe of this woman. She knows what he is capable of. And yet, here she is, sitting down with him, trying to keep the peace between all of us. Or, at least I think that's what she's doing.

"Well, well, *Margaret*, how've you been?" Jeremy smirks and I want to slap it off his face.

"I was doing fine until you showed up," she informs him curtly. Okay. Maybe she's not on a peacekeeping mission after all.

Jeremy just shakes his head, irritating smile still affixed to his face. My mother takes her tea and joins them at the table. I lean on the butcher's block countertop, opting to stay on my feet. God only knows what's going to happen next, and I want to be prepared to move in any direction necessary.

"So, what do you want, Jeremy?" Mom asks in a tone that leaves absolutely no room for small talk.

Now his lips turn down into an exaggerated frown. Like a fucking sad clown face. "It's at times like these when we all need to pull together. We're family, after all. I just wanted to be here to help in any way I can. You know, funeral plans, distribution of assets..."

"No, thank you, Jeremy. I have all of that covered," she tells him as she stirs her tea.

"Well, great! So, when's the funeral? And, more importantly, when do I get my share of the money?"

"What money is that?" my mother wonders, a perplexed expression on her face.

Oh, she is good. Jeremy switches up his own features again, this time trying on his best condescending look. "Poor, poor Mother. You're distraught, aren't you? You know, I'd be happy to handle the estate for you. Who has the will? Ralph Fourquet? Why don't I just give him a call..." he offers, reaching for the old curly-corded phone on the wall.

Mom reaches up to tuck a stray bit of blonde/gray hair behind her ear. She looks tired...no, resigned. It makes me wonder if she expected to find my brother here waiting for us. I notice her hands are as steady as a surgeon's as she sips her tea. When she takes the mug from her lips, her eyebrows knit together and she wags a pink-nailed finger at him dismissively.

"No need. We're just back from his office. It's all taken care of, so I suppose you should just be on your way."

I see his smile slip a little, his eyes cloud over slightly. "Okay. Will he be mailing me my check then?"

"What check is that, Jeremy?"

The last of his smile is gone now. "Don't play around with me, Mother. I'd like to know what to expect as my share of the inheritance."

"You don't have a share of the inheritance," she replies, not even bothering to look at him as she swirls the tea in her mug.

Jeremy draws a long breath, as if willing himself to stay calm. Christ, this is getting worse by the second. I don't know what is going on between the two of them exactly, but Maggie and I are looking back and forth from one to the other, as if we were watching a match at Wimbledon.

It's Jeremy's serve next. "I'm not going to say it again, Mom, don't play with me. I know I'm in the will, and I expect you to honor that. To honor Dad's wishes."

She lobs it back over the net to him.

"No. You're not in the will, actually. I don't know why you'd think that was the case."

"Because I've seen the goddamn thing," he spits, a little too loudly.

That's a deduction for unsportsmanlike conduct right there.

"Oh!" Mom exclaims, as if something has just occurred to her. "You must have been snooping around in your father's office. No, Jeremy, that's an old will. Your father and I had Ralph draw up a new one last year. I think it was right after your last visit here. You know, the time when you tried to break my arm, and your father had to get his rifle out?"

"*What?*"

The single word that comes out of my mouth is, all at once, a question, a statement and a threat. Four little letters convey to my brother that I had better damned well have misheard or misunderstood what our mother has just said.

"Oh, please," he snarls with disgust. "The bitch was asking for it. I just came here to ask them, very politely, to stay out of our business."

I can't believe what I'm hearing. "*Whose* business?" I hiss. "And when, exactly, did this all happen?"

"*Our* business," he asserts, gesturing between him and me. "*Yours* and *mine*. It was when they wanted you to move out of the apartment. I didn't want them getting in the way of what I saw as a mutually beneficial living arrangement between two brothers. But she got her panties in a twist, and Dad overreacted, as usual."

Holy. Fucking. Shit.

"He threatened me," Mom interjects mildly, as if she is correcting him on some small, insignificant point. "I slapped him, and he threatened me again. I told him to get out. He twisted my arm and tried to break it. That's when your father pulled the shotgun out of the pantry. It was the only way he could get Jeremy to leave the house."

"Are you fucking *kidding* me?" I roar from across the table. It's not immediately clear to me which one of them I'm more pissed at—him for doing it, or her for not telling me he did it.

"We had it well under control, and didn't want to bother you with it," Mom continues, reading my thoughts. "But now you can see why we changed the will."

I close my eyes and shake my head a little, as if to shake this conversation out of my head, but it's not budging. I can feel my blood pressure start to climb. My jaw is clenched and I'm breathing heavily through my nose. Any second now I'm going to blow smoke out of my ears like some cartoon character. Maggie sees where this is going and pats the empty chair next to her.

"Come and sit down," she encourages, raising her eyebrows and nodding at me. They're all watching with silent interest as I make my way around the table slowly, glaring at my brother as I do. "I don't see how you could possibly think that your father would even consider giving you a share of his business after that," Mom throws at him after I'm seated.

Jeremy sits up and leans toward me, suddenly more interested. One of his dark brows perks up and I'd swear his hazel eyes are gleaming with excitement now. "Is that what it is?" he murmurs softly to me. "He left you the garage?"

"Money. From the sale of the garage," Mom corrects.

Jeremy looks at her briefly with half a smile. She just swishes her tea around the cup and takes another sip. "How much?" he demands.

"None of your business—" I start to say, but my mother cuts in before I can finish.

"Close to a million dollars, Jeremy."

Fuck! She is *determined* to rub this shit in his face. And she's doing a great job of it. Jeremy looks as if he'd like to eviscerate me with his eyes.

"Yeah, I'll be wanting my share of that," he informs me.

Shit. This is bad. I close my eyes again, forcing myself to calm down. What happens in the next few minutes is going to determine my fucked-up brother's state of mind for the next few years—decades, maybe. I swallow my anger and my pride in favor of the path of least resistance. And least violence.

"Mom, really, I don't need it all..." I sigh with resignation.

"Brett, let me be clear," she warns me sharply. "Ralph didn't mention it, but there is a clause in the will. If you give a single penny of that money to Jeremy, it will all be rescinded and donated to the Humane Society."

"You can't do that," Jeremy snarls.

"I can. And I did."

"Mom, please, be reasonable," I implore, putting a hand on her forearm.

Of course I don't want to give this asshole a nickel, but I know full well the shit storm that's about to rain down on us if he doesn't get his way. For his part, Jeremy looks pleased, believing this to be settled to his satisfaction. The expression doesn't last for long once my mother opens her mouth again.

"Tell him," she demands, glaring at my brother.

"Tell him *what?*" he asks slowly—suspiciously.

""Tell him why you're here. Tell him how you knew your father died," she commands. "No one here called you. The obituary hasn't been in the paper yet, or even online. Tell. Him. Jeremy."

My brother is looking a little less pleased than he was just a few seconds ago. "I don't know what you're talking about," says his mouth, but his expression tells a different story.

Mom raises a challenging eyebrow.

Now, this *is* an interesting question—and one that I hadn't considered myself. How *did* Jeremy find out? Now, we are all three of us staring at my brother, who can barely keep a straight face.

"Oh, alright, alright," he concedes, rolling his eyes as if he's a naughty child caught in a fib. "I came into town a few days ago. I wanted to catch Dad by himself so we could talk. Like Mom said, things didn't end so well last time I was here, and I wanted to try and rectify that. So, I went to the garage...and that's when I found him like that."

"If that's true, then why wouldn't you say anything? Call the police? An ambulance?" I demand.

Jeremy looks at me with irritated exasperation, as if I am too stupid to live. "Because of this, right here." He gestures at us sitting around the table. "This fucking inquisition. Who was going to believe I didn't have something to do with it? Besides, he was dead when I got there."

"Was he?" Mom challenges.

I can see it all on his face—the slight arch to one of his eyebrows, the thoughtful scrunch of his nose and the way his gaze moves, unblinking, across my mother's features. I'm not sure anyone else would recognize it for what it is ... Jeremy's searching for clues.

Does my mother really know something... or is she bluffing? After a long, tense moment, he decides on the latter. "Absolutely," he declares with confidence. "There was nothing that could be done, so I just left. I knew someone would find him soon enough."

"Huh," Mom seems to consider this.

I wouldn't have thought it possible, but there is a palpable shift in the air. Suddenly, the kitchen is a little colder, a little darker. And a lot quieter as Mom takes her time before speaking again. We wait. We watch. And then, finally, it comes.

"You know, Jeremy, I don't think we ever told you that we had security cameras installed in Dad's garage a few years back."

His eyes narrow and he purses his mouth. That, in and of itself, tells me my world is about to explode.

"So, I went back over the tapes with the Police Chief," Mom continues. "We know that you didn't kill your father, but we also know that you were the one who got him so upset that he had the heart attack in the first place. And then, to make matters worse, you stood there and waited for him to die. You didn't lift a finger to call for help. Quite the opposite, in fact. On the tape, you are quite clearly taunting him as he's writhing on the floor."

"You. Fucking. Did. Not." My voice is a caustic whisper. "Jesus Christ, Jeremy, tell me you didn't do that!"

"Oh, he did it alright, Brett, I have the video footage to prove it."

"You sure you wanna go there, Mom?" he whispers as he leans in and puts a hand on her wrist. "I'd hate for you to open up a can of worms you can't close..."

My mother pulls her hand out from under his and offers up a small, bittersweet smile. "Oh, Jeremy. If only I'd opened up that can a little sooner...your father might still be alive today. That will be the greatest regret of my life. That, and giving birth to you."

In an instant, all the air seems to have been sucked out of the room. I can't believe she's said it and, judging by the way he's shaking his head, he can't believe he's heard it.

"Wow. That was harsh, *Mom*. I didn't know you had it in you," he begins, sitting back again and draping an arm over the chair casually. "Oh, but wait...maybe I did. I mean, I have half your DNA, don't I? *Mom?*"

I watch in stunned silence, waiting for her response. And when it comes, it's most certainly not what I am expecting. "You do, Jeremy. And, believe it or not, that means I know you better than you know yourself. So, go ahead, *Son*, tell me again how you had nothing to do with your father's death. Tell me, Jeremy."

Holy. Shit.

My brother doesn't bat an eyelash. In fact, he looks quite pleased with himself when he speaks again. "Okay," he acknowledges, lifting his palms in surrender. "Okay, fine, I did it. But you can't touch me, Mom. I didn't commit any crime."

While I may be without words at this moment, Maggie, on the other hand, is not. "You are unbelievable!" she hisses at him in a rare moment of lost composure. "You think you can let your father die like that, in front of you, and then show up here looking for a share of the inheritance? You fucking sociopath! You're more delusional than even I thought possible!" She jumps to her feet and leans across the table toward him. "I think it's time you left. There are people grieving in this house and clearly, you are *not* one of them."

Jeremy isn't amused. "I suggest you mind your own fucking business, Margaret, or next time it might be—"

"What?" She jumps in with the challenge before he can finish his thought. Before he can finish his threat. Before I can bash his head in with the toaster. "Next time it might be *me* on the ground dying while you stand over me watching? I'd like to see you try it, asshole!"

Oh. This is not good. Not good at all. A steady tide of crimson is rising up her long, lean neck and her hands are balled up into tight fists.

"Maggie..." I start, but she ignores me, turning to my mother.

"Trudy, with your permission, I'm going to call the police now."

My mother shakes her head. At first I think she means Maggie shouldn't call. But I'm mistaken. "No, I don't have a problem with that. The phone is on the wall over there, honey," she directs her.

As she stands up, Jeremy grabs her wrist. "I wouldn't make that call if I were you," he threatens.

But, in a split second he has no choice but to release her, because I'm dragging him across the kitchen table by his collar. "Let go of me!" he sputters, his face darkening to a garnet color.

I push him back so hard that he stumbles and falls over the chair he'd been sitting in only moments before. He lands hard on his ass on the linoleum floor. Suddenly, we are children again, me standing over him, finally fed up with his bullshit threats. Him, looking up at me, finally realizing he has underestimated my wrath. We're both older now. We're both bigger. But I am, by far, the more dangerous—at this second, anyway.

"Don't you *ever* lay so much as a finger on her again, or I swear to God I will *end* you, motherfucker! If you're not out of this house in the next thirty seconds, we'll call the police. And, if that doesn't make you nervous, maybe my call to network stations in Chicago will. They'd be thrilled to break the story and run the video of the Kreisler gold medalist who stood by and watched his father die. Might get them thinking about what else you're capable of."

"You don't have the balls," he spits up at me from the floor. I squat down so that we are closer.

"No? Then try me. Go ahead. I'm waiting." I look at my watch. "Time starts *now*."

At first, he simply sits there, furious and fuming. He's testing me. But he should know better because last time he did this, I broke his arm.

"That's twenty seconds left!" I inform him.

"Fine!" He gets to his feet. "Fine! But we are far from done with this conversation. I'm expecting my fair share, Mom. And you know how I can be if I don't get what I'm expecting."

"Oh, don't worry about that, Jeremy," she assures him breezily, as if confirming she'll handle dinner reservations. "I'll make sure you get *exactly* what you have coming to you."

Her smile as she says this is chilling.

He's cursing under his breath as he ducks out the back door. When she's sure he's gone, my mother gets up and goes to the telephone. She dials information.

"Yes, I'd like the number for a locksmith in Owl Bridge, please."

Chapter 3

Brett

Maggie is nestled in the crook of my arm, her head of soft curls resting on my chest. We lie like that in silence for a long while before she speaks.

"Are you okay?"

"I don't know," I admit into the darkness. "It was bad enough, losing my dad. Now, knowing that Jeremy was involved ... Jesus, the whole thing just makes me sick."

"What do you think he'll do now?"

"Who the hell knows? He might come back here to bully Mom. He might go back to New York. But, then again, he might lick his wounds and head back to Detroit. It could be absolutely anything—because my brother is capable of absolutely anything," I marvel, thinking specifically of Cal Burridge, Jeremy's competitor in the Kreisler International Music Competition who conveniently died from anaphylactic shock just in time for my brother to step into his spot.

"Brett, I'd like to stay here with your mom for a couple of weeks," Maggie declares, looking up at me with her big blue eyes. "Just until things calm down a little. You have to get back on tour, and I don't like the idea of her being here alone so soon."

I stroke the side of her face with my hand. "Maggie, I can't ask you to do that. You've got a lot going on at work right now. You can't just pick up and leave for two weeks."

"You didn't ask, I offered. I've already arranged it with my supervisor. I'll keep in touch with my covering case agent from here. It's going to be okay. She's going to be okay."

Those are exactly the words that I need to hear right now. They may or may not be true, but just to have someone utter the words aloud makes me feel a little better.

"Alright, but you're the one who's going to have to convince my mother. That woman doesn't do a damn thing she doesn't want to do."

"I noticed!" She rubs a palm over my chest. "Wanna fool around?" she suggests with a sexy little lift of an eyebrow.

Actually, I can't think of anything I'm less in the mood for right now.

"I'm kind of wiped out, Mags. Do you mind if we just get some sleep?"

"Not at all. I just thought you might want to live out a childhood fantasy or two in your childhood bedroom." She grins sheepishly.

"Tempting." I chuckle. "But I'll take a rain check if you don't mind. Besides, this isn't the room. I mean, it is, but it isn't. My parents took down all my posters and threw out all the dirty magazines I had stuffed under the mattress."

"Oh, you boys are so predictable!" she groans and rolls her eyes up at me.

"What, don't girls have ... magazines?"

"No! We have romance novels. All 'heaving bosoms' and 'turgid shafts.' We're not as visual as you guys are. We go looking for our steamy stuff in books. If only all those horny little boys knew—it's the girl with her nose in a book they should be chasing!"

"Wait, wait, wait... I'm sorry, back it up a second ... did you say 'turgid shaft'?" I repeat incredulously.

She smiles. "I know! Ridiculous, right? 'Love's sweet spear' and 'molten member' were also two of my favorites. I mean, nothing makes a girl hotter than the thought of a molten spear near the petal-soft folds of her womanhood."

I can't help myself, I burst out laughing. This is easily the most insane conversation I've ever had. And it does exactly what I most need it to do—lighten the mood.

"I'm glad you find my teenage roadmap to 'possessing the lily' so amusing!" she snorts.

In a moment, we're both laughing so hard that we're gasping, tears streaming down our faces.

"You really wouldn't mind staying here?" I ask her once we've caught our breath again.

She rolls over on top of my chest, so that we are pressed, body to body, our faces are only inches apart. Then, she puts her hands on either side of my face, rubbing her thumbs gently

over my temples.

"Brett, it would be my honor to be of assistance to your mother. She is an amazing woman. Besides," she continues, "if Jeremy is stupid enough to show up again, he's going to need someone to keep her from killing him. I'd hate to see Trudy go to jail for killing that idiot."

I pull her close to me so that my arms wrap around her tightly. "Mags, Jeremy is a lot of things, but an idiot is not one of them. I need for you to remember that. Always. Because, the second you underestimate his intelligence or his capacity for destruction is the second that he'll strike."

She studies my expression for a long moment and nods. "I won't make that mistake, Brett."

I give her a halfhearted smile. "I know you won't. You're much too savvy for that. It's just easy to forget who he is. What he is."

"The thing with people like that is they're so good at making you see what they want you to see. Seriously, if your mother hadn't confronted him with the video thing, would you have ever thought he was involved with your dad's death?"

I think about this carefully before answering.

"It wasn't my first thought, but the more I think about it now, the more I'm surprised that it wasn't."

"What do you mean by that, Mr. Cryptic?"

She's half teasing... but I'm deadly serious.

"It was my mother's first thought. She checked the video files, even though it was clear he'd had a heart attack. She made the coroner do an autopsy. She was too smart to take it at face value. It was her first thought. *He* was her first thought."

Even as I say it, it makes me shudder. I can't do this anymore. Not now. Not here. I pull her even tighter into me and give her a long, slow, deep kiss. Suddenly, my body is telling me that maybe there *are* things in which it's interested, after all.

Chapter 4

Brett

Jesus is staring down at me from his cross. He is the face of anguish—the soul of forgiveness. He beckons me to find comfort in his outstretched arms. But I'm having trouble finding any comfort right now as Maggie, my mother, and I sit alone in the middle of the front pew of the church. Behind us, mourners continue to file in until there's no place left to sit, save for our nearly vacant pew. Still, they stand in the back of the sanctuary rather than disturb the grieving widow and her family, such as it is. I take an uneasy look around, half expecting to see Jeremy coming down the aisle to take his place with us. But I don't see him, and I'm grateful for that.

My mother isn't an emotional woman, but anyone who knows her can clearly see she is not herself. She stares up at the crucifix in silence, hands folded primly in the lap of her navy blue church dress. She twirls the plain gold band on her finger absently. This is a faded version of Trudy Corrigan. It's as if some of her vibrancy has died along with my father.

When the Reverend Richard Quillan takes his place on the dais, a sudden hush falls across the congregants. He clears his throat, opens his mouth to speak, and then closes it. He looks down at his feet, takes a deep breath and looks up again.

"Danny Corrigan wasn't just my parishioner, he was my friend," he begins in a choked voice. "Which makes this task both easier and harder. As a clergyman, it is my great honor to celebrate the life of this man. As his friend, my heart is breaking a little more with each and every breath."

Audible sniffs from the pews.

"Danny and I spent many a night sitting on the deck in his and Trudy's backyard, sharing a beer and contemplating the great mysteries of the universe. I wanted to know where he stood on the great Camaro vs. Mustang vs. Challenger debate. Mustang, by the way. He wanted to know if God would forgive him for being a Mets fan. No, by the way."

Chuckles.

"On those nights together, we also tackled more serious topics. I recall one evening in particular, when Danny confided in me his belief that Satan walks among us on this earth in human form. This troubled him.

'How,' he wondered, 'can we possibly fight an enemy who is hiding in plain sight?' My answer came from Ephesians 6:11 'Put on the whole armor of God, that you may be able to stand against the schemes of the devil.'

"I told him that we must put on the spiritual armor that God has given us in order to withstand the schemes of the devil. This special armor includes the helmet of Salvation, the breastplate of Right-eousness, the belt of Truth, the shoes of the Gospel of Peace, the sword of the Spirit, and the shield of Faith. Daniel Dean Corrigan took this to heart, and he wore his armor proudly. He protected his family with the only weapons strong enough to trump evil: love, hope and faith."

I realize that my mouth is hanging open, and I'm not sure how long it's been like that. I have never heard any of this about my father. I had absolutely no idea he was so concerned about good and evil. This might as well be the eulogy of a total stranger.

"Trudy," the Reverend addresses my mother now, "at this point, I would usually recite some homily meant to be a comfort to you. But today, the comforting words come directly from your husband." He pulls the envelope from the pocket of his vestments and withdraws from it a single sheet of paper.

"I don't know if Danny had a sense that his death was imminent, but about a year ago, he gave me this sealed envelope and requested that I read it as part of his eulogy."

What? He was thinking about his funeral... just a year ago?

"I was reluctant to take it," the Reverend continues, "assuring him that he would have more than enough time to tell you all the things he wanted to tell you. But, he was insistent in that quiet way that he had about him. So, I humored him and stuck it in a drawer. I never imagined that I would be holding it in my hands again so soon."

This last bit seems to be more to himself than the congregation.

"My dearest, my loveliest, my Trudy. If you are hearing these words, it is because I have left this earth. I would never do so willingly, because, while I believe in the kingdom of Heaven, I do not believe such a place could possibly exist for me without you in it. It is selfish of me to move on before you, leaving you to stand alone against the darkness of this world. But, then, we've always known that you are the stronger of us, haven't we? So, maybe it's best that you should be the one to see this through."

Reverend Quillan stops and lowers the hand that's holding the letter, raising his other hand to swipe at the tears that have formed in his eyes. After a long moment, he resumes, paper shaking in his hand.

"Please, do not rush to meet me, I will wait for you until your days are done. Please don't stop loving without me. There is enough room in your heart for someone else. Please don't doubt for a single moment that I am with you, by your side, holding you up, holding you close and holding your heart in mine. You will, for all of eternity, be my dearest, my loveliest, my Trudy."

To my left, Maggie has wrapped both of her arms around one of mine, pressing her face into my shoulder as she silently sobs. To my right, my mother sits, hands still folded primly in her lap. All around us are the sounds of sniffling, stifled weeping and blowing noses. The sounds of muted grief. The Reverend carefully places the letter back in the envelope, walks forward and hands it to my mother.

"Trudy, I am loathe to disagree with a dead man, but believe me when I say that you will *never* stand alone against *anything* in this world. The love of your friends and your family, the prayers of this parish and the divine grace of Our Lord, Jesus Christ, will bolster your armor, Trudy. Your Sword of The Sprit and your Shield of Faith."

He pauses for a long moment.

"Let us pray."

* * *

My childhood home appears to have been turned into a de facto bakery. I've never seen so many varieties of cake and pastry in my life. They compete for space on the countertops with the casseroles, fruit baskets and sandwich plates. I hide among the baked goods in the kitchen, trying to avoid the small talk going on in the living and dining rooms.

There must be fifty people crammed into this little house. They linger in the corners, paper plates in hand, speaking in hushed tones. The neighbor ladies have cornered Maggie on the floral couch, grilling her about our wedding plans. My mother has made a job of shuffling the cakes around each time a new one arrives in the hands of a well-wisher.

"So, where's your brother?" comes an unfamiliar voice from behind me.

I turn to see the unfamiliar face that it belongs to. She's not exactly pretty, so much as handsome. She's nearly as tall as I am, with snowy white hair that belies a much younger face.

"He was here a few days ago, but he had an unavoidable conflict that kept him away today." I recite the party line that my mother and I have agreed upon as I try to place her.

A neighbor maybe? One of the teachers from the elementary school where my mother works? Could she be a customer of my father's garage? I feel as if I should know her, but I'm not sure why.

"Hard to imagine a conflict that would trump your own father's funeral," she observes a little coolly.

I'm sure people have been whispering about Jeremy's conspicuous absence all day, but she's the first one who's had the nerve to comment on it. I'm about to reply when my mother walks into the kitchen with yet another cake.

"Leave him alone, Elise. He's not going to tell you anymore than I did," she says as she drops the three-layered German chocolate monstrosity next to an apple strudel.

"Elise?" I gape, a light bulb going off in my head. "As in *Aunt* Elise?"

"It's okay," she reassures, pulling me into her arms for a hug. "I didn't expect you to recognize me after twenty years. It's great to see you, Brett. I've been following your career carefully. I've been to see you nearly every time you've played in Chicago. You're quite talented. And handsome, too."

I give her a weak, confused embrace. "I didn't know you were here. Why didn't you come sit with us at the church?"

"Oh, it seemed as if playing the part of the grieving sister-in-law would be a little hypocritical after I've been away for so long."

"And why *have* you been away for so long?" I inquire with a little more edge than I'd intended.

She gives me a wry smile. "I'm here *now*," she replies by way of a non-answer and gestures toward the kitchen door with her head. "Come on, let's you and I go out onto the back porch. I could use a smoke."

I follow her outside, where cool air and relative quiet are a relief from the stuffy, crowded house. Elise pulls out a pack of cigarettes, taps one into her palm and offers it to me. I shake my head, and she pops it into her own mouth, cupping her hand around the end so she can light it. Finally, she takes a long, satisfied drag before expelling a steady stream of smoke. We stand next to each other, leaning over the rail of the deck and looking out into the backyard.

"Mom called you?"

"No. An old friend of hers thought I should know." She turns to me, blowing smoke out the side of her mouth. "I'm so sorry about your dad, Brett. He was a good man." I nod, continuing to face forward. "Was it Jeremy?"

Now I look at her. "Was what Jeremy?"

"Did he kill your father?"

"*What?*"

The single word implies that I'm shocked by the mere suggestion when, in fact, I'm shocked that she would know it to be a possibility.

Her eyebrows go up as she takes another drag and then exhales. "Oh, I know all about it," she discloses, as if reading my mind. "You could see it plain as day by the time he was four-years-old. That boy was trouble even back then. And that kind of trouble doesn't get better with age. It gets bolder, more brazen and cunning."

For the second time today, I have to will myself to close my gaping mouth.

"So did he?"

"Huh?"

"Did Jeremy kill Danny?"

"I—I don't know. I don't think so. But he was there, and he certainly didn't do a damn thing to help him."

She nods, as if this comes as no surprise to her, before taking one last drag on the cigarette and tossing it to the floor of the porch. She uses her foot to extinguish the butt.

"So, seriously, why *have* you been out of our lives for so long?" I press, more insistently this time.

"You should talk to your mother about that."

"I have. I mean…I used to bring it up when I was a kid, but I never could get a straight answer out of her. Eventually, I just stopped asking."

Elise faces forward again, not looking at me as she speaks. "After your grandmother passed…" she begins, then stops to give me a sideways glance. "Do you remember her? Grandma Ruth?"

"Sure."

"Well, she was like the glue that held us all together. When she died, we all just went our separate ways."

"Are any of you in touch?" I ask, fascinated by this new information. Including Elise, my mother has four siblings. We haven't had so much as a Christmas card from any of them in decades.

"Oh, yeah. Your aunt Patty lives in Memphis with her husband and three kids. Meg is in Tulsa with her husband Jay. They never had any children. And then there's our brother, Clay. He lives up in Elgin with his wife, and they have a daughter about Jeremy's age."

Holy shit! How could I possibly have so much family that I know absolutely nothing about?

"And you?" I press.

"Oh, I live just about forty-five minutes from here. I have a lady friend who I've been with since before you were born."

"Lady friend? You mean you're…"

"A lesbian? Yes. Why, have you got a problem with that?" She's giving me the evil eye.

"Uh, no. No…" I stammer awkwardly.

She breaks out into a huge grin and throws her head back in a laugh. "Jesus, Brett! You should see the look on your face! I'm just kidding with you!"

"About being a lesbian?"

"What? No!" More laughter. I am so confused. She puts an arm around my shoulders. "You're a sweet one. You always have been."

"Unlike Jeremy."

"Yup."

"I don't know where he is," I admit, answering her earlier question. "I'm guessing he went back to Detroit. Wherever he is, he was smart enough not to come here. I think Mom would rather deal with the neighbors' gossip about his absence than with the drama that comes with his presence."

"I'm sure."

We're silent for a few long moments, Elise extracting another cigarette and lighting it, me examining the dirt under my fingernails. "Brett, does your mother ever talk about our father, George?"

The softening in her tone gets my attention. "Not really. Just that he died when she was a teenager."

She nods and blows another long stream of smoke out into the October sunshine. "We had a real hard time of it, growing up. He was a raging alcoholic, and a mean one at that. I think after Mama died, we all went in our different directions because it was just too painful to stay connected. On our own, each of us could reinvent ourselves—make a start fresh. Together, we were constant reminders of the past. We just couldn't get away from the bad memories if we had to see each other. It's not like any one of us ever said that out loud or made an active decision, it just sort of... happened."

"So, will we see you again after today?" I wonder, a little reluctant to hear her answer. Not sure what I want the answer to be.

"Maybe. Depends on what Trudy wants. I certainly don't want to bring back bad memories. But, I have a feeling she's going to need more help than she thinks."

"Why do you say that?"

She shrugs. "There was a callousness to him," she murmurs.

"To my father?" Did she not just hear that love letter he wrote to my mom?

She shakes her head. "No, no, sorry. I meant George. My father. Our father. He was cruel, sadistic even. We were his property, like so much chattel."

Wow. This isn't anything my mother has ever mentioned before. In fact, I can't recall the last time she even spoke his name. It's been decades though, I'm sure. And now I know why. I had no idea.

"I've never once doubted that he would have killed every one of us had he not gotten drunk and landed on his head one night."

For a second, I think I must have misunderstood. But how do you misunderstand a statement like that? Fuck, how are you supposed to *respond* to a statement like that? Another long pause while Elise takes a drag and looks off into the distance.

"Why are you telling me all this?"

My aunt looks at me with those same, dark, penetrating eyes that belong to my mother. And to my brother. "Because, I don't care what that preacher said up there today, or what your father wrote in that letter. You need more than faith to fight some things, Brett. And forewarned is forearmed, my dear nephew."

I don't need to ask to what or, rather, to whom she's referring.

Chapter 5

Brett

When I raise the door on our garage, I'm met with the familiar smells of oil and gasoline. The smells of my father. The chilly fall afternoon spills inside, washing sunlight across a big shelf in the back. I spot what I'm looking for right away, a box with my name on it. I promised Maggie I'd dig up some of my old pictures and my yearbook while we're here.

I'm about to reach for the box when a glimpse of cobalt blue in the corner catches my eye. I leave the box for a moment, drawn to the long-forgotten treasure of my youth: my first mountain bike. It came to me the summer of my twelfth birthday, the summer that my mother's mother spent here with us.

Grandma Ruth was, like my mother and Aunt Elise, a tall, strong woman. One Saturday morning, she shooed us from in front of the television, insisting we go out and play in the fresh air. I didn't mind, especially with that new bike to show off around the neighborhood. Jeremy on the other hand, was irritated at giving up his cartoons, and absolutely furious that I had something he didn't.

We rode around for over an hour before making our way back to the front of our own house. My brother dropped his bike onto the grass and came into this very garage while I practiced tight turns in the driveway. I wondered why he came back out with the big broom. I didn't have to wonder for long. As I rode past him, Jeremy stuck the thick wooden handle right into the spokes of my new bike. I literally flew over the handlebars, hitting the blacktop driveway hard enough to break my arm. Grandma Ruth, who had been sitting on the front porch reading her bible, saw the whole thing.

"Trudy!" she called into the house. "Trudy, come out here, Brett's been hurt!"

My mother was out of the house in a flash, bypassing Jeremy to tend to me as I lay there, scraped up and crying. Grandma Ruth had another destination in mind. She made a beeline for my brother, approaching him with such momentum that he stepped back, for fear she would plow right into him.

"Jeremy Dean Corrigan! What do you think you're doing?" she demanded.

He put on his sweetest, most innocent face and gave her a sheepish smile. "Nothing, Grandma Ruth. Brett fell off his bike."

"Nonsense!" she said sharply enough for my mother to turn and watch. "I saw what you did, young man. Why did you hurt your brother like that?"

"I didn't, Grandma Ruth," he insisted.

"Oh, really? Who am I supposed to believe, Boy, you or my lying eyes? Hmmm?"

"Mama, please," my mother called over to her. "I need your help getting Brett into the car so I can get him to the Emergency Room. I'll talk with Jeremy later."

It might have ended right there if my brother hadn't folded his arms across his chest, put a snide smile on his face, and looked up at the old woman with one defiant eyebrow raised. He was claiming victory.

She laughed at him then. It started out as a stifled chuckle, but quickly escalated into a mocking cackle. My grandmother laughed and laughed, while we all looked on in astonished silence. I was so stunned that I stopped crying. Jeremy narrowed his eyes into little slits and puckered his mouth in disdain, looking as if he'd like to eviscerate her at that very moment.

Grandma Ruth, twice his size, looked down on him, eyebrows raised. "Is that all you've got, little boy?" she asked him mildly.

I could practically see steam coming out of Jeremy's ears. No one had ever dared to challenge him. He was so enraged, that he actually growled at her. And then an interesting thing happened.

Ruth Purdy, widow, mother of five, grandmother of six, set her jaw, squatted down on the lawn so they were face to face, and she growled back at him. He stopped, looking at her as if she was crazy. Mom and I were rooted to the driveway, incredulous to what we were seeing unfold in front of us.

"You listen to me, and you listen good," she hissed, now poking him in the chest with her index finger. "I see you in there. I know what you are. 'For Satan himself masquerades as an angel of light', doesn't he, Jeremy?"

I watched in astonishment as my brother's face turned a deep shade of scarlet, and his eyes grew as big as saucers.

"That's right. You're not invisible. God knows your black and wicked heart. God sees you and keeps an account of every evil thing you do on the face of this earth. But you don't care about that, do you?"

The eight year old shook his head no.

She smiled.

"No matter, Jeremy. No matter at all. 'For they sow the wind, and they will reap the whirlwind.'"

"Mother! That's quite enough!" my mother said, getting to her feet, the spell finally broken.

"No, Trudy. It's nowhere near enough," my grandmother said, getting to her feet again as well. She used her hands to smack at the grass cuttings, which had stuck to her skirt, then turned her back on Jeremy and walked toward where I was still sprawled. "But then, you already know that, my sweet child, don't you?"

My mother didn't answer.

Now, without thinking about it, I reach over and rub my left forearm with my right hand. It still puts out a dull ache when the weather is especially damp and chilly. A regular reminder of what my brother is capable of.

I'm not blind to my own behavior. I look back and I realize that I got over the broken arm... just as I went on to get over the stolen girlfriends, the missing money and the constant, systematic destruction of nearly every good thing that came into my life.

Will I get over this, too? Right now, in this moment, I can tell myself with absolute certainty that I will never forgive Jeremy for taking my father from me. What I *cannot* tell myself with *any* certainty is whether I'll ever be able to put aside the fact that he's my brother. My blood. Only time is going to give me that answer, I suppose.

With a sigh, I take the box of high school memorabilia down from its shelf and head back outside, dropping the garage door as I do. I'll leave Owl Bridge in the morning to rejoin the Walton Quartet on tour. After being here with Maggie and my mother for a week, the thought of it fills me with both relief and dread.

"Hey! What ya got there?"

I look up to find Maggie sitting on the front porch swing. The late afternoon sun casts a halo around her dark curls, reminding me of the day we met ...the day she held my head in her hands while we waited for an ambulance to take me to the hospital.

"Angel head," I utter softly, and feel a smile come to my lips. It's mirrored on her face.

"Angel head. I haven't heard that in a long time, Mr. Corrigan."

"That was the day you saved my life," I tell her as I move down the walkway and up the porch steps. I put the box down and sit next to her on the swing, putting an arm around her

"Well, I wouldn't go *that* far..." she murmurs softly, shaking her head.

"I would. And I'm not talking about my injuries, Maggie. I—I don't know what I'd be doing or thinking or how I'd be acting right now if I hadn't met you."

She opens her mouth to respond, but I press a finger to her lips.

"No, Mags, I don't think you understand. You changed me. You snapped me out of the funk I was in..." I take a deep breath and close my eyes against the tears I can feel coming. "Because of you, my father died knowing that I was a decent guy. That I wouldn't spend my entire life enabling Jeremy to do...whatever the hell he does. It was a gift that I was able to give him because of you."

Maggie reaches up and puts a soft hand to my face, her brilliant blue eyes holding me hostage to her gaze. "Listen to me, Brett. You have always been a decent guy. More than that, you're a good man. A caring and compassionate man."

I tear my eyes away from hers. I can't look at her when I say this.

"Sometimes..." I begin in a whisper, "Sometimes I wish I was more like him."

"Like who? *Jeremy?*" she confirms, her tone turning brittle with alarm.

"Not the crazy shit," I explain, "but ... Christ! Maybe if I could be a little more 'heartless bastard' and a little less 'mama's boy' I could get over whatever the fuck this is with me. This fucking inability to just cut him out of my life. For good..."

Maggie takes a deep breath and takes my face in both of her hands, her grip more forceful this time.

"Okay, so, first of all, I could never love a heartless bastard, so scratch that. And second, have you *met* your mother? In this instance, being a 'mama's boy' is *not* synonymous with 'pussy,' if that's what you were implying."

I can't suppress the smile that's making the corners of my mouth twitch. I put my hands around her waist and pull her close to me. She lets go of my face and puts her head to my chest, as if we're slow dancing, right here on the front porch of my childhood home.

"I just... I hate myself for not hating him more."

There. I've managed to sum-up the biggest quandary of my life in less than ten words. And I can't hold back the tears anymore. They spill down my face in earnest as she shushes me and rubs comforting circles on my back.

Chapter 6

Brett

The stage lights are too bright. The concert hall is too warm. I can't seem to get comfortable in my chair, or in my skin, for that matter. Despite what I had hoped, there's nothing that feels right, or good, or comforting about my return to the Walton Quartet tour.

I'd thought, stupidly, that throwing myself into my music would make me feel a little better. I was very, very wrong. At this moment, it's all I can do to keep myself from bolting off the stage and running back to the only place on this earth where I'm guaranteed some comfort—Maggie's arms. But that isn't an option at this moment.

I strong-armed my way through the light and bright Mozart Quartet. I pushed through the hypnotic Philip Glass Quartet. Right now, as we reset our music, retune our instruments and take an inventory of eye contact between one another, I am finally in the homestretch of this god-awful night. It won't be long now before I can flee the oppressive applause and concerned glances of my colleagues for the sanctuary of my soulless hotel room and its minibar. But, standing squarely between me and that blissful numbness, is Samuel Barber's *Adagio for Strings*.

If only we'd chosen something different to end the program...but then, how could we have known six weeks ago that I would suffer such a devastating loss? As soon as I got into town for rehearsal this afternoon,

Joe sensed this could be a problem. He immediately offered to drop the piece, knowing that it would be difficult for me. But I'd insisted it would be fine—that *I* would be fine. If that wasn't the most idiotic fucking display of pride, I don't know what is.

Now, as Joe begins to play the first violin part, he enters on a note so soft and subtle that it seems to materialize out of the ether. I can't help myself, I commit the cardinal sin of chamber music performance: I close my eyes. Playing in a setting this intimate, with no conductor to direct the ensemble, requires the keenest attention to body language and facial expressions. But if I can't see my colleagues, then I can't see the worry or the sympathy that they've been telegraphing to me silently all night. If I can't see Joe, or Neville, or Philip, I can lose myself in Brett.

I play underneath, listening as Joe spins the lamenting melody that will possess the next ten minutes of my life. The rest of us—second violin, viola and cello, slip in beneath him. We provide a slow-moving blanket of music to catch the sound of the first violin's tears. Not that this is some self-indulgent funeral dirge. This music is raw, unbound emotion—grief at its harshest and cruelest.

It's pining for something forever lost, wishing you could retrieve all that time you wasted, because you now realize that there will never be another hour. Or minute. Or second. There will never be another heartbeat.

As our individual parts melt into one another, we become mourners standing around a gravesite, bound only by our collective agony. Aside from that single thread that tethers us to one another, we are each lost in our own internal suffering—bereft and desolate.

When it's my turn to echo the melody begun by the first violin, I find relief in allowing my viola to shoulder the wordless tune for me. Under my bow, I feel it growing and spreading and building. And then I pull back, allowing the cello to take on the burden of this lament.

Then, little by little, the tension starts to coil and our individual parts weave together into a single intense sound. Our unified agony turns in on itself until we are lost in a frenzy of ragged desperation. This is the sound of a fist, raised and shaking its ire towards the heavens, crying out at the injustice of it.

And then there is silence. It is the silence of the dead. It hangs for one very long moment before transforming itself into the softer, lower chords of acceptance for that which we cannot change. When the original melody returns again, it's no longer haunting... it's haunt*ed*. The jagged edges of sorrow and despair have been rubbed smooth by grudging acceptance. And then Joe is there again, the first violin in its final moments, with the same rhythm but different notes—a lower, tempered play on the opening measures.

As the Adagio comes to its conclusion, the sound stretches thinner and thinner until there's nothing left to hold it together anymore. Just air. And then shadow. And then darkness.

The flame is snuffed. The casket is lowered. And now there is nothing left to prove that this moment ever even existed. That is, except for my broken heart.

* * *

"Join us for drinks?" Joe asks as we head back to the dressing rooms to get packed up. "We're meeting some of the Detroit Phil guys."

Absofuckinglutely not.

"No, thanks, Joe. I appreciate the invite, but I'm pretty wiped."

He nods his understanding. "Do you ... do you want me to tell you if your brother's name comes up?"

"No," I shake my head and then stop. "Yes, actually. No ... Oh, fuck, I don't know, Joe. You decide. If it seems like something I *should* know then please, do. But if it's just the same bullshit he's always up to... then I'd just as soon not. Okay?"

I can see in his expression that he realizes just how wrung-out I am. "Did you tell him you were going to be in town?"

"Oh, trust me, I don't have to. I have no doubt that he knows. And if he wants to find me, he will."

We arrive at Joe's dressing room door, and he puts a reassuring hand on my shoulder. "You're not your brother, Brett. You don't answer to him anymore. You never did—you just didn't know that before. But you do now."

"Well, maybe somebody should tell *him* that," I mutter as I turn my back and keep walking.

I find my way out through the backstage door and into the chilly Detroit night. It's cold enough that I can see my breath, but I'm still feeling warm and flush from sitting under those stage lights. Suddenly my jacket feels as if it's choking me and I stop to peel it off, breathing a sigh of relief when I'm finally free of my leather albatross.

I'm just about to start walking again when I spot him not twenty feet in front of me. It turns out that Jeremy on a bench in Detroit looks very different than Jeremy at my mother's kitchen table. I was certain he'd show up somewhere, I just wasn't certain when or where.

"Bro!" he grins happily as he gets to his feet. He holds out his arms to embrace me, but I just stand there, staring at him blankly. Finally, he drops them to his side. "What? Aren't you happy to see me? I can't believe you didn't mention that your tour was bringing you here to Detroit! I had to read it in the paper."

"When should I have told you? Before you demanded your inheritance, or after you threatened Mom?" I reply icily, shifting away from him.

But a cold reception is no deterrent for Jeremy. "Come on," he coaxes. "At least let me buy you a beer. A one-drink truce, Brett. That's all I'm asking for. If I piss you off, you can just get up and leave. No harm, no foul."

Oh, I passed pissed several days ago. Right now I'm parked squarely in the realm of rage. I consider my state of mind at this very moment, concerned that if I sit down with him for even a single sip, I might just kill him with my bare hands. In the end, I decide I'm more curious to hear what he has to say than anything else. He can see that I'm waffling.

"Please?"

I don't think I've ever heard my brother say that word. He probably spent hours practicing in the mirror so it would look and sound natural coming out of his mouth.

"Fine," I huff in exasperation and follow him in silence to a pub around the corner.

"Bud, please," I say to the waitress once we're seated.

"Make that two," Jeremy adds.

"So, what do you want?" I demand, getting right down to business.

"How was the funeral?"

"Really, Jeremy?"

"I didn't want to upset Mom, so I decided it was just best to stay away. God only knows what she would've done if I'd been at the church and the cemetery."

"Sounds more like you were worried about yourself. About what she might say to you in front of our friends and family."

"Family? What family? It was just you and Melanie, wasn't it?" He sounds perfectly innocent as the waitress sets our bottles down in front of us.

"Jeremy," I growl, holding up my wrist and tapping my watch pointedly, "I don't have the time or the energy for your bullshit. If you keep it up, we might not make it through a one-*sip* truce."

"No, no," he says as he shakes his head. "Sorry. *Maggie.* I meant to say Maggie."

I sigh. "Aunt Elise made an appearance," I tell him at last.

"Aunt Elise? Jesus, I can't remember the last time we saw her. Where the hell has she been all these years?"

"Only forty-five minutes away, as it turns out." He takes a sip of his beer. "And she told me she's a lesbian," I continue.

"Well, *duh*!" He grins at me.

"Wait. What? You knew that?"

"Of course! Don't you remember she brought her girlfriend to Grandma Ruth's funeral?"

"Did she? Jesus! How is it that you can remember that and I can't?"

"Are you kidding me?" He chuckles. "That was one of the happiest days of my life. I hated that nasty old bitch."

I think about her finger poking Jeremy's chest. Yes, I'm sure it did make him happy to see her dead.

We sip in silence as a few locals get loud at the bar, laughing about something we can't quite hear from where we are. One of them walks over to a vintage jukebox and drops some coins in.

"So, are you and Maggie still living together, then?" Jeremy quizzes me over the beginning of Linda Ronstadt's 'Blue Bayou.'

I nod. "Yup. We were at her place for a while, but it was tight. So we ended up moving out of Brooklyn and into a brownstone apartment in SOHO a few months ago."

"Sounds pretty serious."

I shrug noncommittally.

"So...no wedding bells ringing then?" he fishes.

"Not yet."

He faces forward as he takes a long, slow swig of his beer. When he puts the bottle down on the bar, he turns toward me again. "Huh," he muses with the slightest furrow of his brow. "You know, that's interesting, because I ran into Sharon Ginsburg. You remember her from McInnes, don't you?"

Shit. I know exactly where he's going with this, but he doesn't wait for my reply.

"Yeah, she plays with the Broadway touring company of 'Hamilton' now. I ran into her when the show came through town last month. She was pretty hammered. And horny. And chatty. But not a bad lay, as it turns out."

I give him my best *'spit it out'* glare.

"Anyway," he continues, oblivious to my irritation, "she seems to think she's invited to your wedding. The one you're not having."

I hold up my empty bottle for the waitress and she nods that she'll bring me another one. For a second I consider asking for a shot of tequila instead. Or, maybe, in addition to.

"Do you really *not* want me to come?"

His affectation of hurt is nothing short of brilliant. But I know better. My brother doesn't do hurt. "Why? Do you really *want to* come?"

"Of course! You're my only brother. I want to be standing by your side when you pledge your eternal love to your blushing bride."

I'm about to snort when my bottle of beer arrives.

"Thanks," I mutter to the server before turning my attention back to Jeremy. "Oh, please," I hiss. "The only reason you want to come to my wedding is to stir up shit. Not gonna happen. I don't want to see you anywhere nearby. Not at the church, not the reception. And not even God himself will be able to help you if you should somehow pop up anywhere nearby on my honeymoon. Got it?"

I point my bottle at him, making direct eye contact. I need to know that he understands what I'm saying to him. He raises his hands in a gesture of surrender.

"Okay, okay! All you had to do was say 'No, Jeremy, I *don't want you to come.'* That's all."

"Fine. No, Jeremy, I don't want you to come."

An awkward silence settles over us. I offer an olive branch by way of a change in subject. "How's the Philharmonic?"

He accepts the offering. "Not bad, actually. I'd rather be playing first horn, but all things in time."

"I hear Jennifer Ruiz is an amazing player."

"She's not as good as they say," he informs me flatly and takes a long pull from his bottle before continuing. "But the truth is that it isn't her fault."

I nearly choke. "What? Please, are you seriously trying to tell me that you don't hold a grudge against her?" I scoff.

My brother shrugs sheepishly. "Well, maybe a *little* one," he admits. "But, here's the thing...my beef isn't really with her because she didn't want the principal spot. She didn't audition for it. She was trying out for the third horn spot."

"Which *you* now have," I point out.

"Yes, which I now have. I'll admit it, I was ready to make the little twit's life a living hell, but I didn't have to."

"What is that supposed to mean?"

"The afternoon of her first rehearsal, she shows up in tears. She takes me aside and explains that she went to the idiot Orchestra Director and *begged* him to swap our spots."

"She did *what?*" I can't believe what I'm hearing. Nobody turns down that kind of an opportunity.

Jeremy is nodding adamantly. "Oh, yeah. I confirmed it with one of my moles in the administration offices. She wanted out of that spot bad, but the asshole flat-out refused."

"But why? If it was what she wanted..."

"Christ, Brett! Do I have to spell it out for you? She wanted third horn but they gave her principal. I wanted principal but they gave me third. You see where I'm going with this?"

I resist the urge to tell him to fuck off. I want to see if he's going where I think he's going with this. "So you think management is fucking with you," I deduce.

"I don't think, bro, I *know*. The Director is over-the-top pissed off that I managed to sneak into the auditions right under his nose...and actually win. Now the little pussy can't fire me without a huge lawsuit on his hands, so he fucked me over the only way he could."

Holy shit.

If I didn't know how dangerous Jeremy can be, I might just laugh at the insanity of this situation.

"So, what are planning to do?" I ask at last.

"Not much, as it turns out. She's taking care of it all by herself. The stupid bitch is a basket case before every concert and our new maestro hates her. The whole thing is just a ticking fucking time bomb," he declares with a satisfied grin.

That's my cue to leave. I've already heard too much. I drain the last of my beer and slide off the barstool. "Yeah, well, I've had a long day so I'm gonna head back to the hotel..."

He puts a hand on my forearm to stop me. "I heard that Philip Tonka is resigning as cellist of the Walton this season."

Fuck me! I was so fucking close to a getaway...

"Well, he's here in Detroit with us," I begin, choosing my words very carefully, "but this will be his last concert for a while. He's having some surgery that'll have him out of commission for several months, at least."

"Is it true that Julia is taking his place?" I nod slowly, waiting for the other shoe to drop. When it finally falls, it falls hard and fast. "I have to admit, Brett, I'm really surprised. I didn't think you had it in you. I guess we're more alike than I realized."

The mere suggestion of that causes my blood pressure to spike. "What the hell is *that* supposed to mean?" I growl, shifting in my seat so I can be sure to catch every nuance of every twisted word he's about to utter.

"First, you convince Mom to cut me out of the will so you can have it all to yourself. Then, you exclude me from your wedding. And now, you choose Julia—the whore who trashed my reputation—over *me*, your own brother. Dude, how do you sleep at night?"

I make a weak attempt to hold back but it's more trouble than it's worth. Ah, fuck it. I laugh. I throw back my head and continue to laugh until tears are streaming down my face and I'm getting over-the-shoulder glances from the regulars at the bar. Jeremy becomes absolutely still in his rage.

"Are you for real?" I wipe my damp face with the back of my hand. "You want to know how *I* sleep at night? You're fucking delusional, man!"

His lips twist into a sneer and his eyes narrow. This is my second cue to leave, and I aim to take it. "Goodbye, Jeremy," I conclude, getting to my feet. "Thanks for the drink."

"We're not done," he informs me, grabbing my forearm.

I raise my eyebrow. He gets the message loud and clear, releasing his grip. Then I turn and walk out onto the sidewalk outside of the bar, but my brother hot on my heels.

"Brett, I'm not kidding..." he calls out from behind me. "There's more that we need to discuss," he's saying as he catches up to me and matches my brisk pace.

I stop and face him. "That's where you're wrong, Jeremy," I correct him calmly. "We *are* done. And I'm not just talking about this conversation. You and I...We. Are. Done."

"You don't mean that." He dismisses me with his tone and his expression.

"I do," I insist coolly. "There's no coming back for you and me. I'll never forgive you for letting Dad die."

"Oh, please," he scoffs, batting away my words with a flick of his wrist. "Dramatic much, Brett? He had a heart attack. Plain and simple."

Mother. Fucker.

I take a step closer to him, a subtle reminder that I am still bigger and stronger than he is. That I could—and certainly would—kick his ass from here to Grand Rapids if necessary.

"Listen to me, little brother, and listen good. If you're smart, you'll make things work here in Detroit. You've got a great gig, and a nice life for yourself. There is absolutely no reason you can't be happy here. As happy as you're capable of being, anyway."

He seems more amused by me than threatened. Time to change that dynamic. One more step and our chests are touching. My voice drops to a low, menacing rumble that comes from somewhere deep within my chest.

"Stay away from me. Stay away from Maggie. Stay away from Mom."

"Or what?" he challenges, the corners of his mouth now curling up into a hideous grin.

"Believe me, Jeremy, you don't want to find out. If you underestimate me, you'll regret it."

He shrugs with disinterest. "Whatever, Brett. Maybe I *will* stay away from you. Watching you isn't nearly as interesting as, say, watching *my son.*"

I feel my heart jump right to my throat. To hear him utter those last two words is more jarring than anything else he could have possibly said. And he knows it.

"He's getting big, isn't he?" Jeremy continues, knowing full well that he's struck a nerve. "Too bad he's going to look like his Plain Jane mother. But who knows, maybe as he gets older…"

I grab my brother by the collar of his shirt and slam him against the brick wall of the building. Nobody seems to notice or care that there's an altercation occurring right on the street. Just another Saturday night in Detroit.

"You like to think that you know me better than I know myself, right, Jeremy? If that's true, then you will believe me when I tell you that your life won't be worth shit if you get anywhere near that kid," I warn, biting off each word and spitting it in his face. "You *know* I'll do it, Jeremy."

He smiles at me, but I can see the briefest flash in his eyes that tells me he does know. I let him drop to the ground and turn around, starting the walk back to the hotel.

This time, he doesn't try to stop me.

Chapter 7

Brett

"He really said that?" Maggie shrieks. I can hear the creaking of the old swing that we were sitting on just yesterday afternoon.

"Shhhh! Maggie, I keep telling you, my mother has superhuman hearing. You've got to keep your voice down ..."

"Sorry!" she whispers.

"Yes, he said that." I sigh tiredly. "It would just be so much easier if he'd make it work here in Detroit. But Mags, I know my brother. I can tell he's hatching some crazy plan in that twisted mind of his."

She's silent for a long moment. "Brett, here's the thing about sociopaths, they do *not* like to be exposed."

"As what? Sociopaths?"

"As anything. They hate having their plans ruined. They hate being caught in a lie. And, more than anything, they hate being exposed as anything other than what they want you to see them as."

"What are you trying to tell me, Mags? That my brother can throw one hell of a temper tantrum? I know that already."

"Babe, for as many years as you've been subjected to your brother, I'll bet you've barely seen the tip of the iceberg with him. He obviously still sees Julia and Matthew as the people who destroyed his perfectly planned rise to fame and fortune. He resents the hell out of your mother for cutting him out of your father's will. And then there's you..."

"What about me?"

"He perceives you as disloyal. In his mind, you abandoned him to be with me. You cheated him out of the money from the garage. And—probably your worst sin in his eyes—is your disloyalty for befriending Julia and Matthew. You're right to think he might be plotting something. All I'm saying is please keep your eyes open. Someone like Jeremy will go a long way to protect himself. And the rage that comes with that is mind-boggling."

I rub my eyes and stare longingly at the minibar. I've been avoiding it, trying to get by on the two beers that I had back at the bar, but I'm starting to think a teeny tiny bottle of liquid loving might be just what I need to take the edge off and get to sleep. She must sense that I can't deal with this right now, because she softens her manner.

"I'm sorry, Brett, I didn't mean to get you all stressed out while you're exhausted and on the road. What about your concert tonight? Did it go alright?"

I kick my shoes off and flop on the extra-springy hotel room mattress. "Could've been better, that's for sure. I kept glancing into the audience to see if he was out there somewhere."

"And was he?"

"No, not that I could see, anyway."

"Well, no matter. You're done with Detroit now, right?"

"One more show—a matinee tomorrow. The others are hanging for an extra day to catch a concert by the Detroit Phil. They've got a new hotshot conductor from Europe."

"But you don't want to see Jeremy again," she finishes my thought.

"Exactly. So, I'm thinking I'll catch an earlier flight tomorrow evening. Julia will be in Chicago by then, too. I'll take her and David out for dinner or something."

"You've gotten really attached to that little boy, haven't you?"

"More than I ever thought I would," I admit. "Knowing he's half Jeremy should be a repellant, but turns out it's just the opposite. I know it sounds kind of strange, but I think of David as the kid my brother *should* have been."

Maggie thinks about that for a long moment. "I get that," she whispers her reply into the phone. "There's something very familiar about him to you. It's like he's your brother, but better."

"Exactly."

"Have you given anymore thought to telling your mother about him?"

We've had this discussion before, but she doesn't like my answer. So, she brings it up again from time to time, hoping it will change. "I can't do that to her. Not right now."

"But, Brett, I think she needs something like this. Especially right now!"

"It's not like replacing one dead goldfish with another," I snap.

Shit. I didn't mean to do that. I hear her take a deep breath on her end of the line. "Fair enough," she agrees quietly. "I'm sorry. That's not what I was implying."

"No, I'm sorry. I know you weren't ..."

"I'm just saying that your mother has lost her life's companion. And, while having Elise in the picture again is a good thing, imagine what a grandson would do to lift her spirits!"

I'm skeptical and she knows it. "Okay, okay, just promise me you'll give it some thought," she relents.

"Fine. I promise. How's Mom doing, anyway? I thought Aunt Elise would've disappeared again by now."

"Quite the opposite, actually. She's been here twice this week already, once to help us go through your father's things and then she brought Dianne by for dinner last night."

"Dianne?"

"Her partner."

"Oh! Dianne. I didn't know that was her name. Is she nice?"

"I think she just might be the funniest woman I've ever met in my life. I swear, when I woke up this morning, my sides were sore from all the laughing. Your mom really seemed to enjoy it, too. She's actually considering their invitation to come and spend a little time with them at their lake house."

"Seriously? That's really great. I'm glad they're reconnecting. Does that mean you'll be joining me on tour soon?"

"Sorry, no. This working girl has got to get back to the daily grind. I've got young minds to mold and families to reunite. But that doesn't mean we can't have a little fun phone time now," she says suggestively... and a little too loudly for my comfort level.

"As tempting as that is, we probably shouldn't. I told you, my mother hears everything."

"Oh, please! She's all the way over on the other side of the house. And the windows are closed. And the radio is on. And on top of all that, your next-door neighbors are having a very loud spat. Something about the wife, a guy named Buddy, and a chainsaw. Unless your mom's a bat, there's no way she's going to have any idea what we're discussing."

"Okay, fine, then. What is it, exactly, that we're discussing?"

"Mmmm... how much I'd love get naked right now and let you lick strawberry jam off every square inch of my sticky body."

Wow. Well, that's a new one for me. But then, I've been meaning to open myself up to more new experiences. "How soon can we try that one out for real?"

She giggles. It's a sexy giggle. "Well," she considers, "I guess that depends on—" she stops mid-sentence, and the squeaky swing stops abruptly.

"Hold on," she whispers into the phone. "Yes, Trudy?" I can hear muted voices. She must have her hand over the receiver. "Okay, I'm back," she says finally.

"What happened?"

"It was your mom."

"What about her? Is she alright?"

"Yes, she's fine."

"Good. What did she want?"

Maggie clears her throat. "She just wanted me to remind you that strawberries make you break out in hives."

Uh-huh.

Chapter 8

Brett

Watching Julia's nanny walk into the Clarke Hotel in Chicago is like watching a giraffe glide in off the Serengeti, and head in the lobby seems to swivel in her direction. At nearly six-feet tall, Natalie Hughes has long, lean legs, toned arms and a neck that would make Audrey Hepburn's look stumpy. Oblivious to the glances from all around her, Natalie scans the room, giving her broad, toothy smile when she spots Julia and me sharing a couch in the corner.

"Nata!" David squeals from his stroller as he catches sight of her approaching. He's so excited that he bangs his fists on the tray in front of him, sending dry Cheerios flying onto the carpet. "Nata! Nata!"

When she reaches him, Natalie appears to fold in on herself, dropping three-feet of altitude as she squats down to free him from stroller lock-up. She scoops him into her arms.

"Davy Baby!" she croons excitedly. "High-five me big guy!" She holds up one of her long-fingered hands and he slaps it with his tiny corresponding appendage.

As impressed as I am by her ease with my nephew, I'm even more impressed by a certain skill I discovered Natalie to have—a little something her cop father instilled in her as a kid.

"Natalie," I cajole with a conspiratorial grin, "read the room for me."

She glances up at me briefly. "Jeez, Brett, I'm not a circus freak, you know! Didn't you get enough of this the last time I traveled with you guys?"

Oh, Nat, I'll never get enough. Come on…please?"

She sighs and rolls her eyes at me. "Fine …"

Even as she's bouncing the giggling toddler up and down, she's rattling off an inventory of the people in the hotel lobby and what they were doing when she walked in.

"There's a couple holding hands on a settee to the right of the door. A pervy old man is watching them from over the top of his newspaper. There are three clerks at the counter—one blonde man and two brunette women, all in their mid-forties, I'd say. There's a sitting area to the left of the door. A teenager is sitting cross-legged on one of the couches, texting on his phone. His little sister is next to him, brushing the hair of a blonde doll. I'm pretty sure the couple standing at the counter is their parents because the woman keeps glancing back at them every few seconds."

"Amazing!" I slap my hands on my knees. "How the *hell* do you do that?"

She just smiles and shrugs.

"Hell hell hell hell hellllllllll…" David gurgles happily to Natalie.

I get an elbow to the ribs from Julia. "Sorry!" I snicker. "At least it wasn't the F-Bomb."

"Little pitchers have big ears, Unca!" Natalie snorts.

"Unca!" David squeals loudly, now turning in Nat's arms so he can point at me.

Since he's been around our quartet so much for rehearsals, and now on tour, Julia has him calling me Uncle Brett, or *'Unca'* in David-speak. And I have to admit, I kind of like it. A lot.

"How was your trip, Nat?" Julia asks, getting to her feet and brushing the hair from her son's forehead. He's too entranced by Natalie to even notice her.

"Perfect!" she exclaims animatedly as David giggles and tries to stuff his hand into her mouth.

Julia tucks an envelope into the pocket of the stroller.

"Brett and I have to get to rehearsal, but I've left everything you need in our adjoining rooms. I'm 216 and you're 218. Your key card is in the envelope along with the information about the concert hall where I'll be, and our schedule."

Natalie doesn't appear to be focusing on anything but David. But, as she's just demonstrated, she doesn't miss a thing. I know for a fact that she's making a mental note of every detail Julia is throwing at her.

"The crib is set up on my side and his bottles and food are in the mini fridge. There's a diaper bag here in the stroller and one in the room, too," Julia informs her.

Natalie lifts the chubby redhead over her head and onto her shoulders. The kid can practically touch the light fixtures at that height. "No worries, mama," she assures Julia. "I'll drop my stuff in the room, and then Little Man and I are going to take a walk around Chi-Town. I've got every park, zoo, merry-go-round and children's museum in the city mapped out. By the time we get back, he'll be begging for a nap." She's grinning wickedly.

"Bye, buddy!" I wave up to him as we grab our instruments and head for the entrance.

"Bye-bye, Unca!" he responds, grabbing little fistfuls of Natalie's short, blond hair.

"Ouch!" she yips. "Take it easy up there!"

"I love you, baby boy!" Julia blows him a kiss.

"Mamamamamama..." he babbles happily as Natalie takes him toward the room, using the stroller as a trolley for her suitcase.

Julia looks after them a little wistfully.

"Hey, it's okay," I reassure, nudging her arm with my elbow. "Natalie's got this under control."

"I know, I know," she mutters, turning reluctantly and following me out onto the sidewalk for the four-block walk to the theatre. "I can't help it. When he's out of my sight I feel so ... vulnerable."

"I get that, but wouldn't you be even more worried if you'd left him at home in New York? At least this way he's close by."

She shrugs, unconvinced. "Yeah, I guess. I'm fine when he's at home with Matthew. But now that his tour with the Gotham Chamber Players overlaps with our tour, things have gotten complicated. I mean, I knew this would happen eventually. I just have to get used to trusting someone else with my child."

I'd like to tell her that she has absolutely nothing to worry about, that David is safe and there isn't anything out there in the big, bad world that Natalie can't handle. But that would be a lie. Julia and I both know exactly what—or rather who—is out there in the big, bad world. She should be worried. She should be very worried.

* * *

True to her word, Natalie has ensured David is out cold by the time we meet-up again at the concert hall. Julia lifts him gently from his stroller into the playpen she has setup in her dressing room backstage. She kisses the tips of her fingers and then transfers it to his forehead. Natalie has gone back to the hotel for a rest before she's back on duty during concert.

"Looks like it was a big day for the little guy," I comment, watching his chest move up and down heavily through his denim coveralls.

Julia joins me for the Chinese food feast I have assembled for us on a coffee table. "Seems so. And believe me, that's no easy feat! It takes a lot to get him that tuckered out." She smiles and takes a bite of an egg roll.

I dig into a pint of General Tsao's. Chicago is only an hour from my hometown of Owl Bridge. As a result, I know all the good restaurants, including the best hotdog cart, pizza joint and Chinese takeout.

"Have you spoken with Matthew?" I mumble through a mouthful.

She nods. "Yes, they're in Houston tonight then on to Dallas and Austin. He should be home a few days after I get back."

"Will you stay in the city, or head out to your place on Long Island?"

"Oh, I don't know. Since we'll have a break from the Walton, I may go out to the house for a few days, let David play in the leaves and go pumpkin picking."

"Now that sounds like fun." I smile, pointing my fork at her for emphasis.

"You should come!" she exclaims as she sits up straighter, suddenly inspired by the idea. "He'd love it! You and Maggie could stay the weekend and keep us company. That's a big old house to rattle around in, especially when Matthew's gone."

"Yeah, I'll bet it is. Let me ask Maggie when I call her tonight. She's missed some work while she's been staying with my mom. She may need to put in some weekend time to make up for it."

"How *is* your mom, Brett?"

I shrug. "About as well as can be expected, I guess. Her long-lost sister has resurfaced and seems to be sticking around."

"Is that a good thing?"

"Yeah, I think so. My mom is hard to read. But, Aunt Elise seems to get her."

Julia is nodding as she pokes at something in the bottom of a container with a chopstick. "And you? How are you holding up? You came back on tour pretty soon, all things considered."

I sigh and take a second to think about the answer to that question. "I really don't know, Julia. As long as I keep moving, I'm okay. I'm just afraid that once I stop..."

"You'll just collapse," she finishes the sentence for me.

"Exactly."

She looks at me with those emerald green eyes, and I can see the concern that lies behind them. There's something else on her mind and I can guess what or, rather, *who* it is. Better to address it head-on, I suppose. "I saw Jeremy in Detroit," I tell her.

One of her eyebrows goes up. "Oh? And how was that?"

"Awkward. Irritating. Frustrating. Infuriating."

"Sounds about right." She gives me a small, tight smile.

"Yeah, well, he's still a pain in the ass. I knew he'd find me. He just can't help himself. And he's so fucking smug," I grumble.

Julia pulls a bottle of wine out of David's diaper bag and puts it on the table. "Mother's little helper," she says with an impish grin. "I think we need something to help this conversation go down easier, what do you think?"

"Why, Mrs. Ayers!" I pretend to be scandalized. "Are you suggesting that we imbibe before we take the stage?"

"Nope, not at all." she shakes her head as she pours the chardonnay into two paper cups. "I'm *insisting*."

"Oh, well, if you insist, then..." I take a sip and wonder why I hadn't thought of a pre-concert cocktail hour myself.

"So..." she encourages, leaving me to fill in the rest of that blank.

"So, he was waiting for me on a bench outside of the hall. He convinced me to have a beer with him. He wanted me to know that he was aware that I hadn't invited him to the wedding. That didn't sit well. And I got an earful about how much better he is than the girl playing first horn in Detroit. Just your usual Jeremy bullshit."

She nods thoughtfully and sits back on the couch, tucking her legs up under her skirt and swirling the wine in her cup. "Did he say anything about your father?"

I haven't told many people about my brother's role in our father's death—I just can't bring myself to do it. But Julia is different. She can definitely appreciate the depths of Jeremy's depravity. "He asked how the service was, that's all. I mean, what is he going to say at this point? *'Hey, Brett! Sorry I stood by and watched Dad die!'* Yeah, actually, now that I think about it, I'm kind of surprised he didn't say that. But then again, Jeremy doesn't apologize for anything."

"Does he know I've joined the Walton?"

I've been waiting for this to come up. "Yes. But I told him you weren't there in Detroit. I didn't mention you'd be on this stop of the tour either, in case he got the bright idea to surprise us."

"He must see it as a betrayal, you working with me."

"He does," I confirm quietly. No point in trying to hide it from her, but no need to elaborate on how ugly the actual discussion was, either.

From the playpen, David stirs slightly. He gives a faint little whimper, turns his head in the other direction and sighs as he settles back into that blissfully deep baby slumber.

"He didn't say a word about David," I offer quickly, hoping to reassure her with the lie before she can inquire about it. "Honestly, he's so self-absorbed that I think he forgets the kid even exists most of the time."

"Hah!" Julia snorts a little too loudly.

She slaps a hand over her own mouth and we wait to see if David will wake up with his trademark blood-curdling cry—a trait I happen to know he picked up from his father. When it's clear that the toddler has slept through her outburst, Julia starts again more softly.

"You don't have to try and protect me, Brett. I know what we're dealing with. Jeremy Corrigan doesn't forget anything that might be of value to him at some point. It's just a matter of time before he decides that he can use David to his advantage."

"That's not going to happen," I state firmly.

Julia gives me a look that says *'Seriously? Do you think I'm that stupid?'* Shit. We need to get off of this topic. Luckily, I find a diversionary tactic on the table right in front of us. I scoop up two fortune cookies and hold them out in my palm for her to choose from.

"You first," she says.

I get the crinkly wrapper off, decimating the cookie in the process. The paper is fine, though, and I pull it out, peering at the microscopic lettering. "Your shoes will make you happy today."

"It does *not* say that!" she accuses me with a giggle.

I hold the tiny paper out so she can see that I'm telling her the truth. "And you know what?" I prop a foot up on the table between us. "They have! Maggie helped me to pick these out last week."

"Nice!" Julia nods her appreciation of my spiffy new wingtips.

"Your turn." I hand her the remaining cellophane-encased cookie.

She pulls the wrapping apart, breaks open the cookie and pops a piece of it into her mouth while she examines her fortune. Suddenly, she stops chewing, looks up at me, then down at it again, clearly alarmed by what she's read.

"What? What is it?" I prod.

Julia's not laughing anymore. She swallows hard and reads it to me. "Your problem just got bigger. Think what you have done."

Chapter 9

Brett

The Tolliver Theater is a fully restored old-time movie house and every time we play here, I feel as if I've gone back in time. Now, I can see that same wonderment on Julia's face as she takes her seat to perform with the Walton String Quartet for the first time. Ornate columns and gold-encrusted moldings accent row after row of plush red seats. Side balcony boxes seem to float above the house seating below. And above, well, that's the cherry on the sundae. The blue-domed ceiling has been painted to look like the night sky, complete with a blanket of twinkling stars. An old Wurlitzer organ sits off to one side of the stage, a reminder of the days before "talkies."

Now, the four of us tune quickly—Joe and Neville on violins, me on the viola, and Julia playing the cello. We make eye contact and then Joe gives us the nod that starts the musical relay race that is Antonín Dvořák's *String Quartet No. 12*. Each of the four of us has a chance to play the melody before handing it off quickly to someone else. The second movement is a haunting lament, a gypsy melody from the composer's Bohemian homeland. The slow, free flowing beauty gives way to a frenzied Scherzo and Finale. One moment, we're all playing a quick, staccato line, and the next it's a soaring melody.

We're connected to one another not just musically, but physically and emotionally. We watch each other's movements and expressions and listen to every pull of the bow across a string. At times, it feels to me as if we're all sitting in a tiny boat, the four of us shifting and redistributing our weight constantly, just to stay balanced and keep afloat as we move through waters that are alternately choppy and calm in quick succession. It's exciting and dangerous and incredibly powerful and by the time we're done, even *I* want to jump to my feet and applaud.

"You were amazing!" I whisper to Julia as we slip backstage for a quick break.

"Oh, stop it," she mutters, swatting away the compliment dismissively. But I catch just the hint of a smile on her face.

"No, I'm serious, Julia. There's something special about the four of us together. We've got great chemistry."

Now I'm treated to the full smile. "Yeah, it *was* kind of amazing, wasn't it?" she relents, finally giving in to her excitement.

I nod and give her arm a squeeze.

"Hey, you two," comes a familiar voice from behind us. "Fan-freaking-tastic job out there!" Suddenly Ingo Katz is there between us, draping one arm over each of our shoulders.

Strictly speaking, the Walton Quartet isn't always a quartet. There are many times when we expand our ranks to play quintets. That's where Ingo comes in—a double bass player who moves effortless easily between the classical and jazz worlds. He's your stereotypical 'cool cat,' dressed in all black, with a matching pork pie hat and small, round, blue-tinted glasses.

Julia gasps in surprise. "Ingo! What are you doing here?"

"Ah, for me to know and you to find out, Miss Julia!" he replies with a cryptic smile.

She looks at me in confusion. "Brett, what's going on? Why is Ingo here?"

"Beats me." I shrug sheepishly. I can see she wants to interrogate me further, but we're interrupted by our first violinist, Joe Dancy as he walks by.

"Let's go," Joe calls over his shoulder.

"Go on." I give her a gentle push toward the stage.

"Wait, what about you?"

I shake my head and smile. "Nope. Neville and I are sitting this one out. Go break a leg, Julia." I give her a quick peck on the cheek and shoo her forward silently.

While Julia and Ingo get settled, Joe takes a little detour to the front of the stage where a microphone has been setup for him. "The Walton String Quartet didn't start out performing in grand venues such as this one," he begins, using a sweeping hand to gesture across the hall. "Twenty years ago, we were just four guys from Juilliard sharing a tiny apartment in Hell's Kitchen. We played in subway stations, at Christmas parties for drunk Wall Street execs and once, on the observation deck of the Empire State Building on Valentine's Day. Since then, we've crossed oceans and continents to share our love of music and to learn what the rest of the world can teach us about it.

"Tonight, the Walton welcomes its newest member—not to mention its first woman. She is a Kreisler International Music Competition Silver Medalist, and her highly anticipated debut recording is scheduled to be released in just a few weeks. It is my great privilege to share this stage with such a brilliant young talent. Please join us in welcoming the new cellist of the Walton Quartet, Mrs. Julia James Ayers."

Julia's face is beet red as she stands up reluctantly, gives a brief nod and sits again. Joe waits for the noise to die down before resuming his curtain speech.

"What Julia doesn't know, is that I wanted to choose a special piece for her debut concert. A piece that she knows and loves, not to mention one that would showcase the special quality that she adds to the Walton."

I can see Julia shaking her head.

"I can't believe Joe pulled it off," Neville whispers from next to me. "She had absolutely no idea!"

"Not a clue," I agree, smiling.

"I thought about pieces with flashy, virtuosic cello parts," Joe is saying to the audience, "but none of them seemed right. Oh, Julia can play anything you throw in front of her, but it is her warm and soulful sound that makes the biggest contribution to our ensemble. You may have noticed that our colleagues, the wonderful violinist Neville Jenson and violist Brett Corrigan have stepped offstage, and that there is now a super-hip bass player joining us—Mr. Ingo Katz."

Joe gestures back to Ingo, who pulls the hat from his head and does an elaborate little bow thing that makes the audience chuckle. "The change in personnel was necessary because the piece I finally settled on is a trio. Not by Dvořák, or Mozart, or Haydn. But by a contemporary American fiddler and composer by the name of Mark O'Connor."

Julia's face lights up, and all the bashfulness seems to just melt away when she realizes they are going to play one of her favorites. "I hope you'll enjoy hearing *The Appalachia Waltz* as much as we enjoy playing it." Joe returns the microphone to its stand and walks back to his seat, where Julia is shaking her head in amazement.

The Appalachia Waltz isn't a complicated melody. Nor is it intricate or showy. When Joe starts to play it, you realize at once that the strictly metered classical violin is gone, replaced by the unhurried, unmeasured ease of a fiddle. Under his fingers, the theme has a bright sweetness that brings to my mind images of crisp, foggy mornings in the mountains of Virginia, warm glowing fireplaces, and rocking chairs on the front porch.

A few minutes in, the violin hands the melody off to the cello—to Julia. These same notes are so different in her hands. She adds a tone of melancholy that turns my mental images from beautiful geography to poignant history. Suddenly, I'm reminded of young lives lost in service to something greater. As I listen to this tune, I can almost see men and boys walking out of the mountains, rifles in hand, not knowing if they would ever again return home. It doesn't matter how history will ultimately paint them, whether or not they are right or wrong. They are all brave souls in this moment and in this music—in my mind.

I want to close my eyes and explore the story that is unfolding in my imagination, but I can't take my eyes off of Julia as she plays. Her hand barely holds the bow, drawing it slowly and delicately across the strings, as if pulling a delicate silk line. Her eyes are closed, and the fingers of her left hand walk slowly up and down the fingerboard, periodically rocking back and forth to create the slightest vibrato. When she opens her eyes again, she looks to Joe, sending the melody back to the fiddle with just the slightest arch of an eyebrow and nod of her chin. It's a flawless transition as she joins Ingo for the inner harmonies that provide the canvas upon which the fiddle tune is painted.

I know exactly what's going to happen as these three brilliant musicians play out the final notes. Not because I know this piece already, but because I know I'm feeling exactly what the people seated out in the house are feeling at this moment as they listen and look on. And I'm not wrong. There's the briefest silence as the last note fades away, but that is quickly shattered by the applause of an audience so enraptured, that they cannot help but jump to their feet.

All of these onlookers know, as I do, that they've just experienced something very special. They know, as I do, that you shouldn't be able to capture the spirit of an entire country into three soft, string voices. And yet, here it is. We have just had the privilege of hearing the unmistakable sound of freedom.

Chapter 10

Brett

It takes three curtain calls and two encores for the audience to finally clear the hall. This has been one long-ass day, and I'm looking forward spending the next several hours enjoying a stiff drink from the minibar, phone sex with Maggie and a good night's sleep.

I've just gotten my viola packed up and am getting ready to go grab my things from the dressing room when I hear my name from somewhere close by.

"Brett!"

Holy. Fuck. It can't be...can it?

The voice is unmistakable. And jarringly out of context. I turn around and, sure enough, I see my mother making her way backstage. Behind her are Aunt Elise and a short brunette who must be her partner, Dianne. "Mom? What're you doing here?"

"Your Aunt Elise and Dianne surprised me with tickets for your concert. Did you know they only live about twenty minutes from here? Oh, Honey, it was beautiful," she gushes. "I wish your father could have heard you play with the Walton Quartet. He was so proud of you." She steps close to me and puts a hand on the lapel of my tuxedo, patting it gently. As she looks up into my eyes, I can see she's holding back tears.

I put my shock aside for the moment and pull her close to me. For once, I am the soother of nerves, the dispeller of fears and the giver of confidence that all will be right in the world. She allows me to hold her like that for a long moment before disentangling herself and pulling a tissue out of her purse so she can dab at her damp eyes.

"Brett, this is my Dianne," Elise introduces us, stepping forward with her arm around the brunette's shoulders.

I extend a hand to Dianne, but she grabs me and hugs me. "Oh, you! I've seen you perform more times than I can count," she informs me with a squeeze that knocks the wind out of me. I think she might just have cracked a rib.

"Uh, really?" I'm not quite sure what to say to that. It sounds a little stalker-ish, actually. I guess Elise gets that feeling too, because she jumps in to elaborate.

"Over the years, we tried to see you whenever you were playing in town. We've seen you with your high school orchestra, with the McInnes Conservatory Orchestra and we even went to New York when you gave your senior recital."

"Wow, I had no idea. I wish I'd known. I would have liked to reunite with you a little sooner."

"Well, we're here now!" Dianne exclaims happily. "And, my dear, that young lady of yours, Maggie, what a doll! We've already made her promise that the two of you will come spend a little time with us over the summer."

Of course they love Maggie. Everyone loves Maggie. That is, with the notable exception of my brother. "Well, I hope you all enjoyed the concert," I say, hoping they'll take the hint and head home.

They don't.

"Brett, it was amazing. Absolutely beautiful!" exclaims Elise. "Oh, that piece, the trio, it was just mesmerizing!"

"I know," I smile. "I love to stand in the wings and watch them play it."

"That pretty little cellist is just superb," Dianne marvels. "I love the cello. Could we meet her? In fact, I'd love to meet all of your colleagues!"

No. Fucking. Way.

Not a snowball's chance in hell I'm letting them get within a hundred feet of Julia.

"You know what, I think they've probably all headed back to the hotel by now. Why don't you ladies just let me grab my viola and we can go get a bite to eat, okay? I'll come and meet you out front in five minutes."

I'm already turning away from them when my mother starts to follow. "Nonsense, Brett. You haven't been off the stage more than five minutes. I'm sure they must be back there somewhere, and who knows when I'll have this opportunity again? We'll go with you."

I guess hell just got a cold snap.

I know better than to argue with Trudy Corrigan about anything. Ever. So I lead them out of the backstage area to the long hallway with the dressing rooms, holding my breath that no one is hanging around. Meeting Joe and Phil and Ingo is one thing. Meeting Julia is another.

"You know, Mom, it really is possible they've left already. We all like to get out as soon as we can after a performance," I warn her, slowing down considerably, in hopes that this will actually be the case by the time we get there.

But Trudy knows me too well. "I'm quite sure they *will* be gone if you keep moving at a snail's pace, Brett," she quips as her heels click behind me down the hallway.

When we get to Joe's door, I rap gently, praying he'll keep them busy while I slip down the hall to Julia's dressing room. "Come in!" he calls from inside.

We do.

"Hey, Joe, have you got a sec? My family decided to surprise me tonight and they'd like to meet you."

He smiles broadly. Joe loves to play host. "Hello! I'm Joe Dancy. I play violin."

"We noticed!" Aunt Elise replies enthusiastically. They make their introductions and I inch closer to the door.

"Joe, I was just telling my mom how we like to get out of here fast after a concert. And that it's entirely possible the rest of the group has already—"

My sentence is interrupted by a high-pitched shriek from the hallway. It's followed by a small, mischievous laugh. *That* is followed by the sound of someone running in heels. There isn't even time to close the door before the tiny, redheaded tornado comes flying in and crashes into my legs.

"Unca!"

"Oh, my! Who's this?" my mother coos, slipping into kindergarten teacher mode.

Before I can say anything, she's squatting down to see him at eye level as he clings to my leg like a koala bear in a eucalyptus tree. He's being coy, hiding his face from her. Thankfully. Now, if I can just get him to stay this way ... It's a possibility ... until I hear Julia.

"David Matthew Ayers! You come back here this instant! You know better than to run away from mommy!" she's chiding him before she's even in the room with me. And with her son. And my mother.

Fuck. Fuck, fuck, fuck, fuck!

I watch helplessly as the rest of it unfolds in slow motion. David turns around at the sound of Julia's voice, but ends up running right into my mother, who is still squatting down. Instinctively, she scoops him up, and starts to return the wayward toddler to his mother.

Please, God. Please. Please. Please.

But apparently God isn't taking requests tonight—at least, not from me.

Julia doesn't realize who it is that's holding her child. She's not the least bit alarmed by the middle-aged woman with the kind eyes and the teacherly voice. Why should she be? David throws back his head and giggles as my mother stands up with him in her arms, bouncing him the whole way. It isn't until she is fully upright again that I see the briefest flicker of recognition cross her face.

"Unca!" David cries and stretches his arms toward me. He's squirming so hard to get to me that my mother passes him my way before he can jump right out of her hands. "Unca!" he repeats, patting the sides of my face with his hands. And then he twists around, so that he and I are both facing the same way, looking at my mother, side by side.

A dark cloud passes across her face, her gaze turning hard and withering.

Oh, shit.

I know this expression well, but this is the first time it's ever been leveled at me. This is the stare she saves for my brother.

The chill that settles on the room is so palpable that Joe decides this would be a good time to excuse himself. He holds out his arms toward

David and puts a big smile on his face for the boy. "Hey, David, buddy! Let's go find Nata!"

"Nata!" David parrots, blissfully unaware of the Pandora's Box he's just kicked open with his tiny high top sneakers.

"*Really*, Brett?" Mom spits once they've gone. "Is that what you were trying to keep us from seeing?" she demands, pointing to the door through which Joe and David have just left.

"I'm sorry," Julia breaks in quietly, "but I don't think I understand what's happening here."

"Julia, this is—"

"I'm his mother," my mother cuts back in with an off-handed gesture towards me.

Julia is frowning, her lips parted in a questioning 'O'. When it dawns on her what has just happened, her eyebrows shoot up into an alarmed arch.

"And, if I'm not mistaken," my mother continues, "I'm that little boy's grandmother."

She's staring at me, Julia's staring at her, and I'm staring at Julia. "Does Maggie know?" Mom asks.

"Does Maggie know what?"

"Don't play dumb with me, Brett. You're engaged to be married. Does your fiancée know you have a child with another woman? A woman who you're *clearly* still involved with?"

Now, she's dividing her glare between me and a dumbfounded Julia.

"*What?* What're you talking about, Mom?"

"You cannot, for a single second, have thought that I wouldn't recognize that little boy as a Corrigan."

Holy shit. Now I get it, and before I can help myself, I start to laugh. Not a short burst of laughter, either. This is that irrational, near hysterical laughter that consumes you when you realize you have stepped into a cluster fuck of epic proportions.

"You think this is funny?" she hisses at me. I nod, tears streaming down my face, even as her face grows redder with rage. "Brett! That is quite enough!"

Behind her, Elise and Dianne are wide-eyed. I guess they're getting more of a show than they bargained for. The thought of it sets me off again. I try to catch my breath and swipe at my wet face with the back of my sleeve.

"Oh, oh my God!" I gasp, trying to get myself under control. When, I manage, finally, to quash the unruly cackling, I look my mother square in the eye. "He's not *my* son, Mom," I insist with as straight a face as I can muster.

She's just about to lay into me, raising her index finger to poke me, the way she does when she's furious. Exactly the same way that Grandma Ruth did. But then she stops. She realizes what it is that I'm trying to tell her, and now it's her turn to look stunned. Finally, she shifts her attention to Julia, who looks as if she'd give anything to be crushed by a rogue asteroid at this very moment.

My mother's tone softens considerably. "He's yours and...*Jeremy's?*"

Tears have started to slip down Julia's face, too, but hers are definitely not tears of laughter. My mother pushes me aside gently and moves to stand in front of Julia. It's quite an extraordinary sight as Trudy uses her thumbs to wipe the tears from Julia's freckled face, the way that she did for me when I was a child. Then she opens her arms and pulls Julia into her.

"Shhhh. It's alright," I hear my mother murmur in her ear as Julia heaves with silent sobs. "It's alright, Dear. It's all going to be just fine."

Part Two

Chapter 11

Jeremy

If the Maestro had a grenade, the entire horn section would be nothing but a few scraps of metal and bone fragments right now. Luckily, he doesn't have a grenade. What he does have, however, is zero patience, a hair-trigger temper and a strong distaste for women in his orchestra.

Right now, he's standing at his podium, glaring at the empty first horn chair as a low-level buzz starts to spread through the audience behind him. They are, no doubt, wondering what the hell is going on. The orchestra is seated; the Maestro is on the podium. Why hasn't the concert started? From where I'm sitting, I can just make out the music critic for the Detroit Times Herald in his favorite box seat, leaning over the rail in front of him, watching us with interest.

I can hear the frantic clicking of Jennifer's heels backstage as she runs from stage right, all the way around the back behind the curtain to stage left. Finally, she comes out on stage, head bowed down as she shuffles to the horn section and drops into her seat. The expression on her face is a cross between bewilderment, embarrassment and horror. The Maestro hops down from his podium and walks to our section. Up close, his fury is even more evident by the bulging veins in his neck and temples. He's turning redder even as he stands here in front of our section.

Shit. This guy is starting to look like dear old dad did before he croaked.

"Where is your horn?" he hisses at Jennifer in his heavily accented English.

She shrugs and shakes her head in disbelief. "I don't know. It's gone. I'm sure I left it backstage, but it isn't there now. I—I think someone must have taken it."

He shakes his head at her disgustedly. Oh, this does not bode well for Jennifer. The ill-tempered conductor is recently off the boat from a very stuffy, old school, all-male orchestra in Europe. He isn't a fan of female musicians in general, and certainly not ones as young and pretty as Jennifer.

Ever since our misogynist maestro was hired in the spring, poor little Jenny has found herself defending her position as principal horn. He calls her out constantly, making rude and sexist remarks about her ability to play such a 'masculine' instrument. Once, he even suggested she must give an awful blowjob if her tonguing on the horn is any indication. I knew right then and there that he and I were going to get along very well, indeed.

Like I told Brett, I can't hold too much against Jennifer, though, because a lot of it isn't her fault. She's not nearly as good as I am. Even she has said as much. At twenty-one, she's fresh out of Juilliard. When she auditioned for the third horn spot, no one was more stunned than Jennifer was when they offered her principal instead. Just as no one was more stunned than I was when I auditioned for the principal spot and was handed third chair instead.

I was starting to think I was good and screwed when, one day, salvation showed up fresh off the boat in the form of our new conductor. Totally disinterested in orchestral politics, he just wants the best man for the job. And I do mean *man*.

Jennifer is crying now. This is just too much for our no-nonsense conductor. "You! Get off my stage right now!" he growls, pointing his baton at her. She sniffs, nods and scurries off stage, then the Maestro turns to me.

"You can play the part, yes?"

"Yes, Maestro," I assure him, taking Jennifer's vacated seat in an instant.

He returns to his elevated platform and raises his arms. He looks at me with the question in his arched brows. I take a deep breath and give him a slight nod that tells him I am ready. I have to be, because the first horn is the first thing that you hear in Maurice Ravel's haunting *Pavane for a Dead Princess.*

With the conductor's downbeat, my mellow tone rises above plucked strings. It is the sound of molten honey, rich and smooth, golden and opaque. It flows so effortlessly out of my horn... out of *me*, that you'd swear I'd been practicing the solo for weeks. Maybe that's because I have been.

When the piece has ended, the Maestro turns and bows to the audience, then he faces the orchestra again, gesturing to me. I stand, horn tucked under my arm, and give a quick bow from the horn section. The applause swells and I smile. If they liked that, wait till they hear what I've done with Jennifer's part in the Brahms.

* * *

It's well after midnight when I finally leave the hall, and well after everyone else has gone home for the night. I walk around the block and find the kid standing on the corner where I told him to meet me, hoodie covering his head and hands stuffed in his pockets as he hops up and down in the cold night air.

"Good job," I say when I reach him. "Where did you leave it?"

"In the dumpster on Jefferson, where you told me."

"Anyone see you?"

"Nah. Who notices a Chinese delivery boy on a bicycle in that part of town?"

Exactly. And who would ever think there was a five-thousand-dollar French horn in that insulated carrier on the back of his bike rather than containers of Kung Pao Chicken and egg rolls? Certainly none of the dozen or so musicians who ordered dinner in from Wong's Kitchen before the concert. The kid, Jimmy is his name, is at the hall so often that people have stopped noticing him. Security doesn't even look up when he rolls his bicycle through the backstage entrance and down the hall to our break room. Which just happens to be across from the warm-up room. Which just happens to be where Jennifer leaves her horn when she goes outside to call her boyfriend before every concert.

This shit is just Too. Fucking. Easy.

I pull a couple of bills out of my pocket. "Here's the hundred we agreed on. And a hundred to remind you that I can throw a lot of business your way, so long as you don't breathe a word of it to anyone. Ever."

The kid snatches the money from my hand excitedly. "No! No, man, thanks! I promise!"

"Alright. I know where to find you when I need you again," I inform him as I turn and leave him standing on the corner.

I'm sure it won't be long before I do.

Chapter 12

Jeremy

The article that comes out in the Sunday Arts section is a glowing half-page tribute to the orchestra's new and improved sound under its new and improved conductor. There's mention of a *'brief and puzzling delay from within the horn section'* but goes on to note *'whatever held up the horns was well worth the wait. Jeremy Corrigan's hauntingly beautiful solo in the Ravel was matched only by his blistering heat in the Brahms.'*

I'm reading it for the twentieth time when the orchestra director, Doug Lavery, comes into his office and takes a seat behind his desk. There was a message that he wanted to see me first thing this morning. Probably wants to congratulate me on Saturday night's performance.

"This is a great review," I state, not bothering to look up at him. He doesn't respond. "Don't you think?" I prompt, raising my gaze this time.

He's watching me with disdain etched clearly across his face. "Jeremy, I'm afraid I'm going to have to let you go."

I don't think I've heard him correctly. "I'm sorry, what did you say?"

"We know you had something to do with Jennifer's horn disappearing. If you leave quietly, there won't be any reason to get the police involved. We'll cover the cost of her instrument, and no one will press charges. But I want you gone *today*, Jeremy."

I stare at him incredulously. "What the hell are you talking about? I just scored you the best review this orchestra has had in five years! I saved your ass when that teenage twit you hired misplaced her instrument three minutes before a concert. And you want to *fire* me? Are you out of your fucking mind?"

He just gives me his weaselly smile. "Quite the contrary. I've just been waiting for you to pull a stunt like this so I can throw you out of our orchestra. I don't care how good you are, or how much the Maestro likes you. You're nothing but a thug. And, if I'm not mistaken, a murderer, too. I want you out."

This guy has no idea who he's messing with. Does he honestly think that I'm going to let him do this to me? "You can't fire me," I declare defiantly. "I have a contract."

"Oh, but I am firing you, Jeremy—that is, unless you want me to start a criminal investigation. And something tells me the police will look at you a little harder this time around." The pretentious fuck leans forward across his desk and surveys me over the top of his glasses.

"But you know what? I'm feeling generous. In addition to not pursuing an investigation, we'll pay out your salary for the next six months. There isn't a better deal to be had, so I suggest you take it. I mean, if another orchestra were to get a whiff of your latest stunt, you wouldn't even be able to get a gig *selling tickets* at the..." He flips open a file folder on his desk, runs his finger down a page within and looks up again. "At the Owl Bridge Symphony. That's the little piss-ant town where you're from isn't it? Owl Bridge, Illinois?"

"You did *not* run a background check on me," I hiss. He just smiles at me. "You'll never get away with this. Between my attorney and the union rep—"

Now he waves a hand at me dismissively. "Your lawyer can try whatever he wants, but I think you'll find the Union of American Orchestral Musicians to be less than sympathetic to your cause."

"Well, it seems you've thought of just about everything."

He looks proud of himself. "I had to. You may have cheated your way into this orchestra, but there's no way I'm going to allow you to sully its reputation with your sordid behavior. Take the deal, Jeremy," he repeats.

When the rage comes, it is always the same. It washes over me like a rogue wave out in the ocean. I never see it, but I know the instant it hits me. My jaw clenches and my heart starts to beat faster. I can feel the thump of my pulse up in my temples. My face grows hot and my hearing becomes dull. I develop tunnel vision and, what I do focus on, unfolds in slow motion.

Right now, all I can see is this asshole's gloating face. The necktie that makes the folds of his flabby neck spill over his collar. The greasy strands combed over his bald spot. The hair sprouting from his ears and nose. I stand up, reach over his desk and pull him forward by that ugly, soup-stained tie, until he is splayed out and choking. I use my free hand to pull a photograph off the desk and stick it into his face.

"Oh, look! It's your daughter, Denise. She likes to take those late night runs, doesn't she? I've seen her a few times. She starts out east on Lake Street then she cuts through the Michigan Avenue Park and runs down along the canal before heading back home. Gosh, I hope she's careful. A woman out alone like that could get herself gang raped. How horrible that would be!"

Doug is shaking his head while he wheezes. I toss the framed photo to the floor and the glass shatters. There's a second picture. I pick this one up, look at it, and again shove it into his reddening face.

"Your wife, Claire. Does she know you've got a taste for the kink Doug? Because I do! And guess what? I happen to have some photos of my own. Oh, they're not in pretty ceramic frames like this one, and your rent-a-dominatrix doesn't look as sophisticated as your wife does here. But, then again, who looks sophisticated when they're using a riding crop on a fat, bald guy tied to a bed in a hotel room? Gotta admit, I didn't know you had it in you!"

Over my shoulder goes the second frame with a crash. I loosen up my grasp long enough for him to gulp in some air. I don't want the son of a bitch passing out on me.

"You listen to me and you listen good, Dougy boy. I will leave this orchestra when I am good. And. Ready. And on the terms that *I*, not you, set. I expect to be promoted to principal horn in the next week, which shouldn't be an issue, considering Jennifer's recent ... incident Are you hearing me, Doug?"

"Yes," he wheezes.

"Good. Very good, Doug. Because, here's the thing. Anyone, and I mean anyone, who tries to fuck with my career again is just asking to put the people he or she loves in jeopardy. Make no mistake about it, my friend, I don't give a shit about your kids, or your wife, or your ancient mother in Kalamazoo. I will kill your entire fucking family, including your Irish Setter and that stupid three-legged cat you have. Do you understand me, Doug?"

He nods, unable to speak as he starts to sob. I let go of his tie and give him a rough shove back into his chair behind the desk. "Oh, boohoo. What a fucking pussy you are. I just want to be sure we are clear on these points, Doug. Are we clear?"

"Yes!" he blubbers. "Yes, I swear, I'll do whatever you want. Please don't hurt my family!"

I smile and take a deep, satisfied breath. The rage has passed, and I am in control once again. "Good! Now you should get yourself cleaned up. Looks like you had a little ... accident there," I mock as I point to the wet spot on the front of his pants. "You have a long afternoon ahead of you, figuring out how to demote Jennifer and getting a press announcement out about my promotion. And don't forget the bump in salary that comes with that, Doug. I'll be looking for that in my next paycheck."

He nods, wiping his face with the back of his shirtsleeve.

I walk out of his office with the newspaper tucked under my arm and close the door behind me. His assistant, Lisa, looks up from her computer, watching me with interest.

"Everything okay in there?" she asks, tilting her head toward the office I have just exited.

"Oh, yeah, just fine," I assure her with a wave of my hand, continuing on toward the door. I stop just short of the threshold and look back at her over my shoulders. "But...I'd maybe hold his calls for a while," I suggest with a wink.

Chapter 13

Jeremy

"Oh my God! The look on his face must have been hilarious!" Lisa giggles as she lays naked on her stomach in my bed.

"Yeah, it was pretty spectacular," I chuckle. "I wish I'd had a camera. How long did it take for Doug to come out of there after I left?"

I'm lying on my side, running my hands up and down from her bare back, to her perfect ass and back again. She kicks her long legs up playfully. "It was nearly two hours. And when he finally did come out, he was holding his jacket in front of him. He couldn't even look at me! He just mumbled something about not feeling well and going home for the rest of the day."

She rolls onto her side so we are facing one another. The thing about Lisa is that she's a '*Butter Face*.' No, she doesn't have greasy skin. It's what they call a girl who has a hot body, but an ugly face. In other words everything '*But her face*' is attractive. She has a large nose that looks as if it's been broken in one too many bar fights. Her brow is extremely pronounced, giving her a kind of Cro-Magnon look. Add to that a forehead that you could park a jetliner on, and you've got Lisa. It's too bad, really. A little investment in plastic surgery and she could be a seven or an eight. As it stands, her body alone gets her a six, but then you have to subtract four points for the face. Two. I'm in bed with a two.

The things I do to get what I want.

"Jeremy, I'm sorry," she interrupts my thoughts. "I didn't know he was going to do that. There was no mention of it at the board meeting last week. I mean I knew they were trying to get rid of you, but I didn't know it would be like this. Today."

She should be sorry. Thanks to her, I walked right into a fucking ambush. But I can't afford to cut her loose just yet.

"Don't worry about it," I say as I reach over and brush the bangs from the tarmac/forehead. "What's important is what Doug does in the next couple of days. Keep your eyes out for a press release about my promotion, approval for an increase in my pay, and Jennifer's demotion. You'll have access to all that paperwork, won't you?"

"What's it worth to you, big guy?" She smiles suggestively.

"Oh, I think I can make it worth your while," I murmur, closing the distance between our bodies.

"So soon? My, my, Mr. Corrigan, you've got some impressive stamina!" she murmurs, meeting me halfway.

"It's just my *hard* work ethic," I reply just before I take her mouth in mine. I groan involuntarily when I feel her hand on my cock.

"*Very* hard work ethic, I'd say." Lisa chuckles again as she gives me alternating squeezes and strokes. Damn. This girl knows her way around the equipment. Okay, I'll play.

I roll onto my back, flag at full mast, and she follows me across to my side of the bed, starting a trail of soft kisses at my left shoulder and making her way down, down, down. When she reaches her destination, she looks up at me with a dirty little smile. Did I mention her teeth are yellowed, too? Before I can comment, her tongue wraps around me like warm, wet velvet. I arch with the contact and close my eyes.

If I don't have to look at her, I can pretend she's the freshman horn student who took home a sample of my DNA along with an autographed program as a souvenir from our last concert. Yeah. That's who I'm going think about. Lisa licks me gently from stem to stern, building tension little by little. Then, when I think I'm going to have to just flip her over and fuck her to get some relief, she has me in her mouth with the suction of a Hoover vac.

"Fuck, baby, that's good," I moan, getting my hands into her hair. I ball my fists and use it to direct her back and forth, up and down.

She takes every direction immediately. When I feel the nibble of her teeth on me, I literally see stars. And then, her hands are in the mix, cupping my balls, squeezing the bottom of my shaft. Oh, yeah. Easily the best blowjob I've had since Brett's girlfriend blew me in high school. And that was more about screwing him than her.

I'd have banged Lisa even if she'd been some middle-aged cow in spandex. Not because I wanted to, but because I needed to. The key to manipulating Doug is manipulating the person who holds all of Doug's keys. Literally, and figuratively. As his assistant, Lisa is privy to every meeting. She can eavesdrop on any phone call. She sees every bit of paperwork that comes across his desk and has access to the personnel files of every musician in the orchestra. It also works to my advantage that she can't stand Doug, who's done nothing but try and cop a feel since the day he hired her. She's only too happy to stick it to him by letting me stick it to her. Sounds like a win-win to me.

Chapter 14

Jeremy

MUDERER

The word is written in six-inch block letters on my locker at the concert hall. No one says anything as I stand there staring at it, but I can feel the darting glances of my colleagues behind me. I pull out my horn and music and make my way out to the stage for rehearsal without comment. When I arrive at the first horn spot, there's a piece of paper taped to the music stand with the same handwriting, this time spelling out the word thief. I don't bother to tear it down, just put my music folder over it and pull out the Mahler Symphony we're working on today.

"It was there when I sat down," volunteers Graham, our second horn player. "I—I wasn't sure if I should take it down before you saw it..."

"Doesn't bother me," I mumble before putting my horn to my lips and starting my run of scales.

While I play, my eyes move across the rows of musicians around me. I don't think it's any of the string players. They're just too absorbed in their own little world to be concerned with what goes on behind them. That knocks out about half the orchestra right there. It might be a woodwind player, but something tells me I should be looking at the brass players sitting all around me.

I use my peripheral vision to check out Jennifer, now situated down in the third horn chair. She has a brand new horn already, and she looks relaxed for a change—confident even. She may or may not think I had something to do with the disappearance of her instrument, but she's gotten a better one out of the deal and is finally playing the part she wanted all along.

I'm sure I can rule out the other two horns in our section, Graham on second and Latondra on fourth. They do a pretty good job of staying out of the drama—horn players are smart that way. Trombone players not so much. That's where my money is.

Still ripping up and down the scales, I angle to the right just enough to catch two of the trombone players with their heads together, looking my way and snickering. Gus and Terrance. That would be them. Fucking cowards are too chicken shit to accuse me to my face, so they hide behind their music stands like a couple of gossiping teenagers.

The Concert Master stands up to face the orchestra and gives the first oboe the nod to give us an A to tune to. A few moments later, the Maestro comes out and sits down on the podium, reading glasses on as he examines the score in front of him.

"All right," he begins, looking up at us. "We have a great deal of work to do on this Mahler. Horns, there are two extras coming in for the rehearsal this afternoon. They will fill out the section for the concert. Jeremy, I leave it to you to arrange rehearsals for your section. Yes?"

"Yes, Maestro," I agree loud and clear.

From behind me, one of the trombone players gives a loud, fake sneeze that comes out sounding a lot like the word *'Thief!'* I ignore it, and the Maestro doesn't catch it.

"Also, Jeremy, I think I would like the entire horn section to stand for the last two minutes or so of the symphony. That will require all parts to be memorized. This is possible, yes?"

"Yes, Maestro," I repeat.

The sneezer repeats, too, but now with the word *'Murderer!'* as the underlying expletive. This time, the Maestro notices. He takes his glasses off and puts them down on the stand in front of him, peering back to the lower brass section.

"Who is the sneezer?" he growls. It takes us all a few seconds to translate. In his accent the question sounds more like *'who eest zee shneeza?'*

Gus raises a hand slowly.

"Stand up," the Maestro demands. Gus gets to his feet, very reluctantly. I would be reluctant, too. This guy looks pissed.

"You tink dis eesht funny? You tink you are in da kindergarten, yes?"

"Yes. I mean, No! N-no, Maestro," Gus splutters, his face coloring.

"You are zee professional und you vill act as one, or I vill call one of my players from Vienna to take your seat. Yes?"

"Yes, Maestro."

After the rehearsal, I lock up my horn in the defaced locker and make a point of walking past Gus and Terrance. When I stop in front of them, they look up from where they are packing their instruments.

"You know, you're such fucking pussies," I spit as I shake my head at them. "If you want to say something, just say it to my face. But if you insist on taking a page out of the Junior High School Playbook, then at least own it. Jesus Christ. Grow some balls already, will you?"

I walk away before either of them can comment, smiling all the way out the backstage door. Where young Jimmy Woo is waiting for me. My smile heads south, and fast.

"What are you doing here?" I hiss at him, motioning for him to follow me around the corner and into the alley.

"Jeremy, man, I'm in trouble," he whispers.

"What? What happened?"

I'm getting the feeling that his trouble is about to become my trouble.

"It's that horn, man. Someone pulled it out of the dumpster and tried to pawn it."

"*What?*"

He starts speaking quickly, nervously. "Yeah! Someone found it, pawned it, and I guess it was reported stolen."

I take a deep breath and try to stay calm. "Alright. So, what does this have to do with you?"

"My fingerprints were on it."

"And why would that matter?" I'm still not getting what the runt is trying to tell me.

He looks down at his sneakers and then up at me again. "A couple years ago, I got pinched for shoplifting. The police have my fingerprints and they matched them to the horn."

Goddammit! Stupid little shit should have told me he had a record. And what the fuck was he thinking, not wearing gloves? Christ! Does *anyone* besides me have any common sense? I close my eyes in a concerted effort to not strangle this kid. Breathe in. Breathe out. Breathe in...

"Jeremy, the police came around the restaurant asking questions. I got out of there before they could see me. But they're looking for me now, man, and I don't know what to do. You've got to help me!" His eyes are wide with the desperation I can hear in his voice.

"Okay, so you haven't spoken with anyone yet? Is that what you're telling me?"

He shakes his head no. Okay. I can work with this. I put my hands on his shoulders and make certain his eyes are locked on mine. We're going to walk this thing back.

"Jimmy, you just need to tell them that you moved the horn when you brought in the food order. It was in your way and you set it aside. They can't prove anything else. You're in that building all the time. It's not a stretch that your fingerprints would be on an instrument."

"Do you think they'll believe that?" he asks skeptically.

They' better, you little shit.

"I do," I reassure him. "You just act surprised that they would even ask you. The last time you saw the horn, you had moved it over a few inches so you could sort out the dinner orders for the musicians backstage. And, if they start to press, you start yelling about racial profiling. '*Sure, blame the Chinese kid!*' That kind of shit. Do you think you can pull it off?" I ask, looking for any sign of weakness in his eyes.

He takes a deep breath in and nods. "Yeah. Yeah, I can do that Jeremy. I'm sorry, man, I was just...I was just scared, and I didn't know what to do."

"You did the right thing coming to me first. But remember, Jimmy no matter what they offer, or threaten, my name never comes up. *Never* Do you understand me?"

I see the fear return as he stares into my face, which I have made into an icy mask. He should be scared. I can do a lot more to him than the police can.

He nods again, more enthusiastically this time. "I do. I understand.

Jeremy. You didn't have nothing to do with this shit. No matter what. I swear."

My expression thaws, and I reward him with a smile and a playful punch on the shoulder. "Excellent! You're going to get through this just fine, Jimmy. And I promise I will make it worth your while on the back end."

Unless, of course, you fuck this up, and then my punches won't be so playful anymore.

Chapter 15

Jeremy

After my glowing review in the paper, there's an uptick of sales for the Detroit Philharmonic. I peek out into the hall from backstage and see that the hall, usually two-thirds full, is near capacity tonight. I smile. This is for me. Mahler One is nothing, if not an homage to the French horn section. And I am the center of that universe.

So, we play and the audience sits. Through the Mendelssohn Overture. Through the Grieg Concerto. And then, there is the main event. They don't call this symphony *'The Titan'* for nothing. The normal complement of orchestral forces wasn't powerful enough, as far as Mahler was concerned, so he added parts for extra performers in the wind, brass and percussion sections. We all cram onto the stage of the performance hall. It's tight ... but it's so worth the discomfort when we get to the last movement, where the composer decided to pull out all the stops.

The crash of cymbals that opens the finale of Mahler's First Symphony is like the crack of a starter pistol. From that instant, the orchestra takes off and never looks back. The strings take on a frenetic pace, just barely in control as their bows are a blur of sound and motion.

But it's the brass that owns this movement. Alternating fanfares bounce between the horns and the trumpets, with lower brass providing a solid core of support. The trumpets blare so powerfully that they are a hair's breadth away from distorting. It's the most sound the instrument can produce at the highest possible volume, without the whole thing splintering apart.

The horns whoop. The timpani is beating, beating, beating its pounding pulse. It's the heartbeat of the orchestra. Underneath, the strings continue their dizzying, spinning spiral, their bows moving impossibly fast. A brief soft section provides a reprieve. It's an eerie cloud of discord. The horns slip in, unnoticed, at first, then growing more prominent until they are the solid, crystalline core of the orchestra. The trumpets punctuate periodically in a distant echo.

Wind chimes tinkle, adding to the ethereal mood, but not for long before the race is on again, and we are running toward an invisible finish line. The final lap comes in the last seventy-six measures of the movement. For two minutes, the brass blasts, the strings bow and percussion pounds.

This is when we stand. All six horn players, spread across an entire row of the stage with the bells of our instruments raised high, just as Mahler indicated in the score. He wanted to get the largest possible sound out of the horns, and tonight we do his memory proud. The strings sound as if they are swinging from note to note beneath us as we produce a powerhouse of brilliant, brassy sound. The kind of music that produces a physical reaction in the human body, raising goose bumps, sending chills and causing the heart to actually beat faster.

The timpani rolls and rolls.

Now, in these final seconds, the Maestro is only conducting the first beat of each measure, his head tilted back, his eyes closed. And then, he looks up at me, and he nods. That's the signal. Suddenly, we are streaming fire right out of our bells and into the concert hall. Rip-roaring licks spill effortlessly out of me, and my section. This is a hymn. No, it's an anthem. This is the sound of victory. When, at last, we have reached the last note, he throws down his baton, and his hand shoots up in a triumphant fist above his head.

The audience explodes.

* * *

Lisa is standing by my locker when I get there. She must have been waiting a while because it's taken me some time to pack up and get past the throng of well-wishers from the orchestra. Funny how one minute you're a murderer, and the next you're a hero. Not that I give a fuck either way.

"Come to congratulate me?" I ask her with a suggestive smirk.

She blushes as she wrings her hands nervously. "I wish. No, Jeremy, it's Doug. He sent me to give you a message. I got the feeling he was a little too scared to talk to you himself."

I set my horn case down on the floor and stand directly in front of her. I lean over her, bracing my arm on the lockers above her. We are so close that I can smell her shampoo.

"Okay, I'm listening. What does that chicken shit want now?"

"You need to be in the fourth-floor conference room on Monday morning at ten sharp. And you should bring an attorney with you."

I take my arm down, stand up straight and take a step back so I can get a good look at her. Playtime is over. "And why is that?" As my tone sharpens, she suddenly looks very nervous. As she should. "*Why?*" I demand again, more forcefully. That does the trick.

"He w-wouldn't tell me, Jeremy b-but...but I think you're being fired," she quavers.

I smile and pick up my case, not bothering with the locker anymore. "Yeah, we'll fucking see about that."

Chapter 16

Jeremy

The smell of French Roast draws me out of my dreams, and back into my bedroom, where the morning sun is fighting its way around the window shades. I stretch and feel the dull ache of too much repetitive motion—namely, belting Lisa. You see this shit in porn and they make it look so easy. But in truth, the reality of this kind of activity comes with a physical price tag including bruises and scratches and sore, aching muscles. Of course, for some, that's part of the fun. When I make my way to the kitchen, I find Lisa looking way too comfortable in one of the button-down shirts from my closet, sitting at my table, reading my newspaper.

"Good morning, sexy! Would you like a cup of coffee?"

She gestures to the fresh pot, which woke me.

"Sure. I take just a little milk," I say, having a seat.

I look around me and notice that the glass shards have been swept up and the walls cleaned of the sticky beer remnants that I hurled onto them last night. The books that were a jumble on the living room floor have also been returned, nice and neat, to their shelves.

"You cleaned up."

"You noticed!" she smiles, then turns more serious. "I guess you had a pretty rough day yesterday, huh?"

"To say the fucking least," I grumble.

"Well, everyone's talking about it, Jeremy. A lot of the musician's think you were railroaded. Of course, there are some jerks who say you had it coming. I was so angry that I just marched right into Doug's office. I didn't even have his coffee or his messages or anything! I told him he was a fool and that you were the only hope this orchestra has for revitaization and that letting you go was going to haunt him the rest of his career. I told him if he was smart, he'd reverse the decision immediately before you got snatched up by another orchestra."

My brows go up in amusement. "And what was his response?"

Her face hardens in anger. "Oooooo! He made me so furious, Jeremy. That jerk told me if I didn't like his decision then, I should leave, too. So I did."

"You did what?"

"I left."

"Left to come here?"

She smiles. "No, silly! Well, yes, sort of, but I mean I quit and then I came straight here."

"Huh..."

"But, don't you worry about a thing, Jeremy! God, I'm so sorry this happened to you ... but I've got a plan..."

She can barely suppress a giddy smile. My head throbs just looking at it. And her.

"Oh? And what's that?"

"Well, I've already been putting out feelers on openings in other horn sections around the country. A few of the orchestras have administrative openings, too. How great would it be if we could find work together? So, I figured I could maybe help you get your resume together and start making some calls..."

I sit there, without comment, and take a sip of the coffee in my hand.

"Jeremy?"

The smile freezes and then slips from Lisa's horsey face as she realizes I'm not nearly as excited about this as she is. Finally, after a long moment, I turn around behind me and start to pour some more coffee into my cup, speaking to her the whole time.

"Well, hey, thanks for the solidarity, Lisa, and for providing me with all the information I needed to fuck with Dougy." I turn back around to face her. "And, hey, thanks for the terrific fuck last night. I hope you enjoyed it, too because, unfortunately for you, I won't be needing your services anymore. But hey, you've got a real knack for the blowjob. You might want to consider a job in the sex industry."

Her face has gone deathly pale and her lips are trembling.

"Anyway, I've got to take a shower. I'd appreciate it if you were gone by the time I'm done."

She's still staring after me as I leave the kitchen, coffee cup in hand, whistling Mozart.

Chapter 17

Jeremy

You can break many men with psychological torture. You can break most men with physical torture. But, in both these instances, you should keep in mind that the human body has an amazing capacity for self-preservation. It's just a matter of time before the individual either regresses into a dissociative state or loses consciousness in order to protect himself from the ongoing trauma.

Okay, what if you want to avoid those little physiological loopholes? What if your goal is not to manipulate or to extract information, but rather, simply, to inflict as much pain as possible. In this instance, because you have no material motive, there is nothing that the victim can offer up in exchange for relief. There is no amount of begging or bargaining that might convince you to spare him or her. In this instance, you are only governed by your own weakness, your capacity for mercy. If such a thing exists in you on any level, you aren't wired for this sort of activity.

So, let's assume you have the constitution to execute this scenario. How do you proceed, if not using the old standby's like sleep deprivation, beatings or electric shocks? The answer is easier... and closer than you might imagine. As close as the people who surround us every day. What most people fail to realize is that we are most vulnerable through the people we love. As much as a target may be able to endure, as resilient or determined or brave he happens to be, there is absolutely no relief from the agonizing knowledge that someone close to you is in pain *because* of you.

Simply put, the most effective method for destroying a man's psyche, by far, is to cause his loved ones to suffer on his behalf, with no ability to assuage their torture. It's not just the knowledge that your loved one is in trouble, it's the knowledge that she is suffering, and you are helpless to do anything about it. Spouses, children, parents and even pets make a person vulnerable. I keep this forefront in my mind as I start to assemble a plan.

I've been slowly boiling in my rage since I left for Detroit. It was a fine gig, but it wasn't the one I wanted. I should have had my pick of any job in the country. I should be the youngest tenured faculty member at Juilliard by now. It should be *me* with the new CD and touring schedule. Julia and Matthew stole my life and I'm going to make them pay for it.

The first item on my list is anonymity. It won't do to have someone from McInnes spotting me on the subway and calling Julia. So, I find my way to one of those swank salons downtown where I tell the girl with the purple hair, pierced eyebrow and nose ring, that I want a whole new look.

She seems to get what I'm after and assures me my own mother won't recognize me by the time we're done. So, I sit still as she paints paste onto my hair and wraps it in tin foil. When she unwraps me a half hour later, she launches an assault with tiny, sharp scissors. I'm starting to feel like a fucking topiary by the time she's finished cutting. But if I thought that was going to be it, I was wrong. She blasts my face with a hairdryer strong enough to peel the paint off the walls, brushing my hair this way and that. Back and forth and back again. She follows it up with a straight-razor shave.

At last, she stands there staring at me and nodding her approval of my new look. "You ready to see it?"

"I guess," I mutter unenthusiastically.

The stylist spins the chair around so I can see the 'new' me in the mirror. And I'll be fucking damned. This little girl has brought my dark brown hair to a much lighter shade, threaded with golden highlights. My usually shaggy-but-neat haircut has been tailored into a style that looks professional without being stuffy. I can't stop staring at myself. I should have done this years ago. I give her a big tip and take her card for the next time I need to hide in plain sight.

The next item is proximity. I have to be close to my targets in order to study them, so I close up my Detroit house and take a ridiculously overpriced sublet close to the Strathmore Building in New York, where Julia and Matthew live most of the time. I have cleared the big white wall in the studio and covered it with large swaths of butcher's paper. This is where it all begins, my blueprint for revenge, my declaration of war. I call it my War Wall.

With the help of a private detective, I have a glossy stack of candid photos of Julia, Matthew, Brett and Maggie as they make their rounds throughout the city. They were easy enough to track and capture on film. The nanny, though, she's another story, though. Natalie Hughes gave my PI quite a workout as she pushed that goddam stroller all over midtown, in subways and taxis, on the LIRR. She takes the brat to any of a dozen different parks all over Manhattan, never visiting the same one twice in a row.

I affix the pictures of all of them on the wall with notations about their schedules underneath. I have the rehearsal, touring and concert calendars for both the Walton String Quartet, which covers Julia and Brett, and the Gotham Chamber Players, which takes care of Matthew. Where the two ensembles overlap in their schedules is where I can find Miss Natalie Hughes.

Okay. Time to get boots on ground.

* * *

I'm all for a leggy bitch but this girl is ridiculously tall. At least it makes it easier to track her as she pushes the stroller through midtown Manhattan. This is the third time I've followed her, and my PI was right, she never does the same thing twice. Different parks. Different museums. Different parts of town. When she's not working, Nanny Natalie shares an apartment with two other girls in the Flatiron District. And when she's not at home, she's in the law library at NYU. Now, as I sidle up to the bench she is sitting on, I realize she's quite attractive. Maybe this won't be so difficult after all.

"Which one is yours?" I inquire, taking the empty spot next to her.

She gives me a sidelong glance that lasts so long I'm convinced she recognizes me. I'm sure Julia and Matthew have prepped her with pictures of me. But then the long moment passes, and she points to the sandbox.

"Little Carrot Top, over there."

My eyes follow her finger to the child grabbing fistfuls of sand and cramming them into a bright yellow pail. I can't help but notice how much bigger he's gotten since the day I held him in the hospital.

"He's cute," I mention casually. "How old?"

"Toddler going on teenager," she replies vaguely. "Is that one yours?"

She's pointing to a boy in denim overalls. I saw her talking to that one's mother earlier, so she knows damn well the kid's not mine. Obviously, it's a test. Smart girl. But I'm smarter.

"No. I'm waiting for my ex to drop off our daughter," I say and glance at my watch. "She's late, as usual."

She nods but doesn't offer comment.

"Nata! Nata!" the brat yelps from the sandbox as he holds up a plastic shovel for her to see. She smiles at him and waves.

"Nata?" I wonder with some curiosity.

"His version of Natalie."

I fake a chuckle.

"Nice to meet you, Natalie. I'm Kyle," I offer.

She gives me a curt smile and a nod of acknowledgement, but nothing more. Damn, she's a tough nut to crack. I don't think my *Plan A*, hitting on her, is going to fly. Time to move to *Plan B*.

"Hey," I say, as if just thinking of something, "I've been looking for someone to have play dates with my Kyla. She's about the same age as your little guy, maybe we could arrange to get them together sometime?"

Natalie turns to face me fully now, and I can feel her taking an inventory of every square inch of my features. "Why don't you give me your phone number and I'll clear it with his parents?" she suggests.

It's a reasonable request, and one that I wouldn't think twice about if it were coming from anyone other than this bitchy baby bodyguard. It's plain enough to see that she's suspicious, and I'm certain she just wants to get my fingerprints or DNA for some CSI shit. Not gonna happen, baby.

"I was thinking of something more casual, just some sandbox time. Are you here every Tuesday?"

She smiles and stands up, preparing the stroller for action.

"Sometimes. We'll keep an eye out for you and...I'm sorry, what did you say your son's name was?"

Nice try, bitch. "Daughter," I smile up at her. "Her name is Kyle, after me, Kyle."

"Sweet," she says without a hint of sincerity. "We'll see you around, *Kyle.*"

Within a matter of seconds, she has the kid out of the sandbox, strapped into the stroller and sucking on a bottle.

"Yes, you will," I mutter as I watch them roll down the path and out towards 59th street.

Part Three

Chapter 18

Julia

MANIFESTO

I used to be painfully shy, hiding in the shadows. I used to be silent, watching as the rest of the world went by. I used to be scared, scurrying from place to place, like a tiny mouse, praying not to be seen. I used to be lonely and lost and confused. But I am none of those things anymore, and I haven't been for some time.

It's nothing short of miraculous, the instantaneous transformation that occurs when you bring a child into this world. Suddenly, hiding is not an option. Nor is silence. You no longer have the luxury of fear or insecurity. Because your job—your *sole* job on the face of this earth—is to love and nurture that helpless little soul who sleeps so innocently under the blanket of your protection.

Not so very long ago, a charming and handsome man came into my life. He swept me off my feet, showering me with love like I'd never known ... like I'd always longed for. There was passion and fire, laughter and tears...and it all seemed so real. But it wasn't. What *was* real was the pain that came from his intentional cruelty, practiced manipulation and carefully orchestrated abandonment. What was real were the smoking, crumbling, ruins of my life after he'd decimated it.

But he left something behind in that wreckage ... my son. And, with the birth of that child came the rebirth of his mother, a strong, confident woman who stands in the light and raises her voice. A woman who loves and is loved as wholly and completely as any person on this earth could be. A woman who is not afraid to go up against the evil of this world and toe-to-toe with the force that created it.

Get thee behind me Satan, or you're going to be sorry. Because I am not afraid anymore. Because I will descend into the depths of hell itself to protect that which is mine. Because I love and I *am* loved and there is no greater weapon than that.

Chapter 19

Julia

The day I met Natalie Hughes, I was interviewing six nanny candidates. She wasn't one of them. David was four months old then, and I was desperate for some help. So, in they marched to our apartment in the city and our home on Long Island. It was an incredibly varied pool of applicants, ranging from a very mature eighteen-year-old, fresh out of high school and looking to start her life, to a very youthful seventy-three-year-old, fresh out of the convent and looking to reinvent hers. And, while all of the final six candidates were ready, willing and able, there was just something missing. Something I couldn't put my finger on until that afternoon in the coffee shop.

On a particularly lovely afternoon, I packed up my boy, put him in the stroller and wheeled him out through Lincoln Center, around the Revson Fountain a few times and to a coffee shop a couple of blocks away. I'd often noticed the striking young barista—at nearly six feet tall, she was hard to miss. But it wasn't just that. She had a calm easiness about her.

On that particular afternoon, I ordered my coffee at the counter and then rolled the stroller to the other end to wait for it. The girl gave me a bright smile and a nod, offering David a quick wave. I was exchanging texts with Matthew a few minutes later when she yelled so loudly that I jumped.

"STOP!"

Her unexpected demand was so forceful that we did just that; all of us. Every single person in the shop stood perfectly still as all eyes swung to the barista. I looked at her, perplexed, but it took just a split second to see what she saw. There was this man. His back was to me. He had been speaking with his companion, walking backwards with a piping hot cup of coffee in one hand, uncovered, as his other hand felt for a sugar packet behind him. To my horror, the entire scene unraveled in my imagination. One more step backward and he'd have tripped over the stroller, causing a shower of scalding hot coffee to rain down on my child.

Even as she was preparing several coffees at once, listening to the incoming orders, and acknowledging the customers, Natalie Hughes spotted the potential danger in progress. With one single word, she commanded two-dozen people to stop dead in their tracks. Any other action—saying a polite 'excuse me, Sir' or 'watch out' or trying to get the guy's attention would likely have gone unnoticed by him—at least for that single, irrevocable step—and the results would have been catastrophic. But the one word, uttered with such force, commanded us all and suspended time for the one brief second she needed to keep my son out of harm's way.

I realized in that instant what it was I couldn't put my finger on with any of the other candidates. I wanted the person who would, in the midst of all the chaos around her, never lose sight of David and the potential dangers all around him. I wanted the woman with the sharp instincts and lightning quick reflexes, coupled with the confidence to trust and use them both.

Ten minutes later, she was on her break and sitting across from me at one of the tables. I discovered she was the only girl in a large family. Along with her father, all five of her brothers were police officers. Her father had raised her to be street smart and hyper-aware of her surroundings. She was taking a year off after undergrad to study for her LSATs. All she wanted was a job that would pay her enough to live, while affording her the flexibility and the time to study.

She didn't have references from any of the best families on the upper eastside, nor did she have a degree in early childhood education. She wasn't fluent in three languages and she hadn't attended Wellesley.

But I knew then and there that she was exactly the right person. She was the one who would keep my son safe.

"So, what was it about him that gave you a bad feeling?" I ask now as I wrap my long red hair into rollers the size of coke cans. David is down for a nap in the nursery and Natalie is sitting cross-legged on my bed, folding one of his dinosaur t-shirts.

She shrugs. "I don't really know. Instinct, I suppose."

"You said he had a daughter..."

"That's what *he* said," she corrects. "That he was waiting for his ex to drop her off."

"But, you never saw the ex-wife or the kid?"

She shakes her head and pulls a sweatshirt out of the laundry basket. This one has Spiderman on it.

"Julia, I don't know why, but the guy ... he just gave me the creeps. It was the way he was looking at David. He was being subtle, but he was definitely trying to pump me for information. At first he was all charming and a little flirty. Then, when he realized I wasn't interested, he tried to sell me on the play date thing."

"Okay," I say thoughtfully, moving on to my make-up. "Have you ever seen this guy before? At the park? Or anywhere else?"

"Well, not exactly." she says, pausing her folding for a moment.

I freeze my blush brush long enough to look at her in the mirror behind me.

"I know we haven't met before and I'm pretty sure I haven't seen him anywhere around, but there's just ... there's something very familiar about him."

Oh, I don't like the sound of that. "What did he look like? Exactly..."

"He was tall..."

Yup, Jeremy's tall. Check that box.

"Lean..."

Check that one, too.

"Brownish green eyes...

Shit. Check.

"Sort of dirty blonde hair and clean-cut. Very Wall Street, but in a hipster kinda way. Oh, and he had a pierced ear."

I breathe an internal sigh of relief. Jeremy Corrigan could pass for hipster, but not Wall Street. And he isn't blonde...or clean-cut, for that matter. And he would *never* wear an earring. Way too effeminate for his testosterone-fueled ego.

"Well, maybe you should take a break from that park for a while," I suggest. "And if you see him anywhere else, please let us know right away."

Natalie nods her understanding, and I turn back around, rummage in my bag for the eyeliner that will miraculously transform my eyes from invisible to arresting.

"Julia?"

"Hmmm?"

"That guy you and Matthew warned me about when you first hired me ... Jeremy? You were worried it might be him, weren't you?"

I look up at her again in the mirror to find her watching me intently.

"Yes, I thought maybe, but he doesn't fit the description," I say after a long moment, turning around to face her.

"I saw the look on your face. You were really scared there for a second." I give her the briefest of nods. "Do you think he might want to hurt David?"

I should tread very carefully here. There's a fine line between caution and hysteria ... I should know, I've crossed it enough times.

"Nat, Jeremy Corrigan is Brett's brother. He and I were together for a while. As it turned out, he wasn't a good guy. He ... he hurt me. And when he did, Matthew fought back in a way that damaged Jeremy's career. Thankfully, he's been gone, working in Detroit for more than a year, and I haven't seen or heard from him since. But..." I pause and close my eyes for just a moment, forcing myself to say aloud the words that I hide from every day. "But he's not the kind of guy to forgive and forget."

"Still! You don't think he'd hurt a child..."

"The single worst thing you can do with a guy like that is to underestimate him—to assume that he plays by the same rules that the rest of us do. He doesn't. So, yes, I was scared there for a second, thinking he might have come back. But, from what you've told me, it doesn't sound like him." I give her my brightest, most reassuring smile. "I *love* that you're so alert. There's no one that I trust with my son more than you."

This makes her smile and blush just a little.

"What about Brett?"

"What about him?"

"You said this Jeremy guy is his brother. But you seem to trust him ... and Maggie."

I nod, thoughtfully.

"Yes, you're right, I do. There was a time when that wasn't the case. But Brett was there for me when I needed him."

This is, of course, the understatement of the year. Had Brett not intervened, my son might not have ever been born. Not if Jeremy had had his way, anyway. But Natalie doesn't need to know those kinds of gruesome details. Nobody does.

"Yeah, so, he proved himself to be someone I could count on. And he and Maggie have become like a surrogate aunt and uncle to David."

"Will they be at this event you're attending tonight?"

I roll my eyes. "I wish. If this party is anything like the other fundraisers I've been to, we'll be eating rubber chicken and trying to convince people to part with their hard-earned cash. I'm sure it's not the kind of parties you go to," I grin.

She snorts and tosses a ball of tiny socks into the laundry basket "Yeah, well, believe me, I've been very happy to trade in the loud sweaty mob scene for a standing Friday night pizza date with David He's always happy to see me, never makes ridiculous demands and never complains about staying in and watching TV. He'd be the perfect man if I could get him to wipe his own backside!"

As I shake my head and laugh with her, a sudden wave of gratitude washes over me.

"You know, Nat," I say, my tone turning serious. "We don't have any family, Matthew and I. So, when we come across people like you, and Brett, and Maggie...we just kind of assimilate them into our lives. They *become* our family

"Assimilate! Ohhhhh, I like the idea of that!" she beams at me with her big, toothy grin. "Like you've sucked me up into your pod, or something! I just love SciFi, you know."

I didn't. But I'm glad I do now.

Natalie Hughes is a welcome addition to the Ayers pod.

Chapter 20

Julia

When he wraps his arms around me, the whole world melts away. The people dancing around us just seem to fade into the background. All at once, the sounds of loud chatter and clinking glasses are drowned out by the crickets and the wind as it whispers through the leaves. I look up, at him and at the sky beyond him. It isn't until right now that I truly understand the meaning of the phrase 'blanket of stars.' There are millions of tiny, glittering points of light winking at us from every direction. If I could just find a way to affix a sound to each of them, they would create a beautiful, celestial symphony.

I sigh contentedly as I snuggle in closer to my husband, putting my head against his chest. The beat of his heart nearly matches the beat of the music swirling around us. Matthew holds me tightly, guiding me gently from side to side and in a circular motion around the dance floor created just for this occasion on the back lawn of a spectacular mansion. We are in Nassau County, in an area known as 'The Gold Coast,' where some of Long Island's most affluent citizens call home.

Michael and Danielle Milano are huge arts patrons and are hosting this gala as a fundraiser for The Walton String Quartet. From where we are dancing, I can see the young couple as they make their rounds to every table. With his height and dark good looks and her blonde hair and stunning features, they're hard to miss ... as are the two perfect little boys who chase around after them. What are their names? Mark... no, Mason. Mason and Steven...the little guy runs like David...

"I know what you're thinking, Mama Bear." Matthew says, resting his chin atop my head. "You'd like to have our little monster running around out here too."

"Well... maybe a little..." I confess.

"Are you having a good time, or are you counting the minutes till we can leave?"

I stop dancing and look up at him with a disbelieving smile.

"Are you nuts? Dancing with you under the stars on a beautiful night? I can't think of any place I'd rather be right now!"

He leans down and gives me a sweet and gentle kiss. "How about the Gold Coast Inn?" he asks when he pulls away.

"Ah, well, yeah, that might give this a run for the money. They say that place is amazing, with a fireplace in each room..."

" And don't forget about the hot tub for two," he adds.

"Well, I guess I'm not the only one who's seen the ad on TV," I tease "Why?"

"Because we have a reservation there tonight."

"What?" He cannot be serious. The most modest room at the Gold Coast Inn starts at five hundred a night. And, if I know Matthew Ayers he didn't give the modest room a second look. "I was right the first time You *are* nuts!" I exclaim, shaking my head.

He just smiles and shrugs.

"And what about David?"

"No worries there, I booked Natalie for an overnight with him weeks ago. She'll stay in our room tonight and make sure he gets to his play date in the morning so you and I can enjoy a late check out ... in the hot tub, I hope."

He's giving me his most suggestive grin.

"And what am I supposed to wear?"

He leans close and whispers in my ear. "Well, you won't be needing any clothes tonight, I'll make sure of that. As for tomorrow, Nat packed an overnight bag. It's already in the car."

That little Mata Hari! She didn't drop so much as a hint!

He stands back and surveys me with a very self-satisfied smile on his face. I'm about to comment when I feel a hand on my shoulder.

"May I cut in?"

It's Philip Tonka, our friend, and a fellow cellist. It was his spot that I took in the Walton Quartet.

"Of course," I say, stepping back to leave him and Matthew together with a giggle.

"Oh, *no!*" Matthew groans, shaking his head and waving his hands. "The last time I danced with this guy, he stepped all over my toes. I think you'd better take this one, Julia."

We're all laughing as Philip whips me around in a dazzling spin that makes me dizzy, but impresses, nonetheless.

"Wow, Philip, I had no idea you can dance!" I marvel.

He gives me his big, kind smile.

"My mama raised me right," he says, suddenly lowering me into a deep dip.

"Hey, stop making me look bad!" I hear Matthew call from the sidelines.

The band has moved on to a slower song by the time I'm upright again. *'Moonlight in Vermont'*, I think.

"Oh, this is an oldie but a goodie," Phil murmurs appreciatively, pulling me a little closer for the low-key melody. He hums a few bars of it under his breath. "You're too young to remember this."

"Oh, I know it, it's just been a long time since I heard it. Hey, how are you feeling?" I ask, my tone turning more concerned. "It hasn't been that long since the surgery. Should you be out here ... doing stuff like this?"

"Like what? Dancing with a beautiful woman?"

He makes this sound lecherous, and I swat him on the arm.

"Dancing with a *married* woman, Mr. Tonka!"

"Oh, of course! Good thing you reminded me," he chuckles, then becomes more serious. "I am. Feeling better, that is. And you're right, I shouldn't be able to be out here dancing. But it's a sign that the surgery was a success. If I were having balance problems, it might be a sign that there are still problems with my ears. But so far... so good!" he says, dropping me into a deep and unexpected dip.

I laugh and snort all at the same time. Definitely not my most lady-like appearance. He brings me upright again after a few moments and we return to our gentle glide around the parquet tiles laid in the grass, my long silvery dress swishing around my ankles with every spin.

"How's David?" he asks after our first full rotation.

"Wonderful. He's so funny and sweet ... that is, when he's not being cranky and horrible." I laugh.

"I hear he met some Walton fans when you were on tour," Philip says, gently approaching a topic he's clearly unsure about.

"Yes he did," I confirm, giving him the confidence to continue.

"How was that? For you, I mean?"

He's never come right out and said it, but I'm certain that Philip knows Jeremy is David's biological father. Maybe from something Brett said. Maybe Matthew. Maybe he just saw the resemblance between the two of them and put it all together. I don't mind. This man is a gentle soul who has genuine affection for my family.

"To be honest with you, Philip, it was pretty horrifying," I admit. "I was totally blindsided by Trudy Corrigan. I had no idea she'd be there, or I would've made sure David was back at the hotel with Natalie."

"Why? Would it have occurred to you that she would recognize him?" he asks, genuinely curious.

"Of course, she's a mother. And a grandmother."

"So?"

"So, there's no doubt in my mind that *I'd* recognize my own grandchild, even if I didn't know he existed! It's not just a physical thing—it's an instinctual thing. You know how it seems like some mothers have eyes in the back of their heads? They do! I call it the *'Spidey Sense'* but some people say it's a mother's intuition."

"Huh," he says looking down at me with great interest. "Still, maybe it's best that you were blindsided. Sort of just tearing the Band-aid off, if you know what I mean. It had to happen sometime, and it might have been better this way, rather than you agonizing about it forever."

I think about this for a moment as we circle the floor again.

"Yes, you're probably right about that. Still, it was really...unsettling." I sigh with exasperation and roll my eyes. "Oh, who am I kidding? It was terrifying, Philip!"

"I'm sure it was. Have you heard from her since then?"

I shake my head. "No. We were both pretty emotional and decided it would be best to take some time to consider things. She'll be here next month to help Maggie with some of the wedding plans. We're going to get together then."

"And what about *your* big day?" he asks.

"What big day?" He's looking at me expectantly and I suddenly realize what he's referring to. "Oh! The CD release party? Yeah, that might as well be a wedding. The guest list gets longer every time I turn around. They've changed the venue twice now to accommodate everyone. I tell you, Philip, I'd just as soon skip it."

"No, no, don't say that. This is huge, Julia. You need to revel in this, because these moments are few and far between for most of us. Enjoy the spotlight for once," he says with a grin.

"You'll be there, won't you?"

"I wouldn't miss it for the world!" he says emphatically.

"Afraid I have to steal her back, my friend," Matthew says, gently cutting in on us. "The lady and I have to make the rounds and be on our way."

"Madam, it was my honor," Philip says, giving me his most chivalrous bow.

"The honor was all mine, kind sir," I return with a gracious bow of the head.

"Good night, Philip!" Matthew calls over his shoulder as he puts his hand on the small of my back and leads me off into the cool breeze of early fall.

Chapter 21

Julia

Did I say five-hundred-dollars a night? The suite I'm standing in must cost upwards of twenty-five-hundred a night. It has a marble entryway which leads into an exquisitely decorated sitting room with plush, velvet sofas in a rich plum color and gleaming mahogany tables. There's a huge gas fireplace with a mantel on one side of the room. I follow Matthew into the bedroom, which is outfitted with a mahogany four-poster bed draped in sheer, gauzy panels. A delicate chandelier casts a warm sepia glow across the entire room. Matthew tosses his suit jacket onto the bed and grabs my hand, pulling me excitedly through another doorway.

"Come on, this is the best part!"

He leads me into a bathroom that must be as big as our entire bedroom at home. Maybe our entire apartment in the city! It's marble from floor to ceiling, with a soaking tub big enough for four people. "Watch this," Matthew grins excitedly, dropping my hand and opening the door to the huge, glass-enclosed shower. "Flip that light switch next you," he points.

I do as he asks, and we are in total darkness, but only for a moment. Just as I hear the gentle rain of the water as it's turned on, I see the glow of a brilliant cobalt light from above the showerhead. Matthew pushes a button and now, it's a soft pink. Again, and we are bathed in a tawdry crimson. I step closer and realize there are showerheads mounted all over this thing. When you stand in the middle, the warm pulsing jets massage while the lights cast a vibrant wash of color over you.

"Matthew," I marvel, "this is *amazing!*"

He turns the water off and, with it the light show. We're in total and complete darkness and, while I sense him close to me, I can't quite tell where he is. That is, until I feel his hands on me, moving over my body, his lips on my neck and my face and my shoulders. He's tugging impatiently at the zipper on the back of my dress, but I'm too mesmerized to help him. Finally, he manages it, and the gown falls to my feet. I can hear my breath growing louder and faster to match my rising pulse.

It's as if his hands are everywhere at one time. The straps of my bra are slipped off my shoulders and he's cupping my breasts in his hands. I hear him breathing hard now, too, as his lips return to my neck. Suddenly, he's behind me, groping my left breast gently but firmly.

When he takes my earlobe in his mouth, I gasp. I don't even notice his other hand until it's under the waistband of my lace panties. He doesn't waste a single moment as he slips his long, strong fingers into the cleft of my sex, dipping into me, feeling my wetness. A deep, appreciative moan rises from his throat. I almost collapse back onto him as he spreads me and runs a single finger up and down, slowly. Up and down, up and down in a rhythm so hypnotic, that my hips are beginning to sway with his movements.

"Oh, Matthew..." I murmur, my breath growing more rapid with the maddening pleasure that is building. Just when I think I can't take another second, he is gone.

Wait! What happened?

I can barely formulate the thought when I realize exactly what has happened. He is in front of me now, in the pitch-blackness, on his knees, his palms on each of my thighs as he widens my stance.

"Lean back on the vanity, Julia. It's just behind you," he whispers into the darkness.

When I reach back, I realize that the marble countertop is right there. I put my hands flat on it and shift my weight back. In a split second he is lifting me so that I am sitting on it. The surface is smooth and cool. It, like everything else, has a heightened sensuality to it in the strange, lightless space.

God, this is so sexy I can't stand it. He doesn't even bother to take my panties off. Instead, he just pulls the crotch aside and slips his tongue into my moist folds. I let out a garbled cry as he manages to hang my legs over his shoulders. Again he is there, this time deeper, finding the spot that makes my entire body tense on contact.

"Ahhhh..." I moan loudly, savoring the added sensation of his clothing as it brushes against my naked thighs. His voice comes to me from below.

"I haven't been able to think of anything but getting you to myself all night long," he says and plows into me with a renewed fervor. I'm writhing on the marble, the lace panties allowing me to slip and slide without friction. Things are happening fast, very fast, and I love it.

"God, yes, yes, please, Matthew. Please..." I beg and he doesn't disappoint. His mouth finds the sensitive nub and latches on with a suction that makes me ball my hands into his hair and throw my head back so it touches the mirror behind me.

The sound of my orgasm echoes across every inch of the hard-walled room. When I have finally stopped shaking, he pulls away from me and stands up. There are no words between us, he just walks into me and my legs wrap around his waist, my arms around his neck. Still breathing heavily, I rest my face against the shoulder of his dress shirt. The fine silk blend feels soft and cool under my cheek as he carries me to the four-poster bed.

I sink six inches into the soft plushness of the pillow top mattress and watch, lazily as Matthew makes his way around the room, turning out lights and slipping out of each article of clothing he is wearing, one by one. I'm feeling chilly and I start to pull the duvet out from under me so I can get under it, but he holds up a finger for me to wait.

"You'll be warm in just a second," he promises with a sexy smile.

Oh, my. I don't know that I can take much more of his warm-up, but I'm willing to give it a try. It doesn't take long to find out. The room's dwindling light is finally extinguished when he reaches a small lamp atop the ornate writing desk. I expect to feel his familiar weight in the bed next to me, but instead I hear him shuffle toward the door to the sitting room.

"What are you doing?" I ask from the bed.

"Give me a second," he says. "It's somewhere right around...there it is!"

I hear the flick of a switch and the corner fireplace comes alive, casting its coppery glow across the room and wrapping cozy plumes of warmth around my naked body. I sigh with the comfort of it. Now he joins me on the bed, naked and slightly disheveled from the evening, not to mention what I did to his hair in the bathroom.

He lies on his side and I roll onto mine so we are facing one another. "I have loved you since the day I first laid eyes on you, you know," he says softly.

I smile. "I know."

Part of Matthew is always going to wonder why it took me so long to see what was so obvious to him. But, I can't worry about what I cannot change. I put a hand to his face, smooth and soft from his earlier shave, and he moves his own hand to meet it.

"I want to...I think we should..." He stops abruptly, closes and reopens his eyes and starts again. "I'd like for us to have another baby. Soon."

"Really?" I say sitting up suddenly, unable to control the excitement in my voice. "I thought you wanted to wait until David's a little older."

"Yeah, I know...but God, if we're this crazy about David, how much happier do you think we'd be with another one around the house? Maybe a little girl this time. Or a little brother for David. They could be 'our boys.' What do you think?"

"*What do I think?*" I squeal, bouncing the bed up and down. "Matthew, I wanted to get pregnant right after David was born. Of course, I want to have another baby! Your baby. *Our* baby!"

It's a little hard to know exactly how to phrase it without it sounding like David is anything less than our son. But he understands, and he is smiling, still holding my hand to his face.

"What would you name her?"

"I don't know, I really hadn't given it much thought since we were putting this on hold. How about if we create a name after we've created the kid, okay?"

"Fair enough, Mrs. Ayers," he murmurs, rolling onto his hands and knees so he can snake his way over to my naked body.

I slip back down so I'm lying on the mattress again and he climbs over me, resting one palm on either side of my head. His knee finds a break between my legs and coaxes them apart so he can align himself with me. I can't take my eyes off of his face as I reach up and hook my arms under and around his strong shoulders so I can feel them; so I can pull him close enough that his skin is touching mine. He drops down, his forearms flush with the mattress, and I wrap my lower body around him. I rub my calves against the backs of his thighs, loving the feel of his taut muscles across my soft skin. His head drops and his lips find my face. Tiny little kisses rain down on my forehead, my cheeks, my eyelids and my neck.

"What did I ever do to deserve you?" he whispers in my ear.

For him, it's a rhetorical question uttered in a moment of passion. For me, it's a sentiment that deserves expression.

"You waited for me to come to my senses," I whisper.

Matthew stops and raises his head to look down at me. I can see his face clearly against the moonlight streaming through the window. When he pushes his hardness into me, his eyes are fixed on mine. He likes to watch. The more excited I get, the more excited he gets.

"Ughhh..." I let out a reflexive groan with the unexpected fullness of him.

When he starts to move, slowly at first, every inch of me is wanting for every inch of him. In my husband's arms, the tender and the gentle live side by side with the heat and the full-hearted yearning. To him, sex is never just sex. It's always an expression of his love—his desire to be as close as two human beings can ever be.

"Oh, Julia," he whispers, his hands running the outer length of my body from the swell of my breasts to the curve of my hips and thighs. "Oh, God, Julia," he murmurs against my ear.

Ah, I see we're on the express train tonight. Works for me! With one swift movement, I manage to roll out from under him and over, until I'm straddling him from above.

"Holy shit, that was impressive!" He smiles up at me, pleasantly surprised.

"Oh, yeah, I've got a million moves," I brag. "In the morning, I'll show you my Reverse Cowgirl!"

I'm sure he'd have a comment about that, but as it turns out, I don't waste any time working my hips in circles around him. His mouth opens into a perfect 'O,' and his eyes get big. Time to blow his mind. I close my eyes and throw my head back, rocking back and forth against him.

"God, you are huge," I murmur, and feel an immediate twitch from within me. I get a little louder as I grind myself into him deeper and faster.

His hands are on my waist now, guiding me in the motion and rhythm he needs at that second. And a second is about all it takes.

He throws his head back...and promptly bangs it against the headboard. "Owwww! Fuck, that hurt!"

"Oh! Matthew!" I cry out, more in concern the ecstasy, then slap a hand over my mouth to keep myself from laughing. It doesn't work. For either of us.

I roll off of him and land on my usual side of the bed, facing him, both of us howling with laughter.

"I'm fine, I'm fine," he rasps. "I just got a little...over enthusiastic."

"I understand," I say with a coy smile. "Hey, can we take a blue shower now?"

Chapter 22

Julia

"Good, I wish Brett would take a few notes from Matthew," Maggie mutters over her shoulder as she models for me. We're in the living room of the brownstone apartment she and Brett share—which suddenly felt a whole lot smaller when she entered wearing the puffy, sparkly confection that is her mother's wedding dress. "The Gold Coast Inn—I mean, that's like a second honeymoon, Julia!"

"Well, we never had a *first* honeymoon," I point out as I tilt my head from side to side, adjusting the angle from which I'm looking at her. And the dress. And her in the dress. "But it was certainly the most romantic night I've had in a long, long time."

"Oh, I'll just bet," she grins knowingly. "Okay, so, what's the verdict?"

"Turn around," I instruct her, making a little circle with my index finger.

She does. Wow. This thing makes the very slender Maggie look like she's got a Mack truck for a butt.

"And this is what your mom wore?" I ask skeptically. I'm having a hard time imaging any woman who could pull this look off.

Maggie nods miserably. "It's awful, right?"

"Well..." There's just no way around it, the dress is hideous and I can't find a single redeeming quality to point to. My non-response confirms her suspicions.

"I knew it! I was hoping it was just me being a brat about wanting my own special dress, but it's *not* just me, is it?"

I take one last, long look from neckline to hem and make my way back up to her eyes. I shake my head no. No, it's not just her. She puts a hand to her forehead and falls back onto their overstuffed denim blue couch with a puff of taffeta and crinoline.

"Holy crap! What am I going to do?" she whines.

"Is it possible that once she see you in it that she'll realize that it's..." oh, how to say this tactfully? "That it's not a good fit for you?"

Maggie is shaking her head emphatically now. "No. No way. I can't even let my mother see me in it. I mean, I can just hear my mother now, *'Oh, Maggie, you look so beautiful! I just can't believe my baby is going to be a married woman!'*" She puts her head in her hands. "I am *so* fucked," she mutters then looks up and we both burst out laughing at the same time.

Before I know what's happening, she's slid onto the braided rug on the floor, holding her stomach, and I'm howling so hard I'm crying. It takes us several minutes to regroup from our untoward display of wedding attire hysteria. Finally, Maggie sits up again, wiping at the tears on her cheeks.

"Seriously!" She wheezes. "What am I going to do? I cannot walk down the aisle looking like the Barbie birthday cake from when I turned six, Julia."

It's all I can do to keep myself from falling back into a fit of giggles over the thought of the birthday cake, so I bite my tongue and consider her plight. And then it comes to me.

"Trudy!" I declare excitedly.

"What? What about her?"

"Brett told me she sews everything, including her own clothes. I'll bet she'd be able to whip that dress into something a little less..." I wave a hand at the garment as I search for an inoffensive adjective.

"Tacky? Fluffy? Garish?" Maggie offers.

"I was going to say *dated*." I laugh. "But seriously, why don't you ask her about it? I'll bet she'd love to do it for you, Maggie."

"That's such a great idea." She sighs in relief. "I'll call her this afternoon."

She hoists herself up off the floor with considerable effort. "You know this damn thing weighs thirty-five pounds? I'm not kidding! It's right on the shipping label. What bride wants to be thirty-five pounds heavier on her wedding day? Here, will you please unzip me so I can get out of this thing?"

I never had any friends, aside from Matthew. Maggie's become my sounding board, my confidant, and a damn fine aunt to my son.

"Have you spoken with her?"

Her question interrupts my thoughts and, for a moment, I'm not sure what she's talking about. "Spoken to who?"

"Uhhh... your child's *grandmother*?" she teases.

"Oh, her," I reply sheepishly, tugging the zipper the last inch. Maggie shrugs the dress off her shoulders and it falls to the floor with an audible thump.

"So. Much. Better," she murmurs, closing her eyes in relief. "Sorry, go on..."

"Um, no. No I haven't. She was very kind, but she was obviously stunned. It's hard to say what her true feelings on the subject are. Unless, of course, you're able to provide me with some insight into that..." I fish.

She steps out of the pool of fabric and turns to face me in nothing but her bra and panties.

"I know she was pissed at hell that Brett didn't give her a heads-up on that little tidbit. He's been in the doghouse with her since you guys got back from the tour."

"It's not his fault. He was respecting my wishes. There was just no way around it...she may be Brett's mother, but she's also *Jeremy's* mother."

She's still talking to me as she makes her way to the bedroom. "I get that. But now that it's out there I think you should consider the implications and how you want to proceed with her."

"What implications...exactly?"

She hops out of the bedroom again wearing a Journey T-Shirt and trying to get her other leg into her jeans.

"Like... do you want her to be David's grandmother? You know, to have that relationship with him? And how will you feel if she's not comfortable with that? And, if you don't want her to have a relationship with your son, how will you tell her?"

"All good questions," I admit thoughtfully. "I hadn't really considered them."

"Julia, you've had enough *Mama Drama* to last you a lifetime. Trudy's an amazing woman... and the total opposite of Jeremy. But she's a tough cookie. And she'll tell you exactly what's on her mind."

"So I noticed!" I snort loudly, recalling our catastrophic run-in backstage at the Walton Concert. "Well," I sigh after a long moment, "I actually would like David to know his grandmother ... especially since he already has a relationship with Brett. It'd be awkward to have one without the other ... but I'm not going to force myself, or my son, onto her. She has an open invitation to get to know us a little better, and she'll either take me up on it, or she won't."

"Fair enough," Maggie agrees with a nod that makes her black curls bounce. "If you think this is bad," she says, pointing to the discarded wedding dress, "wait till you see the lampshade my mother used as a headpiece!"

Chapter 23

Julia

"Julia!" Matthew bellows from his office.

I guess this is what they mean by 'the honeymoon's over.' It's hard to believe I was enjoying naked room service this time last week. My trip down the hall is about as far away from chocolate covered strawberries and blue showers as you can get.

"Did you need something, my love?" I ask sweetly, from the doorway. But his exasperated expression tells me sweet's not going to cut it right now.

"Julia, David got into my filing cabinet. *Again.* Everything has been pulled up and out and shifted around, it's a mess!"

This is only the thirty-eighth time we've had this conversation, and I'm not particularly interested in having it a thirty-ninth time.

"Matthew, you know he likes to pretend he's working in there, like you. You thought it was cute a month ago," I point out, appealing to his 'daddy ego.' But he doesn't bite.

"Yeah, well, a month ago there wasn't grape jelly on my bank papers," he snaps, waving the offending sticky documents at me.

"Why didn't you lock the cabinet?"

"Why should I have to? It's *my* office!"

I shrug. "Well, then, I guess you'd better lock the door to *your* office where *your* unsecured documents are stored, because our son can turn doorknobs now, in case you hadn't noticed."

He throws his hands up, turns around, and walks away shaking his head. I try, unsuccessfully, to stifle a giggle, and am punished with an Evil Eye over his shoulder.

It's been an adjustment, having this tiny person running around the house. Since he's been mobile, I've played more games of hide-and-seek with my cellphone than I can count. In fact, I'm still waiting to find it from the last time David got his sticky little fingers on it. I sigh and try my best to be more sympathetic.

"Matthew, you're right, he's been getting into a lot of things lately. But he's at that curious stage when he wants to investigate everything. We just need to be more careful about what we leave lying around."

No sooner are the words out of my mouth than he reaches into his top desk drawer and pulls out... Oh. No. He *cannot* be serious right now. The blade on the knife he's holding must be six inches long. The thing looks like a prop out of a Vietnam War movie.

"What. Is. *That?*" I manage to ask in a horrified whisper.

My husband looks up smugly. "*This* is what David might find next time he's in my office if we don't teach him some boundaries. He's old enough..."

"No," I interrupt him flatly. "No."

"No, what? No, we can't teach him not to..."

I shake my head. "No, you can't keep that thing in this house."

His normally sexy lips turn up into an incredulous, condescending smirk. "I'm sorry... I can't keep it? What's wrong with you? It's just a little hunting knife."

"You don't hunt. And there's nothing *little* about it."

"Well, no," concedes, "but still, don't you think you're overreacting just a little?"

Okay, Julia keep your cool. Take a breath. Count to five and Do. Not. Strangle. Your. Husband.

"Matthew, *honey,*" I grit out, "I get the sentimental value of the knife. And maybe, someday—a long, *long* time from now—you can share it with David. But I'm sorry, I'm just not comfortable having a weapon like that in the same house where our child plays."

"It's not a gun, Julia," he scoffs, dismissing my concerns. "David isn't going to accidentally stab himself to death..."

Okay, well, so much for keeping my cool. Clearly I'm not getting my point across, because Matthew still seems to be under the impression that he has a choice in this matter. Time for the big guns. The 'Guilt' guns.

"Oh? Are you sure about that, *honey*? Because, you know it happens all the time. I mean it's not hard to imagine a scenario where something tragic happens! He runs with it and falls on top of it, it impales him." I smack the back of one hand into the palm of the other as I paint the image for him. "Or, he runs with it and slips down the stairs, it impales him. Maybe he's out by the pool with it..."

Matthew jumps to his feet, holding up his hands in surrender. "For God's sake, please stop saying it's going to impale him! That's *so not* fair!"

All is fair in love and guilt and the sooner my dear husband realizes that, the better for both of us. But especially for him because this is a battle I do not intend to lose.

"Julia, please, how about this, I'll buy a lockbox for it. You know, the secure kind that people use to secure their handguns? Then I'll keep it up high, in the very back of the closet."

"Kids get into closets, Matthew..." I point out. "You don't think an incredibly active, incredibly bright little boy will eventually find his way to something like that? To him, it looks like a big, shiny toy."

"Toddlers don't get things that are seven feet off the ground. I *swear* to you, I will buy a lockbox for it before we come back here next weekend. When he's a little older, I'll find someplace else for it. And you have my word, if David even catches sight of it, I'll get rid of it."

I sigh heavily. "Fine. But I'm going to hold you to that, Matthew Ayers. There'd better be a lockbox here by next weekend or I'll turn right around and take David back to the city until you get one."

He nods mutely, realizing at last that this is a game he will never win.

Chapter 24

Julia

Later, after the dust has settled, I'm enjoying a cup of coffee as I sit at the long farm table, watching through the slider as a doe and fawn pick their way through the backyard, periodically stopping to munch on some mums. They're a stark contrast to the mother/child scene playing out here in the kitchen as David contentedly mauls his macaroni and cheese. He flattens the sticky elbows against the tray of his highchair, using an airplane-shaped spoon. When he has sufficiently crushed them, he grabs a fistful of the gooey mess and stuffs it into his mouth. About a third of it stays in there.

"Sweetie, let Mommy help you..." I offer, reaching for the spoon.

"*No!*" he screeches. "*No, Mammmmmmaaa!*"

I hold up my hands in surrender. Since this little boy came into the world, I've learned all about the art of picking my battles. Squashed mac and cheese I can deal with.

"Hey! What's all the yelling about in here?" Matthew asks as he breezes into the kitchen, considerably more relaxed now that I'm off the warpath. He pours himself a mug of coffee from the carafe on the counter and comes to give me a kiss on the cheek. Then it's David's turn. Matthew sneaks up behind our son, still preoccupied with his dinner, and delivers a sloppy, sneak-attack raspberry on the back of his neck, making the boy chortle uncontrollably. When he stands up again, Matthew has macaroni stuck to his face.

"You have a little something ..." I point out, gesturing to the spot on my face that reflects where the food is on his face.

He swipes at it with his hand and examines the rogue noodles before popping them into his mouth.

"Yummmmmmmmm!" he says, picking another off of the highchair tray.

David's belly laugh fills the kitchen. When I look at the two of them, I see father and son ... which makes me think about Jeremy...which makes me think about Trudy.

"So, Maggie's going to take the train out from the city tomorrow morning with Trudy. She'll stay here and watch David while Trudy and I have a bite out," I inform him, trying not to sound as unsure about the plan as I feel.

Matthew musses the top of David's hair and comes to sit with me at the table. "Yeah? That sounds nice. Where're you going to take her?"

"That little cafe on Love Lane in Mattituck." He snorts. "What? What can you *possibly* find amusing about that?" I challenge.

"Let me guess, you picked."

"Yes. And...?"

"*And*, I'm just struck by the fact that you're a nervous wreck about having this conversation with Trudy and, yet, you're still thinking about pancakes."

"What?"

He pokes me in the arm. "You. Love. Pancakes. You especially love *their* lemon ricotta pancakes."

I think about this for a second. "Oh my God," I groan and roll my eyes, smacking a hand to my forehead. "You're right! What's *wrong* with me?"

I'm horrified, he's laughing. "Nothing! I just think it's hilarious that even at this seminal moment in your life, you're thinking about breakfast."

I shake my head at him, starting to laugh at myself. "Matthew, what do you think that is?"

He shrugs, still smiling. "Honestly, Julia, I think it's your comfort zone kicking in. Besides, if things don't go well, the day won't have been a total bust..."

I slap his hand playfully and am about to say something when the blaring sound of a foghorn filters into the bright, white kitchen from outside.

"Boat!" David yells proudly from the highchair.

"Yes, baby, very good!" I praise him and then turn to Matthew. "Can't we do anything about that? The new foghorns on the ferry are so loud!"

"It's already on the agenda for the next civic meeting. At the very least, we should be able to get a curfew, so there won't be anymore of those midnight wakeup calls. I don't think it'll be an issue, honestly. The ferry company likes to be a good neighbor.'"

"I'd settle for having them be a *quiet* neighbor right now," I grumble.

"Okay, so let's square away the plan for the rest of the week," he says, pulling his phone out of his pocket to consult his calendar. I reach for mine and realize it's still missing, thanks to the redheaded imp sitting next to me. "Lunch with Trudy for you," Matthew is reciting as he scrolls from date to date. "A date with Maggie for David. I've got a rehearsal for the Montauk Music Festival gig I'm doing, so I won't be home till dinner. And then...?"

"And then we have a down day on Wednesday before we head back to the city Thursday. I gave Nat those two days off. And then Friday..."

"And then Friday is Mommy's big night!" Matthew says excitedly, scooping up David from the highchair and spinning him around the kitchen.

"Matthew, put him down before he throws up on you," I warn him, already envisioning the gooey, orange mess.

"Mommy's a worry wart," Matthew informs David and delivers him back to his seat.

"More!" he demands, pounding his chubby fists on the tray. "More!"

"Finish your dinner first," Matthew tells him. It seems to do the trick and peace is restored in the kitchen—at least for the moment. "As I was saying, your big night. Is everything ready?"

I roll my eyes and groan. "It's a nightmare. I spoke with Lester Morgan this afternoon. The guest list is up to a hundred and fifty!"

Matthew waves away my alarm with a dismissive hand.

"Oh, come on now. You've played for audiences ten times that size!" he reminds me.

"Yeah, well, this feels different. God, it's *all* about me, this time."

"Julia! It's supposed to be all about you. This is your first commercial release—it's a very, very big deal!"

"I know," I whine, "but all those people...they'll be wanting me to sign their CD's and they'll want to talk with me and ... well, you know playing for an audience is one thing. Interacting is another."

He seems to consider this. "Yeah, I can see that. But still, it isn't as if you'll be alone. I'll be there, Dr. Sam, Maggie, Brett. You'll be among friends. Just go and play. The rest will take care of itself."

"You think?"

I can hear the skepticism in my voice, and so can he. He stands up, faces me and reaches down, taking my face in both of his soft, warm hands. "I know. If I had even an iota of doubt, I wouldn't let you do it I swear, Julia."

I smile up at him and his amber eyes fill me with the confidence I'm lacking. "You know I love you, right?" I murmur and watch as his smile makes his eyes crinkle.

"I do," he says, leaning down and giving me a soft kiss on the mouth. "Now, where's the rest of that macaroni and cheese?"

Chapter 25

Julia

I poke at the pancakes, awkwardly. Funny, I'm not very hungry now that they, and Jeremy's mother, are sitting in front of me. She's looking at me intently and I feel the need to look away. Finally, I bring my eyes back to her face. She smiles at me kindly.

"Julia. Please don't be nervous. I promise you, I don't bite."

I feel a rush of warmth to my cheeks. "I'm sorry," I mumble. "I just—this is awkward."

She nods. "Yes, it is. But it doesn't have to be. Why don't you tell me a little about yourself? How did you come to play the cello?"

"I was at the Children's Home—kind of an orphanage here on Long Island."

"Your parents are dead?" Her face wrinkles with concern.

"Yes. Uh—no..."

She raises an eyebrow. "I don't think there's much wiggle room in there. They're either dead...or they're not."

"Right. Well, my mother is alive. My father is dead." She swishes her coffee around, waiting for me to elaborate. "My mother was a drug addict. She left us when I was five. After she'd gone, my father was abusive...physically," I hurry to add, not wanting her to think it was anything darker than that. "I—I look a lot like her, you see. And he was so angry…" I break off for a moment and look down at my half-eaten breakfast. When I glance up, she's still waiting patiently.

"Anyway, I was taken away from him when I was eight. That's when I went to the Children's Home. And that's where I met Matthew. His parents died in a boating accident. He was my only friend and he's the one who introduced me to music. I didn't speak, so the cello was my voice."

She looks startled, then confused. "You were…mute?"

"Yes. Well, sort of. For more than a year, anyway. I stopped talking the day I went to school and the teacher realized what was going on at home. I was afraid to answer questions from the police and the doctors and the social workers. I thought if I told them what was happening, my father would get mad at me and hurt me. So, I didn't speak then, or for more than a year afterwards."

Trudy Corrigan puts a firm, reassuring hand over mine. "You were a strong girl. And you've grown into an even stronger woman," she informs me.

I shrug. "I wasn't always so strong. I became strong after…" I stop cold, but she knows exactly where I was headed.

"After Jeremy destroyed your life," she finishes for me. I nod dumbly. "He's good at that, my son."

Another silent nod from me. I'm afraid if I open my mouth I'll fall apart.

Trudy clears her throat and continues. "Brett came to see us a while back. He was very upset…said he'd just stood by and watched Jeremy hurt some poor girl. He didn't help her, and he was having a hard time living with that." Piercing, hazel eyes consider me carefully. They are Jeremy's eyes, I can't help but notice. And David's. "Was that you? Were *you* that girl?"

"Yes," I whisper. "That was me."

Trudy's lips draw into a tight line and her brows draw in toward the bridge of her nose. This expression, too, is a carbon copy of Jeremy's.

"Well, you should know that it was eating him alive."

"We've talked about it," I assure her. "He—he's more than made up for it since then."

"I'm glad," she says with some relief before she changes her tack.

"Now, what of your mother? Where did she go after she left you? If you don't mind me asking, that is ..."

"Umm, no, no, that's fine," I say, my voice a hair uncertain. "She ended up as a...uh...prostitute," I finally spit out with great difficulty. "She tells me she was an addict and often exchanged...sex acts...for drugs."

The concern on Trudy's face is so deep—so sincere—that she makes me feel as if she understands, even before I've told her everything. It gives me the courage to finish. "Somewhere along the line, this guy managed to get her off the streets. He married her and now she has a new life, complete with a new daughter."

"Oh, my. Well, it sounds like she pulled herself out of a bad situation. It's easy to see where your fortitude comes from, Julia." I don't quite know how to respond to that, so I don't. She notices. "You're not happy for her, then?"

The question isn't an accusation, so much as a curiosity.

"Happy? No. She left me to rot in an orphanage while she started a shiny new family, not thirty miles down the road."

"I'm so sorry, Julia. Have you been in touch with her?"

"Yes. I finally gave in and sat down with her for a cup of coffee about six months ago. I was curious more than anything. I wanted to see how she could possibly justify leaving me...with him. She knew the kind of man my father was and she left me with him anyway. Trudy, the man burned me with a car cigarette lighter. He broke my ribs and scalded me with hot coffee. There was no one to protect *me*."

At some point during this hellish little narrative, the tears started to fall and I feel them drip down my cheeks and under the collar of my blouse. Trudy reaches into her purse and hands me a tissue, which I accept with a grateful sniff.

"Anyway," I continue after a minute, "we met, and I asked her, point blank, why she didn't take me with her."

"And what was her reply?"

I scoff and roll my eyes as if it's too unbelievable to even say out loud. But then, I say it out loud. "She told me that she knew that as bad as my father could be, I would still be safer with him than with her. That she knew she might end up doing something awful if she took me with her and that she'd make the same decision again if she had it to do over again. Can you believe that?" I ask incredulously.

Trudy seems to give this some thought. "I know you don't want to hear this," she begins slowly, quietly, "but I have to say it makes perfect sense to me."

"*What?*"

"Julia, one of the hardest things for any parent to comprehend is that there are times when the best thing you can do for your child is to *leave* him."

I shake my head. "No. No, I don't buy that..."

She holds up a finger to stop me. "Please, just hear me out. I have been a kindergarten teacher for more years than you've been alive and I've seen my share of family dysfunction. Bitter divorces where the children are pawns, abusive parents, abusive children, homelessness, abandonment ... and some of the most vile atrocities one human being can inflict upon another.

"But I've also seen incredible acts of heroism in some of those situations. And in that category I include the father who threw himself between his daughter and an oncoming car and the mother who gave full custody to her ex-husband and committed herself to an institution for psychiatric care."

"Trudy, how can you compare those things to what my mother did? There was nothing heroic about her actions. She wasn't saving my life or protecting me from what she might do..."

"Wasn't she?" Trudy asks. "Now, believe me, I pray to Jesus you never have to face a situation like that, but until you do, then you'll never know the agony that your own mother felt in making the decision to let you go."

I can feel the shock that must be telegraphed across my face...slack mouth, wide eyes, flaring nostrils. I simply *cannot* believe what I'm hearing.

"When something like that happens," she continues, "you have to fight yourself, every instinct you have as a mother. You have to make a decision you may very well be hated for, during the rest of your life. But you'll do it. And you would do it again if you had to, because you know in your heart that it's the best thing you can do for him."

I lean forward across the table so that eyes are locked together. "Are you telling me that she abandoned me because it was the best thing for me? Trudy! How can you possibly..."

"I don't know your mother or her situation. But, based on what you've told me, I'm guessing she felt leaving you was a better option than what you might have endured had she taken you with her that day. She was a prostitute ... and a drug addict to boot."

I nod miserably.

"Well, it's my understanding that the kinds of people who move in those worlds would think nothing of offering her a fix for...use...of a beautiful, innocent little girl."

"I—I don't understand..."

She closes her eyes for a brief second and then answers. "I'm saying, that desperate people do desperate things, Julia. And that somewhere, deep in her addled mind, she knew that taking you with her was not an option that day because ... because she wasn't strong enough to protect you from *herself*."

"More coffee?" a perky young waitress pops in and I practically jump out of my seat.

"No!" I say a little too harshly. "I'm sorry," I say more softly. "No, thank you. We'll let you know if we need something else."

The girl can't get away from our table fast enough. I turn back to Trudy, unsure of whether or not I'm offended.

"Even if I can come to some understanding of that," I concede at last, "of her decision to leave and not take me, how can she possibly justify not coming back?"

Trudy sits back in her chair and folds her arms across her chest. In this light, I can see that her light brown hair, cut to chin length, is threaded with silver. She looks tired suddenly. And, if I'm not mistaken, just a little bit sad. Oh, hell. I have to remember that this woman just lost her husband ... and here I am bringing up my ancient baggage.

"Trudy, let's just talk about something more pleasant..."

She puts a warm, delicate hand over mine. "We will in just a moment, I just want to finish this. To answer your question, I don't know why she didn't come back. Perhaps she wasn't secure enough in her sobriety or didn't trust herself ... I wish I had the answer for you, but I don't. There's only one person who does ... your mother."

"So, you think I should reach out to her?"

She gives me a small, sympathetic smile. "I think that there's no wrong answer here, Julia. And, there's no time limit on this. You may not be ready to hear her now ... but possibly later you'll feel differently. The best advice I can give you, dear, is to consider the circumstances around her ... departure ... and try, *as a mother*, to see if her actions are redeemable, or even explainable, in any situation. Then, listen to your heart, Julia. It won't steer you wrong."

I want to snort, but it comes out more like a hiccuppy sob.

"Oh, but it did, Trudy," I sniff, using a napkin to dab at my damp eyes. "My heart steered me right into Jeremy."

I don't know where the strength to say that to her came from, but there it is. My words are like a living, breathing thing at the table with us.

"Yes," she says at last. "Yes, I suppose you're right about that."

Chapter 26

Julia

"Are you alright?"

I pull the pillow over my head and scream into it.

"Okay, then. Not so much alright," I hear Matthew say as he climbs into bed with me.

I feel the palm of his hand under my nightgown, rubbing my back gently. Left to right. Up and down. Circle, circle, circle, just like he does to calm David. He doesn't say anything, just rubs until I gradually stick my head out from the cotton cocoon that envelops me. He is lying with his head on his own pillow, facing me.

"Hi," he says with a smile.

"Hi," I echo.

We lie like that a little while, just looking into one another's eyes. He runs the back of his hand along my cheek.

"What can I do for you?" he asks.

"Not unless you'd like to represent me at the CD launch party so I can stay home and play with our son..."

He tips his head back and laughs. "Hah! You'd like that, wouldn't you? Well, too bad, Mrs. Ayers. I'm not the one the public is clamoring to see!"

"Ugh! God, this like one of those weddings that keeps getting bigger and bigger and bigger. You know, they've temporarily cleared out one of the sculpture exhibits at the gallery to make room for us?"

"Wait, wait, wait…" he begins, scrunching up his face like he's trying to process this information. "The Beau-Radcliffe is a huge space. How many people we talking about here?"

"Two-hundred," I mouth with exaggerated enunciation.

"What?" He props his head up on his elbow so he's looking down at me now. "How is that even possible? Who are they inviting?"

"Oh, let's see … per the Kreisler Competition office, it's an assortment of donors, press, Kreisler competitors and, of course, my personal guest list."

"Which is all of what? Like a dozen people?"

"If that!"

"Now. .. when you say Kreisler competitors, you don't mean…"

"Jeremy? No. I asked that he be excluded from the invitation list."

"Still…"

Now I'm up on my elbow, too, a wave of panic washing over me. "What? You don't think he'd show up, do you?"

Matthew shrugs and shakes his head, his dark hair falling over his eyes. I reach over and brush it back and he grabs my hand before I can pull it away. "No. I don't think so, but it wouldn't be a bad idea to ask Tony to be there…"

"Well, he's on my list anyway…"

"I know, but as a guest. I think I'll ask him to come in a more 'professional' capacity."

"You really think that'll be necessary?"

"I know I'd feel better."

A horrific thought occurs to me and I can't keep the panic out of my voice. "What about David? Should we leave him home with Nat? I mean, just in case?"

Matthew sits up fully now, his back against the headboard. I follow suit and we're side by side, as we often are for these serious conversations. "No. I think we should stick with the plan and bring him. Nat will be there, and Tony and Maggie and Brett. We'll have a lot of eyes on him at the gallery."

I consider this and nod slowly. "Yes, you're right."

"I know," he grins at me cheekily. "So, there it is. You'll show up, hide in the back until you're ready to play, give your performance and then sign a few CD's. There'll probably be a champagne toast in there somewhere so you might want to prepare a few words in response."

"Oh, no! You think? Really? They'll want me to speak in front of all those people?" I'm utterly horrified by the idea. Matthew shrugs and grabs my hand.

"Probably. But all you need to say is 'thank you for coming' and 'thank you to the Kreisler International Music Competition for their support.' That's it. You can manage that much, can't you?"

"I suppose," I sulk. "But I'm not happy about it."

"I'm sure you're not." He chuckles. "But, you know, the party's not for another couple of days. Perhaps we should do something to take your mind off it for a little while."

He leans over and starts to pull me toward him, but I put a hand to his chest to stop him. "What? Are you okay?" he asks, his impending lust replaced by immediate concern.

I take a deep breath and tell him what I've been wanting to say for three days now... but haven't dared. "Matthew... I'm late."

His brows scrunch in confusion for just a second before they arch in understanding and surprise. "Really?" he whispers excitedly. "We've only been trying a month... do you think...? So soon, I mean?"

"It only takes once, Matthew! And we've 'tried' more than a few times in the last month," I giggle.

Suddenly, he looks like a kid in a candy store. His eyes are bright and wide, a goofy grin plastered across his face as if he can't believe his dumb luck. "Okay, so...what now? How soon can you see the doctor to find out?"

"The doctor? Oh, honey, we don't have to wait that long," I assure him with a pat to his cheek. "I've got a three-pack of pregnancy tests in the bathroom."

"Jesus, Julia! What are you waiting for, then?"

He jumps out of bed and pulls me with him into our en suite bathroom. When we're situated on the fluffy blue bathmats, he looks at me expectantly. "What now?"

"I pee on a stick."

"Ohhh... huh..." he says, suddenly looking a lot less enthusiastic.

"You know what? I'm nervous enough without you watching. Why don't you just wait out there and I'll do the test myself? It takes like three minutes to process."

"You sure you don't want me to stay?"

"Pee. On. A. Stick."

He holds up his hands in surrender as he backs out of the bathroom, closing the door behind him.

* * *

I stare helplessly at the bomb in my bathroom. Oh, it doesn't look like a bomb. It looks like an ordinary kitchen timer, but with each tick, it brings me one second closer to a life-imploding blast. I'm waiting for it to go off in my face, raining down debris and rocking my perfect, orderly little world. One way ...or another.

Tick, tick, tick, tick.

I'm perched on the side of the tub, unable to move or speak. Helpless to stop this collision with destiny.

Tick, tick, tick, tick.

The house is absolutely still. I can't even hear Matthew pacing the floor anymore. He must've finally sat down. Somewhere in the distance I can hear the Long Island Railroad as it makes its way into Port Jefferson from points further west.

Tick, tick, tick, tick.

With every passing second, I know I'm closer to my fate, my new reality. This little bomb has the power to change everything. Or, it may be a dud. It may simply end its countdown with nothing more than a reminder that anything may change at any time.

DING!

I jump up and stand, staring. I take a deep breath. "It's okay. I'm okay. I can do this," I whisper to myself as I take a tentative step toward the vanity, where the pregnancy test is resting, face down, on a washcloth. I close my eyes for just a moment and then open them again with resolve. Here goes nothing. Or everything.

I don't pick it up all at once. Instead, I carefully lift the edge of it, tipping it back little by little until I see a tiny bit of color. Blue. A little more and I see part of a dash. And a little more, a line crossing it. A dash with a line crossing it. It's a plus sign. A beautiful, bright blue plus sign.

I rush to the door and throw it open, ready to propel myself through the bedroom, but I stop short. He's already there, standing right outside the threshold, waiting ... almost fearfully. I hold up the blue plus sign for him to see. He looks from it and to me, and then back to it again.

"Is that... a plus?" he asks, as if he doesn't trust his eyes.

I nod.

In an instant, he's twirling me around, and we're both laughing. When we stop spinning, he puts me down, but doesn't let me go. His lips find their way to mine in a kiss that is as light and soft as feathers.

"Are you happy?" I ask him when he finally pulls his mouth from mine. I see tears start to well in his eyes. He can't speak; he only nods. "You're going to be a daddy," I whisper.

Now comes his smile, making the skin around his eyes crinkle. "I'm already a daddy, Julia," he reminds me.

"Yes," I say, putting a hand to the side of his face.

As if on cue, a high-pitched shriek comes over the baby monitor. Matthew sets me back down on the floor and delivers a kiss to the top of my head. "That would be our firstborn, in need of a diaper change, judging by the sound of it," he says. "I'll get him, you relax. It's time to start taking better care of yourself, Mrs. Ayers."

"Matthew," I protest with a laugh, "we've still got a long way to go. Please don't start treating me like I'm made of glass already."

"Oh, so the idea of a nice long bubble bath before bed isn't appealing to you then? Would you rather put on the hazmat suit and get David into a clean diaper yourself?"

Well, since he put it like that... The corners of my lips twitch with the threat of a smile.

"Uh-huh," he says, pointing to my face. "I saw that. Go! Soak until you're a shriveled little prune."

He doesn't have to tell me again. I start to head back to ground zero so I can immerse myself in lavender bubbles, but I stop in the doorway and turn back to him again.

"I think it'll be a girl this time," I say.

"Really?" I nod. "Well, I think we should pick a boy's name too, just in case."

"I want a musical name this time," I blurt.

"What? You mean like Johann Sebastian or Wolfgang Amadeus?"

"No, silly!" I giggle. "Maybe Coda or Symphony."

He's looking at me as if I've lost my mind. "*Coda* Ayers?"

"Or... Symphony Ayers," I counter.

He shakes his head. "I don't even know what to say to that, Julia," he groans as he turns around and walks out of our bedroom, still shaking his head.

"Your mommy is crazy!" I hear him say to David through the baby monitor. "Crazy, crazy, crazy!"

Our son's deep laugh tells me there's some tickling going on a few doors down the hall. I rub my belly gently and smile. These are good minutes, I think. That's the way I used to measure time as a child. But I had good reason—my entire life was lived minute by minute. One minute my father was fine. The next minute, he was beating me with his belt.

On this particular evening, the good minutes turn into a good hour. By the time I put on my robe and head back into the bedroom, I find Matthew and David both in our big bed, sound asleep. I stand in the doorway and watch my husband, on his side, with David snuggled into the crook of his arm. Their chests rise and fall, almost in unison.

Over the last two years, I have marveled at his capacity to love a child who isn't his. A child who, with every passing day, grows to look more and more like his biological father. It seems as if so much of my life has been one disappointment after another, so to find myself in a happy marriage with a beautiful child and a flourishing career, well, it's just that I never dared to think we could be this happy. Even now, I reach over and rap the wood doorframe, just to be on the safe side. I wouldn't want to tempt fate.

But, then again, even I know that fate doesn't always need a reason.

Chapter 27

Julia

I'm feeling considerably better about the CD release party when we're back in the city the night before. Matthew is busy getting David down for the night while I unpack the suitcase I made him haul here from Long Island. I love having the best of both worlds, the country and the city, but it can be a real juggling act, getting three people packed and organized to move from one location to the next every other week.

I unzip the roller bag and start the inventory process. I have less than twenty-four hours to go and this would be a good time to find out if I need to pick up hairspray or lipstick or something. One by one, I pull the items out of the jam-packed case. Stockings. Extra pair of stockings. Extra *extra* pair of stockings. Favorite nail polish. Incredibly uncomfortable, incredibly expensive, incredibly gorgeous shoes. Velvet wrap. Sparkly hair clips. Extra sparkly hair clips ... and so on, and so on, and so on. When I get to the bottom of the bag, I notice something unusual ... something wrapped in delicate tissue paper.

"What on earth?" I mumble as I pull the sheets apart to find my 'special' nighty. The one I keep wrapped in tissue, so its gossamer-thin fabric won't pull. I take it from its paper nest and hold it up by its delicate, lace straps. I'd forgotten how beautiful it is. What I haven't forgotten is how insanely expensive it was. I bought it for the honeymoon we never took, though it did make a very brief appearance on our wedding night. But how did it get in here? I didn't pack it. Which means that...

"Oh, you naughty, naughty boy," I gasp to myself, shaking my head and grinning at the same time. "Hoping to get lucky, are we?"

I glance at the alarm clock on the nightstand. It's nearly nine o'clock. David should be out cold before Matthew even finished reading him 'Goodnight Moon.' That doesn't leave me much time.

I quickly toss everything back into the roller bag and push it around to the other side of the dresser out of sight. After that, I run around the bed, quickly turning down the sheets and fluffing the pillows. Then, I head into the shower for a quick hosing-off and leg shave.

When I finally slip the whisper-soft negligée over my head, it falls in all the right places. Next comes the matching thong. I *hate* the matching thong. It's like butt floss. But he loves them, and I suppose I should be grateful he's not into garters or corsets. Finally, I pull the ponytail holder from my hair so that it falls into soft, auburn waves around my shoulders.

A quick check in the full-length mirror, and I know I'm good to go. And not a moment too soon, as I hear Matthew checking the locks and turning off the lights... the last thing he does before settling down to read in bed. The bed upon which I'm lying when he opens the door.

He stops dead in his tracks.

"Wow," he whispers appreciatively, eyebrows arched. "Julia, you look ... incredible. Is that what you wore on our wedding night?" he asks quietly. As if he doesn't know *exactly* what it is!

I nod, pretending not to know that he put it in the suitcase and allow a sultry little smile to play on my lips. I'm not usually the instigator when it comes to sex, so this is a nice treat for us both. His willingness to participate is, shall we say, suddenly very pronounced as he comes into the room and shuts the door behind him quietly. By the time he gets to the bed, he is minus one sweatshirt, two socks and he's already got one leg out of his jeans. I get up and help him to dispense with the other leg and his briefs. And since I'm in the neighborhood...

"Oh, Julia," he moans, when I take him in my mouth. His hands stroke my hair from above where I'm kneeling on the floor. I'm gentle, but firm with him, alternating sucking and licking and nibbling. Once upon a time, this wasn't on the top of my to-do list, but my Matthew seems to cherish and adore everything that I do for him. To him, and me, this isn't just an act of physical pleasure—it's a gesture of my love for him. This is the love of my life and *that* is what makes this so hot for both of us.

"He gasps in surprise when my hands come up from under to massage his testicles. This man is mine, I think, as I take him deeper into my mouth, my eyes peeking upward to catch a glimpse of him with his own eyes closed, head lolling back on this neck, as if praying to the heavens.

"Julia," he whispers down at me after a few more seconds of this. "Julia, let's go to bed."

Uh-uh. Not this time. This time I get to be turned on by his mewling and moaning and begging. I get the vicarious thrill of his pleasure and the high of controlling it. I redouble my efforts, using more inward pressure as I wrap my mouth around his shaft.

"Julia... please... I don't think I can—"

I'd smile if I could. I know that tone in his voice intimately, and I put him out of his misery with some fast in and out across my slick lips. Suddenly, his hands are balled in my hair, and I can feel the tremors wracking his body at the same moment that I taste him. When, at last, he is able to open his eyes, he finds me, still on my knees, watching him with complete adoration. His pleasure is my pleasure.

Before I can get a word out, he bends down, scoops me up and takes me to our bed. Oh, he can't possibly be ready to go another round! But, as it turns out, that's not exactly what he has in mind. At least, not yet, anyway. I'm on my back, lying across the bed as he climbs up with me. He is lying on his side next to me when he takes my face in his hands and kisses me. It's a long, deep, kiss that makes me feel as if he's trying to inhale me, to drink in my essence, my soul.

I feel his fingers exploring me through the thin fabric of my soaking thong. When he nudges his index finger past the elastic at the crotch and makes contact with me, I gasp into his mouth and arch off the bed. But he is relentless. His mouth will not leave mine—as desperate as I am to moan out loud—to call out his name. His tongue continues its soft caressing of my cheeks and teeth and all around my tongue as his fingers pull me apart, wantonly rubbing and pinching and thumbing, as if my body were his to play with as he pleases. Turns out, it is, actually.

I think I'm going to lose my mind when he stops suddenly, both the touching and the kissing. But it only takes him a second to pull my right nipple from the cup of the nightie and attach his mouth to it. At the same time, his arm makes itself at home as it lays between my breasts, all the way down to my abdomen so he can lodge his entire hand into the front waistband of my panties now, with full, unrestricted access to every part of me.

My mouth is free once again, but I can't even moan, I'm too busy taking in one surprised gasp after the next as he manipulates me with expert precision. He runs his hand languidly up and down, up and down, from one end of my slickness to the other, ever so slightly brushing against my clit, as if by accident, but just to tease. The torture is exquisite, and then, with no warning, his mouth finds mine again with even more hunger and passion, and he concentrates his efforts on rubbing just the right spot while dipping into me again and again.

He was right to cover my mouth with his because I'd be screaming at this point if I were free to do so. Instead, I moan and plead and groan against his lips as if they're a gag. All the while, he pushes me further and further over the edge with his relentless rubbing and thrusting until my body is writhing left and right and up and down, unable to control itself.

When the wave comes, it takes my breath away, wracking my limbs with shuddering intensity until I'm reduced to a few residual twitches of ecstatic electricity. I'm panting and practically in tears when he takes his mouth away from mine. My eyes are closed as he kisses my forehead, then my eyelids and my cheeks and lips. I'm unable to speak when he adjusts himself on his back and pulls me into his strong arms so I can feel his heart beating through the wall of his chest.

Oh, yeah. This nighty was worth every penny.

Chapter 28

Julia

When I was fourteen years old, I became entranced by the winter Olympics. At the North Fork Children's Home, I'd beg our housemother to let me stay up late to watch the figure skating. I didn't see pretty costumes or romantic stories. I didn't care about the athleticism or the difficulty of the programs. Watching the skaters was like seeing music in a physical manifestation. I could see the music. And I was enraptured by what I saw.

Now, from next to me, my accompanist starts the rippling undercurrent of Bach's *Prelude No.1 in C Major*. The composer wrote it for piano. And then, nearly a century and a half later, a composer named Charles Gounod superimposed his own melody on top of Bach's...his setting of the *Ave Maria*. It became known as the Bach/Gounod *Ave Maria* and it is the last piece that I will play tonight. It's the encore that the audience has demanded of me and, with the heavy lifting of Vivaldi and Brahms behind me, I allow myself to be lost within this sublime music. I allow myself to skate.

In my mind, I glide effortlessly across the smooth, unmarred ice, stretching my arms and delicately turning my body so that it faces in the opposite direction even as it continues its forward trajectory. And then I slip into a spin. Not a blinding, blurring spiral, but the most delicate of circular motion before I fall back effortlessly to where I began. Up down. High low. My body flexes with the music, which flexes with my body.

As the piece starts to its climax, I see myself as a skater in the 'spread eagle' position, both feet on the ice, toes pointed outward in opposite directions, heels facing one another. My arms are outstretched, my chest laid open as if awaiting embrace. As the music builds, so does my speed, carrying me into a series of intricate jumps strung together. A toe loop, an axel, a camel spin. I can practically feel the gentle swoosh of air blowing through my hair as I sail effortlessly through the boundaries of gravity.

After much too short a time, I feel the *Ave Maria* coming to its inevitable conclusion. Even as I pull bow across strings, I am like a gold-medalist at the end of an emotionally powerful routine. I come out of one final, languid twist, sinking down and down and down, until my knees hit the glassy surface and I simply slide across the ice with eyes upturned toward heaven and arms open in welcoming adoration.

When I come back to myself once more, to this tiny room built around a concrete floor, I am breathing hard from the effort and spent from the satisfaction. The audience jumps up in rapturous applause for a performance that they don't even know they have seen.

* * *

My sublime experience is quickly forgotten as I step out into the main exhibit hall of the Beau-Radcliffe Gallery and into a swarm. It's clear that the Kreisler Competition has really gone all out with its huge PR and marketing departments.

Every horizontal surface is littered with my new CD. There's a banner outside the gallery, over the front door, and then, there's the cardboard cutout. Right now, I'm standing in front of it, tilting my head from side to side, trying to decide what to make of my super-sized doppelganger. It's me, but it's not me. I'm considerably more statuesque in the image in front of me, easily six-feet tall compared to my more diminutive five-foot-one. And-a-half. My teeth are the size of subway tiles and my God, you could literally drive a truck through those pores!

"Wow, has anyone ever told you that you look like her?"

Matthew has sidled up next to me. Both of me.

"You read my mind!" I say with a delighted smile. He leans down and gives me a long, slow, soft kiss. "Again, you read my mind."

He wraps an arm around my waist, pulling me closer to him. "You did the skating thing again, didn't you?" he guesses with a knowing smile. I give a little shrug, amazed by his ability to see through me every time. "Well, you were spectacular," he murmurs in my ear.

"If you think that was good, wait till we get home. I've got quite an encore planned." I offer a suggestive raise of a single eyebrow.

"I'll look forward to multiple curtain calls," he counters with his own bit of naughty thrown in.

I put my head on his chest and lean into him as I survey all of the people swirling around us. It almost feels as if we are standing still while they continue to move in fast forward. They're taking signed copies of my CD from a big display table and chattering animatedly to one another as they survey the beautiful paintings and sculpture around them.

"They're all here for you," Matthew reminds me, following my eyes around the room.

He's right. I recognize most of the people here. Some are from the Kreisler International Music Competition, including Lester Morgan, the director. Several friends from McInnes Conservatory are here as well—I spot Mila Strassman with her boyfriend, they're sneaking kisses in the corner and it makes me smile. Brett and Maggie are here somewhere, too. I debated about whether or not to bring David, but it would be way past his bedtime and my little firecracker of a son gets very testy when he doesn't get enough sleep.

My eyes are drawn to an abstract painting by a hot new artist, Vanessa Shogreen. I suspect by the time this event is over, half of her paintings will have 'sold' stickers on them. I've been eyeballing one called 'Still Life in French Toast,' though I'm sure Matthew will just tell me my breakfast food obsession is out of control. I'm just wondering if I can sneak the four-figure price past him in the checkbook when I hear a familiar, squeal.

"Noooooo, Nata, nooooo!"

I cringe as I watch David squirming to get out of Natalie's iron embrace, surrounded by several extremely expensive pieces of sculpture. Maybe bringing him wasn't the best idea.

"What on earth is all the fuss about?" A moment later, Trudy Corrigan steps out from behind a life-sized rendering of a winged woman with a beanie on her head. David stills instantly at the sound of her voice.

"Holy cow..." I gape.

"More like holy shit," Matthew chuckles from next to me. "That woman is like a baby whisperer or something."

He's hit the nail on the head. My boy's huge hazel eyes track on the tall, lean woman as she makes her way toward him—the woman with the identical, huge, hazel eyes. When she's close enough, he holds out his arms to go to her. Nat shoots a questioning glance our way and I nod my okay.

Trudy says something to her that I can't hear, and it makes Natalie smile. She hands him over and I watch in awe as David immediately wraps his arms around her neck, snuggling his little head against her chest. It's as if he's known her his entire life.

"If I weren't seeing it...I'd swear it wasn't possible..." Matthews marvels. "That kid *never* goes to strangers."

"Oh, it's possible," Brett quips from behind us, putting an arm over each of our shoulders. "My mother has never met a toddler she couldn't tame."

I watch in awe as she bounces him gently, whispering something in his ear and kissing his carrot top. In a moment, Maggie joins them, and he perks up, excited to chatter at her.

"You were great, Julia," Brett says, and I get my own smooch on the cheek.

"Thank you, Brett, I'm really glad you guys could come...and that you brought your mom."

"Oh, that was all her," he informs me. "She hasn't stopped talking about what a remarkable woman you are since you had breakfast."

"Really? I was afraid maybe I'd put her off a little. We talked about some serious stuff, and I didn't agree with everything she had to say."

Brett shrugs in his navy suit jacket and runs a hand through his hair, a slightly darker shade than his mother's. "Trudy doesn't take many things personally, Julia. And she's not one to hold her tongue, so she's used to having difficult discussions. Still, she seems eager to spend more time with you and Matthew and the chubby tornado over there."

He nods in David's direction with his chin an instant before my spots him.

"Uncaaaaaaa!!!" he screams, making Maggie, Trudy and everyone in a three-block radius wince from the volume.

"Uh-Oh! I've been summoned by the prince," Brett says. "Hey, are we still having dinner at Tucci's after this?"

"I hope so," I groan. "I was too nervous to eat all day and now I'm starving. Will your mom be joining us?"

He shakes his head. "No, she's going to head back to the brownstone. In fact, I was hoping maybe she and Nat could share a cab...just so I know she gets home safely."

"Oh, of course!"

"Hey," Matthew interrupts, "why doesn't she just go back to our apartment with Nat? David would love it and you know how interesting Natalie is. They can order some dinner in."

"Now that is a great idea," Brett agrees. "I won't have to worry about her sitting in my apartment all alone. Let me go suggest it."

No sooner is he gone than I smell Old Spice close by. I'd know that scent anywhere. When I turn around, Dr. Sam is smiling at me, drink in one hand, overflowing plate of goodies in the other.

"Dr. Sam!" I exclaim as I gingerly try to navigate around his perishables so I can get close enough to give him a kiss on the cheek. He's grinning from ear to ear.

"Julia, your playing was breathtaking, as always. You make me so proud!"

I can feel the familiar warmth of color rising to my cheeks.

"Oh, you, stop being so bashful, already! Don't you know you're the toast of the classical music world right now?"

"Stop it," I mumble. "You're embarrassing me!"

"You two sound like a teenager and her father," Matthew grins with a chuckle.

"Well, you *are* the closest thing I have to a dad," I say softly, putting a hand to his lapel.

Just then, Lester Morgan, the Kreisler Competition Director, and host of this oversized soiree, breezes past on his way to the other end of the room.

"Julia," he says over his shoulder. "Don't go too far, please, it's nearly time for your toast."

He's gone before I can respond, but he somehow manages to send a waiter our way with a tray of champagne flutes.

"Oh, just seltzer for me," I tell the young man. He nods and slips away again.

"My dear girl," says Dr. Sam with alarm in his voice, "don't you know it's bad luck to toast with water?"

"I'm not drinking right now," I reply and give him my best, Mona Lisa smile. He gets it.

"Oh. Oh! Julia, you're not...are you...?"

I nod and Matthew gives me another side squeeze.

"I am. We're expecting another baby in the early spring. I was hoping to get through all of this before we told anyone."

He's beaming, like the proud grandpa that David already knows him to be. "I'm so glad things have finally settled down for the two of you."

"Shhh! Not too loud," I caution, only half-kidding. "You'll jinx us, Dr. Sam!"

"Ah, good point! Now, then, where did that lad with the champagne go?" he mutters as he wanders off in search of another drink.

"Hey, Mrs. Ayers," Matthew says as soon as he's out of earshot. "No more talk about jinxes, okay? Everything is going to be just perfect from here on out. Understood?" he asks, putting a hand on the camouflaged swell of my belly.

I put a hand to his face in response. "I love you, Matthew Ayers."

He smiles so broadly and once again I'm struck by how handsome he looks in his suit. Those amber eyes, the tousled brown hair. He looks hot as he leans down and gives me another kiss, this time deeper and longer. I find myself standing on tippy-toes just to be closer to him. I'm tempted to take this man and sneak out the side door, but it's too late. I catch sight of Lester, waving at me frantically from the other side of the gallery.

"Do you want me to go with you or wait for you?" my husband asks.

"With me. Always, always with me."

He gives a quick bow and offers me his arm like some chivalrous suitor out of a Jane Austen book.

"I'd kill for a drink right now," I mutter, forcing a smile as they all start to applaud my success.

Chapter 29

Julia

The wineglass is almost to Brett's lips when it stops short, sending tiny waves of Shiraz spilling over the rim and onto his shirt. "Oh, fuck!" he says, looking down at his newly bloodied chest briefly before looking back at Matthew. "You're making that shit up," he accuses with a laugh.

"I shit you not," Matthew responds, shaking his head solemnly. "I wish I was. Julia is determined to get my kid's ass kicked on the playground."

"What? Stop it!" I protest, smacking his arm. "God! What is with you and the baby names? I make a few original suggestions, and suddenly I want our child to be bullied?"

"What was it again? Bass Cleff?" Brett teases.

I put my hands on my hips. I'm not amused.

"Crescendo," Matthew corrects.

"Oh, no! Poor little *Crescendo!*" Brett wails in a tortured voice. "God, those kids can be such douchebags! Julia! Why, Julia? Why?"

I roll my eyes. "Okay, okay, knock it off already."

We're two bottles of wine too many into this little 'after party' at Tucci's, down the street from the Beau-Radcliffe Gallery. Well, more accurately, Matthew and Brett are. Maggie's a bit tipsy, too, and I'm finding it's not as much fun being the only sober one at the table.

"I'm thinking Glockenspiel," Matthew says, ignoring me.

"Are you sure?" Brett counters. "Dude, how about Cadenza or Allegro or maybe Forte..."

"Okay, okay! Enough already!" Maggie laughs as she passes the basket of bread in my direction. "Leave Julia alone. She's just trying to find an original name that has some meaning to her."

Brett leans over and kisses her cheek sweetly. "That's my girl. Always coming to someone else's defense," he murmurs.

She swats him with a linen napkin. "I'm serious, Corrigan, knock it off!" she says more sternly, and then, she smiles and rolls her eyes. "Ugh. I knew Julia and I should have gone out and left the two of you at home!" she groans.

"No, no. I'm sorry, Maggie," Matthew says with a contrite smile. "Julia knows I'm just teasing. I don't care what we call the baby, I just want to get him or her into the world safely."

"Good answer," I agree.

There's a whirl of activity around us as two servers deliver beautiful plates, piled high with Italian delicacies meant to be shared family-style. My mouth is watering.

"Dig in, everyone!" Maggie says, starting the circulation of the platters and plates and bowls filled with our Italian feast.

"Wow, this all looks so amazing," I murmur as I ladle a river of sauce onto a mountain of pasta. "Good restaurant choice, Maggie."

"Thanks, I love to come here so I can try a little of everything."

"Oh, yeah. And she means *everything*," Brett teases. "Careful! You can run-up a bill that's more than your bow is worth here, Matthew."

"No worries there," Matthew says, holding up the empty bottle for our server who hurries off to find an opened one. "Julia's got the tab tonight," he grins.

"Hmm?" I ask distractedly, having been caught glancing at my phone.

"Don't you worry, Mama Bear, Baby Bear's doing just fine," he says, nudging my arm with his.

I nudge back and smile.

Brett points a fork in our direction. "You know, if I were you guys, I wouldn't be worried about what's going on now. But I *would* be losing sleep over what David will do when he has an accomplice!" he chuckles

Matthew looks at me, his face suddenly panic-stricken. "Shit, Julia, he's right," he says with deadly seriousness. "We are *so* fucked."

Chapter 30

Jeremy

"**T**wenty bucks," I offer, pulling my wallet out of my pants pocket.

"Dude, I can't ..."

"Fifty."

"Fifty?"

Ah, there it is. The pimply kid scratches his head underneath the ridiculous baseball cap with the meatball on it.

"Come on, man," I coax him with faux male bonding. "I want to surprise my girlfriend by putting her engagement ring in the box and delivering it myself!"

He looks uncertain. Last chance before I knock you over the head with a brick and take it from you, you little shit. "Seventy-five. It's all I've got, but you have to give me the hat, too."

Sold! The hat is on my head, the box is in my hand, and he's strolling back down the block counting the cash in under five seconds. I pull the hat a little lower down on my forehead in case there's someone in the lobby who's seen me before. But when the doorman opens the door to let me in, I see that won't be a problem.

"Delivery for 16D," I announce matter-of-factly to the rent-a-cop at the front desk. He nods and calls up to confirm they're expecting me. They are. Well, they're not expecting me. Just the pizza. I smile once the elevator doors slide closed and I'm on my way up to the place where it all began for Julia and me.

I walk to the door and keep my head down to the peephole when I ring the bell.

"Papa Paulie's delivery," I call out cordially.

"Just a second!" comes the muffled response.

I hear her thumping around in there, presumably getting my payment and tip. When I hear her pull the peephole cover aside and hold my breath but then I hear the deadbolt unlock and I exhale. Then comes the doorknob lock. I shift the pizza box to my left hand and make a fist with my right.

The door opens, inch-by-inch, as if in slow motion. The bitch is smiling at the top of my hat, cash in hand. I lift my head and see the immediate light of recognition on her face. Her mouth opens to say something, or maybe to scream, I'll never know which, because she never gets it out. I punch her so quickly, and with so much force, that she's knocked back through the tile foyer and onto the carpet of the living room. I step inside, quickly locking the door behind me. She's groaning from the floor.

I drop the box on the breakfast bar and lose the hat on my way to squat down next to her. Before she can even think about doing anything, I pull the hypodermic from the case in my pocket and jab her arm with it. She's out cold within a matter of thirty seconds. Nice. I wasn't a hundred percent certain this shit would work. You never know when you order online. I put the case away with the remaining hypodermic. This one's got Julia's name written all over it.

There's no way I'm picking this chick up, so I grab her from under the armpits and drag her into Julia's bedroom. The bedroom where we spent many a sleepless night. I'm able to get her up onto the bed and leave the room, closing the door behind me. That's when I hear him.

"Nata!"

I walk slowly to the other side of the hall, to what used to be Matthew's bedroom. I notice the new blue color from here. A few steps more, and I spot elephants on the walls. When I stick my head in the room, there's the big white crib with more elephants hanging over it. And there he is, I can see him lying down through the slats. I can't decide if I care enough to get a good look at the brat. Oh, what the hell.

He doesn't seem at all alarmed when I peer down at him, quite the opposite, actually. He gives me a big sloppy smile, and I spot a few tiny white teeth. Well, there's no denying it, this kid is mine. I see myself all over his face. The eyes are the same and he even has my arched eyebrows—though his are red. Really not a bad looking kid, as far as rug rats go.

"You be quiet. You hear me? I don't want to deal with a screaming kid," I say down to him.

He just smiles and laughs, kicking his legs up and down excitedly. I reach above the crib and wind the mobile, so the elephants start a slow spin above him, to the strains of Brahms' Lullaby. He fixes his tiny mini-me eyes on the mobile and his lids start to droop immediately.

"Well, that was easy enough," I mutter. "Let's hope for your mother's sake that she's as cooperative as you are."

Chapter 31

Julia

The apartment is dark when I come in. Why is it so dark in here? I drop the cello case next to the door and hang my purse on the hook.

"Nat?" I call out.

Silence.

"Natalie?"

I glance at my watch. It's nearly midnight. Maybe she's fallen asleep? But that's not like her. I walk into the kitchen, no note. In fact, there's no sign that anyone has been in here since I left this afternoon. I walk out into the living room, which is totally still, totally silent and totally empty. I flip the switch for the lights but nothing happens.

"Dammit!" I mutter to myself.

Well, just two more places they could be, if they're anywhere in this apartment. I take a left down the hall to the baby's room, which used to be Matthew's room when we were just roommates. I stick my head in the door first and can clearly see David in his crib by the glow of the elephant nightlight in the corner. I breathe a sigh of relief.

Okay, she must be taking a nap in my room. Not like her, but not out of the realm of possibility either. But before I confirm my suspicion, I need to confirm that all is right in David Land. I slip my shoes off in the hallway and pad silently into the room so I can peer over the rail of his crib.

And there he is, my sweet little boy. He's on his back, looking up at me with a smile. He gurgles softly, kicking his legs as if he's riding a bicycle. I can tell he's sleepy, but he wants to play. If I keep things low-key enough, he'll just go back to sleep. Or, I could just pull him out and smother him with kisses, which is what I want to do. But he's going to have to wait a second while I track down Nat.

"You stay put, little man. You hear me?" I say softly, and am rewarded with his big, sloppy, gummy grin.

I take a step, continuing to wave at him as I make my way out of the room backwards. I'm almost to the door when I hear a familiar squeak behind me, the hinge of the closet. But I'm a split second too late. From behind me come two strong hands, one grabbing my waist and pulling me back, the other clamping down over my mouth. I try to pull away, but my stockinged feet slip uselessly on the hardwood floor.

Oh my God! Oh my God!

All I can think about is getting away from whoever this is and getting David out of here. I start to struggle, kicking at the person behind me, clawing at his arms, slamming my head back against his chest. But I'm only succeeding in wearing myself out. Then I feel breathing, hot against the side of my face.

"Shhh," his voice whispers soothingly in my ear.

I shake my head violently, defiantly, but I'm no match for his strength. *Jeremy's* strength. Who else could this possibly be? Just the thought of it makes me dig my nails into his arm around my midsection.

"Hey, knock it off, Jules!" he demands, and my suspicion is confirmed.

Son of a bitch! He's in my home! He's been in here with my child. I'm not scared now, I'm furious. I twist and writhe and try to slam my weight down on his instep, but he's too fast.

"Enough!" he hisses in my ear as I try to get a garbled scream past his hand. He pulls me hard up against his body, his face so close that I can smell the beer on his breath.

"Listen to me, if you don't settle down *right now* and do what I say, little David isn't going to be smiling for very long. Do you understand what I'm telling you?"

Oh, Christ. My heart sinks as I realize I'm totally and completely stuck. It's not just me anymore.

"Do. You. Understand?" he repeats, more gruffly this time.

I take a deep breath through my nose and try to calm myself. I give him a slow, grudging nod.

"Good!" he chirps, his tone suddenly pleased. "Now, if I take my hand off your mouth, can you keep quiet?"

I start to nod but he stops me.

"Wait. Think about it for a second, because you screaming is the difference between life and death. Do you need a second to calm down?"

Strangely enough, I do. Though how he could have possibly anticipated that, I have no idea. I nod again. Yes, I need a second.

"Fair enough," his voice says softly. "Go ahead and breathe in through your nose."

I do as he instructs. One breath. Two breaths. The third time, I feel my breath catch in my throat and I start to cry.

"You're going to suffocate like that," he informs me coolly.

He's right. Without use of my mouth, the crying is causing my nose to run.

"Can I take my hand away now?"

I nod and he very slowly uncovers my mouth. I don't move.

"Okay, good. I'm going to let go of you but so help me God, if you try anything—and I mean *anything*, Jules—I'll kill both of you. Him first so you can watch. Do you understand me?"

I close my eyes and nod again, not trusting myself to speak yet. Jeremy lets go of me just long enough to grab ahold of my shoulders and spin me around so we're facing one another. His newly blonde, clean-shaved image smiles down on my tear-stained face. So, Natalie's instincts were right. I want to kill *myself* for not paying closer attention.

"Hello, Jules!"

"What do you want, Jeremy?" I rasp, my damp eyes meeting his.

"Everything, Jules. Absolutely everything. And you're going to give it to me."

"Where's Natalie? Did you..." I swallow hard. "Is she alright?"

He's still smiling. "Oh, she's just fine. She's passed out on your bed. I put her there after I shot her up with a sedative. She'll wake up in a couple of hours with a nasty headache."

I close my eyes and take a deep breath, trying to steady my frantic pulse and concentrate on the situation at hand. I have to keep my baby safe. "Okay, what's next?"

"We're going to leave now. All three of us. Like a happy little family."

I look over my shoulder to the crib where I can see David pulling on his feet and hear him chattering nonsense to the mobile animals hanging over his head. I feel the fear rising in my chest. "Where?"

He doesn't reply.

"Jeremy, do you have any idea how much work he is? He'll fuss and cry and whine. He runs all over the place now, and he throws temper-tantrums at the drop of a hat. You don't want to take him anywhere, believe me. He's more trouble than you need," I entreat him, trying to sound sincere and reasonable even as the panic within me is starting to reach critical mass.

I see him considering this. He looks at David, then at me, then back at the crib again. "Fine. He stays here. Let's go."

"But we can't just leave him here alone!" I exclaim a little too loudly He gives me a warning look. "I'm sorry, I'm sorry."

"He'll be fine," he says, grabbing my forearm and pushing me toward the door of the nursery.

"Jeremy, please..."

"Now, Jules," he orders, clearly starting to lose what little patience he has.

I notice the diaper bag on top of the changing table, a bottle sticking out of one of the front pockets. Jeremy wasn't bluffing—he'd been prepared to take us both.

"Let me just give him his bottle..." I say, reaching for it, but he yanks me back hard.

"Uh-uh. I don't know what the hell you and Xena Warrior Princess have hiding in that bag."

Dammit! Think, Julia. Think.

"Then you get it," I blurt. "Please, Jeremy, it'll keep him quiet, and then he'll probably fall asleep."

From the crib, David is starting to become agitated.

"Mama!" he calls to me, peeking through the slats of the crib. In another second he's going to pull himself up to a standing position and once he does that, I won't be able to get him back down to sleep. I turn back to Jeremy and put a hand on his arm, meeting his gaze squarely.

"Please. Just do this for me and I swear I'll go with you without a fuss. Please. You know me well enough to know I'm not lying," I plead.

He scrutinizes my face, as if he can see something written across it that will confirm what I'm saying to him. At last, I see the acquiescence in his eyes. "Alright," he mutters, reaching around me and sticking his hand into the bag. He pulls the bottle from its pocket and hands it to me. "You have thirty seconds."

"Thank you," I say sincerely.

He lets go of my arm and I rush to the crib and help my son to lie on his back again. He smiles up at me. I put the bottle in his mouth and his chubby little hands latch onto it as he sucks happily. I brush the hair off of his forehead and watch as his eyelids grow heavy.

"It's okay, baby," I whisper. "Everything is going to be just fine."

"Yeah, I wouldn't count on that this time," Jeremy mutters right behind me. He grabs my upper arm and pulls me from the crib while pushing me toward the door.

I swipe at the tears, which are running down my face again, looking over my shoulder every inch of the way down the hall, through the living room and to the front door, where we stop short.

"I'm dead serious, Jules. Don't even *think* about sending a signal, making a run, screaming, anything." He holds up Natalie's key ring for me to see. "I can be back in this apartment and snapping his little neck before you can even get someone to notice you. And you know I'll do it."

"I understand, Jeremy," I assure him quietly. "I just don't know if I can get through the lobby looking like nothing's wrong."

"Yeah, well, we're going out the back, so that won't be a problem."

"I—I don't have a key for that elevator..."

"I do," he cuts me off as he opens the front door, sticks his head out and looks both ways down the hallway. It's silent.

He gestures for me to step out ahead of him. I do, and before I know what's happening, he's ushering me all the way down and into the service elevator, which he does, indeed, have a key for. We're out of the building in under two minutes. There isn't anyone back here in the alley, but I look up and around, hoping the security camera will catch me and the security guard will notice. But no one comes as we approach a nondescript white commercial van.

"Where are we going?"

"Right here," he says, pulling the back door open. He nods for me to get in. When I look over my shoulder one last time, he gives me a rough shove. I scramble inside on my hands and knees, him following close behind me, pulling the van doors shut and securing them from the inside. Then he turns around and gestures to a mattress I hadn't noticed.

"Lie down on your stomach."

"What?"

"You heard me."

I do as he says. "Jeremy, you don't have to do this," I plead desperately, but he doesn't respond. I hear the rustle of a plastic bag, and then I feel his weight next to me on the mattress.

"Put your hands behind your back," he orders.

"What?" I repeat.

"I'm not going to keep repeating myself, just do it the first time I tell you or I'm going to get pissed off. And you know what I'm like when I'm pissed off, Jules."

I do. I put my hands behind me, and he pulls them together roughly before fastening my wrists with a zip tie. "Ouch! It's too tight," I complain as the plastic bites into my skin.

"Oh, come on, Jules. You don't fool me, I remember how much you like to be tied up," he teases me as he repeats the process with my ankles

I have no response, so I just bury my face in the soft pillow in front of my face. But he doesn't allow me that luxury for long. Without warning, Jeremy grabs a handful of my hair and yanks my head up with one hand, while holding a cotton bandana in front of my face with the other.

"Open your mouth," he barks.

I just stare at it, realizing what he intends to do. My panic is renewed, and I start to struggle again. He jams his knee painfully into the middle of my back, his weight pressing me hard down into the mattress.

"What the hell are you thinking? Huh? I'm more than twice your size and you're tied up. Who do you think is going to win this little tussle?" I fight back a sob. "Okay, you know what? Maybe little David should come with us. It seems as if that's the only way you're going to do what I tell you to do." He starts to get up.

"No! No, no, please, wait!" I beg, twisting my head and trying to catch his eye over my shoulder. "Please, I'm sorry. You just—you scared me with the gag. I'm so sorry, Jeremy. Please leave him here. Please."

He seems to consider me for a moment before holding up the bandana. "Last time, Jules."

"I know," I agree quickly.

This time, when he pulls the bandana around my face, I open my mouth wide, and he ties it tight around the back of my head. He's close to my face again.

"Excellent," whispers against the shell of my ear. Then, I feel his hand on the back of my bare leg. He runs his palm up and under my skirt. It's all I can do to keep from recoiling.

"Don't you worry, Jules, we'll have plenty of time to play later, you and I."

I cringe at the implication. His hand keeps moving upward. When he reaches my panties, he gives the elastic waistband a snap and squeezes my flesh. And then, suddenly, there the unmistakable pinch of a hypodermic needle. I grunt in surprise.

"Oh, yeah," he drawls, back in my ear again, his breath warm on my face. "I've missed fucking you, Jules. You get your rest now, and when you wake up, I'll show you a real good time. I promise."

He kisses my cheek, and then his weight lifts off the mattress. I don't know what it is that he's just injected into me, but it's only a few seconds before I start to feel its effects. He climbs over me and into the driver's seat, starts the van and turns the radio on. But it's not the radio. This is my new CD.

"Off we go!" he calls back to me cheerily, as if we're off on a road trip.

I realize as I feel the van pull away from the curb that I am totally and completely on my own. The thought terrifies me for the thirty seconds more that I'm awake, and then it doesn't matter. Nothing does.

Chapter 32

Matthew

Clusterfuck. It's a highly improbable and extremely destructive confluence of events that transpire in the same brief period of time, rendering the victim well and truly fucked.

What's unfolding right now, onstage with the Gotham Chamber Players, is a textbook clusterfuck. It started with Vivian in the horn section. After using an aluminum mute earlier in the concert, she left it sitting on the floor next to her chair. Which wasn't a problem ... until the player next to her accidentally kicked it over during a super-soft section of the Brahms Serenade No.1. The mute, which is essentially just a large, hollow, metal cone, fell over onto the stage floor, bounced once and then ricocheted off the leg of Vivian's music stand. It then rolled—loudly—under the chair of Bill, the bassoonist sitting in front of her.

It was bad, but maybe if it had stopped there, it would have just been an unfortunate disruption of an otherwise uneventful concert. But it didn't stop there. Not by a long shot.

Rather than waiting for us to finish the Brahms, Bill the ever-helpful bassoonist tried, unsuccessfully, to fish the mute out from below his seat. While half the audience, most of the orchestra, and the conductor looked on in horror, Bill leaned as far to the left as he possibly could. A triumphant smile lit his face as his fingertips grasped the neck of the mute. That's when the strap that holds his bassoon in place slipped out from underneath him. As if in slow motion, the top of the instrument, a tall, wooden pipe known as the bell joint, slipped and swung to the left, hitting Marie, the second chair oboist who happened to be sitting next to him.

Marie's oboe jammed back into her face, its hard reed smacking into her mouth and splitting her lip. Poor Marie started to bleed like a stuck pig.

It was bad, but maybe if it had stopped there, it would have just been a *really* unfortunate disruption to an already eventful concert. But it didn't stop there.

The first chair oboe, Sarah, tried valiantly to continue playing, even as she turned a sickly shade of green. Finally, she pulled the oboe away from her face and slapped a hand to her mouth in an attempt to keep from vomiting. She failed in her attempt and, sickened by Marie's blood as well as her own bile, she simply slid out of her chair and onto the floor, as if she had suddenly become liquid.

Inexplicably, with only a couple of minutes more in the piece, the maestro stubbornly continued to conduct even as a half dozen orchestra members got up to tend to the two oboists. By the time the Brahms came to a weak and sputtering finale, the double doors at the back of the hall burst open and a pair of paramedics came rolling in with a stretcher, radios squawking, having been summoned by an alarmed audience member.

That would be a clusterfuck.

* * *

"I don't know, I don't think it was *that* bad..." Brett is saying as we cross the parking lot to his car.

"Dude! It *was* that bad!" I can't help but laugh and shake my head.

It's been really nice, this new, friendlier relationship I have with him. After nearly a decade of being fierce rivals and enemies, I find I'm enjoying this time he's spent subbing with my ensemble. I'm also enjoying the time he's spent building a relationship with Julia and me. And with our son, David, who is Brett's own flesh and blood.

"How long do you think it'll take us to get back to the city?" Brett wonders, glancing at this watch.

I shrug. "Depends on whether or not there's construction traffic. But, if you've got to pee, I'd go now..." I smile.

He holds up a hand. "Nah, I'm good, thanks," he laughs and then jumps a little in surprise. "Oh, hey, my pants are vibrating!"

"Excuse me?"

"My phone, Matthew. Please, as if *you'd* be the one to make my pants vibrate!" he chuckles and shakes his head as he pulls the phone out of his pocket and looks at the screen briefly. "Hey, give me just a second, okay? I need to take this," he says, turning his back and walking several feet away.

I glance at my own watch and see it's quarter till ten. If we hit it just right, Julia and I could be curled up on the couch laughing our asses off over tonight's debacle before midnight.

When I look up again, Brett has the phone to one ear and his hand to the other ear, blocking out the extraneous noise around us.

"Alright already!" I call out. "Can we put the phone sex on hold so we can get on the road already? I'd like to be home before tomorrow morning!"

Brett ignores my teasing. When he ends the call, he continues to stare at the screen in his hand and I get the distinct sense that something's not right. That's when he looks up at me slowly. Too slowly Brett's eyes are wide, and his jaw is slack. I can see the phone shaking in his hand.

"What? What is it?" I ask calmly and quietly, preparing myself to jump into damage control mode—whatever it is that's happened to him.

Brett just shakes his head. He seems to be having trouble finding the words. I walk to him and put a concerned hand on his shoulder.

"What is it, Brett? Tell me."

The look in his eyes... Oh, Christ. A look like that can only mean someone is dead. His mother, maybe? I hope not ... not so soon after his father. Or ... no! It couldn't be Maggie, could it? And then it strikes me with the force of freight train. My breath catches in my throat, and I feel my blood run cold even as a film of perspiration breaks out on my face.

"It's not ..." I close my eyes and shake my head. I can't look at his face when I ask. "Is it Julia?" My voice is barely a whisper.

The half-second delay in his response answers my question. My eyes fly open now, and I can feel them darting, squinting, looking for answers. "Oh, God, no... the baby?"

"Matthew," Brett begins, leveling his eyes on mine, "It's my brother. It's Jeremy ..."

My grip on him tightens as the panic seizes me from within. *"Tell. Me!"*

"He forced his way into your apartment and knocked Natalie out. He was waiting when ... when Julia got home tonight. He took her ... somewhere ..."

Suddenly his voice sounds so far away, and the starry sky above me has started to spin. I can't stay upright for a single second longer, so I drop to my knees as my viola case slides off my shoulder and into the grass. Brett is there, squatting in front of me, shaking me.

"Oh, God. Oh, my God," I whisper. "When? Is David with them?"

"No," he says firmly. "No, David is still with Natalie. She wants to call the police ..."

"*No!* No police!" I hiss, grabbing his arm and staring at him in wild-eyed desperation.

I don't know what's happened yet, but I know enough—I know *him* well enough—not to get the police involved. He'll hurt her... No, he'll *kill* her before he lets himself be caught by the police. Besides, the fucker's brilliant in that crazy, cunning, dangerous way. He's most likely got a fool-proof back-up plan in place, should he have to make a run for it. And then Julia is dead for sure.

No. My only chance to do this myself.

"Matthew?" Brett is shaking my arm.

"No. Police," I grit out.

He takes a deep breath and nods. "Okay, man, no police. I promise. But we need help. Come on, you have to stand up now so we can get moving. I'll tell you everything in the car, but we have to leave *now* Matthew. Do you understand?"

I swallow hard and nod. He extends a hand to help me get back up on my feet. I take it and allow him to lead me by the shoulder toward the parking lot. In the meantime, he's dialed someone else and seems to be waiting for a response.

"Mom," he utters into the phone, after a long moment. "Mom, I need you to do something for me. It's really important."

I fight back the wave of panic and fear that threatens to unravel me. But it's too late. The destructive events are already transpiring and the clusterfuck is imminent.

Chapter 33

Julia

I fight my way back to consciousness in stages, first taking a physical inventory. My head is throbbing, likely from the drugs. I don't think he hit me. Yet. My neck, shoulders and arms are achy and stiff from being tied up. Tied to something... a chair. I'm sitting in a hard-backed chair and each of my ankles is tied to one of the legs.

I struggle to clear my head, grasping for any tiny snippet of memory beyond the van. But there are no snippets. I have no idea what's transpired in the last...what? Hours? *Days?* No. It couldn't be days, so I can't be that far from home. I listen carefully, trying to discern if Jeremy is nearby before I let on that I'm awake. Nothing. I don't sense his presence in my immediate vicinity, so I open my leaden eyelids slowly against bright lights. I squint and wait for my pupils to dilate.

As the room finally comes into focus around me, I recognize it as a kitchen. Stove, fridge, cabinets. Breakfast nook... Suddenly my eyes are wide open and my breath hitches in my chest. I fight back a whimper. This is *my* kitchen! My kitchen in our Port Jefferson house on Long Island!

I take a moment to concentrate on slowing my runaway pulse.

Do. Not. Panic.

I stop and take a long, deep breath, in my nose, out my mouth, which no longer has a gag in it. That's an improvement, anyway. But why on earth would Jeremy bring me here of all places? I mean, it's my house. If you want to kidnap someone, you take them someplace where no one will look for them. Of course. I realize I've just answered my own question. It wouldn't occur to Matthew to look for me here. He thinks I'm somewhere in the city.

Damn! Okay. That's the bad news. The good news is that this is *my* house. I know it inside and out. Every baby-proofed crevice. The fog is lifting slowly and I am focused enough now to hear him moving around close by. He's opening and closing doors, moving things around down the hallway.

I take another deep breath and gather my courage.

"Jeremy?" I call out tentatively. He doesn't answer.

"Jeremy? What are you looking for? Maybe I can help."

He's quiet for a moment and then I hear his voice from behind me "I want a drink. Where do you keep the liquor?"

Okay, that's easy enough.

"There's a cabinet in the living room, it's just to my right." I point with my head. "Against the wall, next to the big window. Since the baby's been walking, we keep it locked. You'll find a key sitting on top of it and glasses on the shelf above. There's also beer and wine in the fridge if you prefer."

I'm not certain that he's left the kitchen again until I hear the clink of bottles in the next room. When he returns, it's with a bottle of vodka and a glass. He puts both on the counter and sits next to them on a stool, swiveling so he's facing me.

"This is some place you've got here, Jules. No wonder Matthew wanted to relive his pathetic little childhood here."

"It's a good place for a family," I say softly. "A good place to raise the baby."

He smiles, shakes his head at me and knocks back a shot.

I know how Jeremy thinks. I know what makes him happy and what makes him angry. He's not wired all that differently than my father was. If I can make him feel powerful, flatter his ego without fawning over him, I might be able to reason with him, convince him that he doesn't have to hurt me. I don't have a lot of time here, and the more he drinks the shorter my window gets. I take a slow, deep breath. I'm okay. I can do this.

"Did you look at him?" I ask.

He furrows his brow. "Who?"

"You know who! The baby," I tease him a little.

"No," he mutters without even looking at me.

"Oh, come on. You must have," I coax. "I know you did."

Now he's looking at me. In fact, he's glaring. It's a warning that I'm on thin ice here. "You must have seen it."

"What's that?

He's trying to sound disinterested.

"How much he looks like you."

"I hadn't noticed."

"He has your eyes. And the way his brows arch, that's all you. Your chin, too. When he was born, he looked more like me. But as he gets older, he looks more and more like his father."

Jeremy doesn't respond, he just slips off the stool he's been occupying, and gets some ice from the freezer.

"It makes Matthew crazy," I murmur, as if to myself, but loud enough for him to hear.

When he turns around, there's a half smirk on his face. Well that certainly got his attention. "Yeah, I'll bet it does," he snorts as he pours more liquor over the ice.

"I..." I trail off and pretend to try again. "I kind of like it."

Another snort. He takes a sip, all the while looking at me as if I'm full of crap. "No, really," I say as earnestly as I can. "I was afraid, because I'm so ... plain looking. But now I think he's going to be an incredibly handsome man. A redheaded version of you."

Jeremy puts the glass down on the counter hard and comes to stand in front of me. Shit. Have I pushed too far, too fast? I guess we're about to find out.

"What are you trying to do here, Jules?"

I shrug as best I can without use of my hands. "It's not anything I can say to anyone else, Jeremy. No one else knows about you being his father. And the people who do know, would be horrified to hear... to hear how I really feel."

"And how is it that you feel, Jules?" he mocks.

"Like... I'm glad. I'm glad he's your son. I'm glad he looks like you. I hope he grows up to be as talented and smart as you." The words come out of me in such a rush that, suddenly, I'm not so sure they're just words anymore. I keep going before I can think about it too much. "A small part of me wishes that things had been different with us," I profess, looking down at my lap as I feel my face coloring scarlet.

He has no comment, just returns to his spot on the stool and spins around so he has a view of the lights out in Port Jefferson harbor. We sit in silence for what feels like an eternity.

"What do you want me to do?" I ask at last. He swivels back around to face me, one eyebrow cocked in surprise. "I'll do whatever you want Jeremy. I'm not going to fight you. Just tell me what you want me to do and I'll do it."

"Well that's quite an attitude adjustment."

"Maybe, but now that I'm past the initial shock of...all this...I realize that I'm better to my son alive than dead. I'm not going to give you any reason to hurt me. I swear to you."

He leans forward and, for a split second, I think he's happy with my acquiescence. I know better as soon as his mouth twists up again.

"Oh, Jules," he whispers, shaking his head at me pityingly. "Is that what you think? That if you behave yourself, I won't hurt you? That I won't kill you? You're not getting this, you stupid girl. It's not about me hurting you because it makes me feel good—although it does—it's about me hurting Matthew. And the best way to hurt Matthew, is to hurt you."

That's when the reality of this situation dawns on me with crushing certainty. I'm not going to live through this night if Jeremy Corrigan has his way. I must look incredibly alarmed suddenly, because he makes a concerted effort to soften his tone a little. Not, I'm sure, because he wants to comfort me, but because he doesn't want to spook me into doing something desperate and making his job harder.

"That being said, if you do what I tell you to do, when I tell you to do it, then you might just spare yourself a little grief." I nod, as if to indicate my acceptance of his terms. "Although," he continues, getting up and going back to the fridge again, "I don't think you're going to like what I have in mind for you."

I see him pluck something out from under a magnet. He comes back to stand in front of me, holding the small card close so I can see what it is.

Oh, no. God, no. Please. No, no, no!

I fight back the bile that rises to the back of my throat even as the blood drains from my face. Jeremy is holding the appointment card for my next OB/GYN appointment. The one that says 'four-month sonogram' on it. He tosses the card up onto the counter, then squats down on his haunches, putting his palms on my knees so we are face to face.

"Congratulations, Jules! I can't tell you how happy I was to discover you're expecting another rugrat," he crows brightly. "So, *so* happy! Because, you see, the only revenge better than hurting you, is hurting you *and* your baby. Matthew's baby."

He puts a hand to my bloodless face and locks his eyes on mine. "Now, I'm not sure how you're going to come out of all this, Jules, but there's one thing I can tell you with absolute certainty. You won't be needing that appointment."

Chapter 34

Brett

When we arrive at the apartment, my mother is holding David to her chest, while Natalie is holding a bag of frozen peas to her swollen face.

"Matthew!" Natalie cries out, jumping off the stool, tears running down her face. "Oh, God, Matthew, I'm so sorry! I thought he was the pizza delivery guy. He had his uniform and the box... he punched me... so hard, Matthew... I was unconscious. Then he shot me up with something... I just woke up in your bed. That was hours ago," she sobs in one, long miserable breath.

Matthew pulls her into his arms and pats her back—an extraordinary gesture, considering the desperate panic I know he's experiencing at this moment. "I know. I know, Natalie. I know. It's not your fault," he somehow manages to comfort her. "Is David okay?"

"He's fine," she sniffs. "When I finally came to, he was in his crib crying."

We turn to my mother, who is silently bouncing the sleepy child. She nods her agreement that he's fine.

"Oh, thank God," I whisper.

"But, you should know that he was ready to take David, Matthew. The diaper bag was packed, the stroller set up. I think Julia must have convinced him to leave David behind," my mother informs us.

Matthew puts a hand to his face and shakes his head. He looks as if he's about to start crying himself until Natalie speaks again.

"Matthew," she says softly, "he left a note."

I watch as he swallows hard, and I know exactly what he's thinking, because I'm thinking it, too. This is one of those moments. He's sitting on the very edge of his world. In a matter of seconds, everything is going to change, and this may very well be the last second of ignorant bliss that he'll ever have. The last moments when his life is intact. He takes a deep breath, and walks to the breakfast bar, where the single sheet of white paper sits, my brother's unmistakably meticulous handwriting in bold, black marker. The instant Matthew picks it up and reads it aloud, he has slipped into the abyss.

Matthew, no police. Wait for my call and think about what I'm doing to her right now.

And with that, I slide right into the void with him.

Chapter 35

Jeremy

"Mama!" David whines as I hold him in my arms, rocking him like I used to do in the middle of the night when he was just an infant. Now, I'm resting my head against his as he cries. He's the only person on this earth who can bring me any solace right now. And clarity. This isn't just about me bringing my wife home safely, it's about bringing David's mother back to him.

"I know, baby," I murmur, holding him even tighter. I look up when I hear a quiet knock from the doorway to the nursery. It's Trudy.

"Matthew, may I come in?"

"Of course."

She comes in and sits in the armchair next to his crib. "I'm so sorry …" she begins.

I shake my head. I know this can't be easy for her either. "Please Trudy. This isn't your fault any more than it's Natalie's."

She doesn't respond at first, only looks down at her hands, folded in her lap. "It took a while for us to see it, Matthew. Danny and I... we couldn't believe... we didn't *want* to believe that our child was... was...' She has trouble finding the word.

"Mentally ill?" I offer softly.

"A monster," she corrects me.

Holy shit. Well, there's some self-awareness for you.

"I should've done something sooner, before it got to this point," she explains. "But, I was selfish, Matthew. I wanted Jeremy out of my house. I wanted him out of our lives. It didn't occur to me that it might be my job to..."

"To what, Trudy? To beat it out of him? Have him committed to some mental institution? There isn't a damn thing you could have done to prevent him from becoming who he is," I assure her, trying to assuage her guilt.

But, guilt is not the emotion I see on Trudy Corrigan's face. No, it's more like regret. Regret for things left undone that have now come back to haunt her. I can tell she's about to respond when Brett sticks his head in.

"Hey, so, I've been thinking, it probably wouldn't be a bad idea to get David out of here."

"Surely you don't think your brother's going to come back for him ..." Trudy gapes, looking from her son to her sleeping grandson, and back again.

"I don't know what to think as far as Jeremy's concerned," he admits. "But, Matthew, you need every bit of energy you have right now, and I don't think you'll be able to give it your full attention until you know that David is somewhere safe."

He's absolutely right. I look to Trudy.

"What can I do?" she offers without hesitation.

I stand up and walk to the crib, putting David down, and then turn to face her. "Trudy, will you please stay with him? Will you take him to our house on Long Island? It's far enough out of the city that we won't have to worry about him being anywhere near Jeremy."

"Yes, Matthew, of course."

"Mom," Brett says, picking up where I've left off, "There's a midnight train out of Penn Station. You'll have to take a cab there, and then another one to the house when you arrive. Are you okay with that?"

She raises an irritated eyebrow at him. "Brett, I've been wrangling five-year-olds for more than twenty years. I think I can manage to get in and out of a couple of cabs with a sleeping baby." For the first time in hours, I find my lips twitching with the hint of a smile. "You two go do what you need to do, I'm going to pack a few things for him. Are there any bottles made up, Matthew?"

"Uh, yes, in the fridge. I'll pack them in the insulated bag. You can load it all into his stroller. As soon as you're ready, I'll call downstairs and they'll hail a cab. I'll go get you a key and write the address for you. His nursery is upstairs, just turn left at the top and go down to the end of the hall. He'll probably sleep the entire way," I assure her, getting up to set this plan in motion.

She nods, and I follow Brett out into the hall.

"Okay, that's David squared away, he says. "What the fuck do we do now?"

I look at him for a long moment before speaking.

"We do exactly what Jeremy told us to do. We wait."

Chapter 36

Julia

He's holding the phone in his hand, poised to dial it. "Last time, Jules," Jeremy warns. "Not a word, not a clue or a hint about where you are. Understood?"

I try to glance at the clock without being too obvious. Two minutes. I have to ensure that, in two minutes, Matthew is on the phone. But I know Jeremy isn't going to want to speak with him for that long, so I've got to stall the start of this call.

"May I ask him about David?" I ask. "How he's doing, if he's eaten, that sort of thing?"

"You're not going to have time," he informs me flatly. "The only reason I'm even going to let you talk is because I know that idiot is going to demand to hear your voice before he'll listen to me."

I take a deep breath. "Okay then, what, *exactly*, would you like me to say to him?" I'm trying to feed into his need to have control and it seems to be working.

"You'll tell him you're safe. You'll tell him not to call the police. You'll tell him that I'm going to hurt you..."

"Are you?" I interrupt.

"Am I what?"

"Are you going to hurt me?"

He looks at me as if I'm the dimmest person on earth. I have to be careful here not to play *too* dumb, or he won't believe me. God only knows what's going through that twisted mind of his. "What do *you* think, Jules?"

I think I've got another thirty seconds or so to kill before I can let him make that call. Time to improvise.

"I think that I'm hoping I can convince you not to hurt me."

"We've already been through this," he grunts out with some irritation.

"I'm sorry, you're right. If I do this well, will you untie me so I can make us something to eat?"

"What? And let you loose around the steak knives?" he snorts. "I don't think so."

"You can stand right next to me. There's food in the fridge that I can throw together and microwave. Mac and cheese, David loves that you know...and you do too if memory serves. I think there's a frozen pizza..."

"Jules, we're not going to plan a fucking menu right now."

"But I'm really hungry, Jeremy and I'll bet you are, too. Plus, I really need to use the bathroom and that's a little hard to do when I'm attached to a chair." He's glaring at me, but I keep my face looking hopeful and innocent, so he won't suspect I'm stretching. "Please?" I throw in for good measure.

He rolls his eyes. "Fine. If this goes well, I'll get you to the bathroom. If it doesn't go well, then it won't matter because you'll be dead anyway."

My earnest face slips and I gulp so hard I'm sure he's heard it. One more surreptitious glance at the clock. Okay, it's now or never.

"It'll go well, Jeremy," I assure him. "I'm ready. I can do this."

He nods, dials and activates the speaker function on his phone. I hear the phone in our apartment ring once. Twice.

"Julia?" comes Matthew's breathless voice through the ether.

"Guess again, Matty!" Jeremy jeers.

"You son of a bitch!" he spits back at him. "What the hell have you done? Where is she?"

"That's for me to know, and you to not find out until it's too late," is his mocking retort.

"I want to talk to her," Matthew demands.

"You and I have few things to discuss first."

"No," Matthew says. "Not until I know she's alright. Otherwise you can hang up right now."

Well that was a bold move, but it works. Jeremy puts the phone close to my mouth and nods his chin at me as an indication to speak.

"Matthew?" I whisper hesitantly.

"Julia, Honey, are you okay? If that bastard's hurt you ..."

"I'm okay, Matthew. How's the baby? How's David?" I interrupt him, keeping eye contact with Jeremy.

"He's fine, Julia, don't worry about him."

I'm getting the sign to wrap it up from Jeremy and I nod my understanding. "Listen to me, Matthew, do whatever Jeremy tells you to do and, for God's sake, do *not* call the police, okay?"

"Okay," he sniffs.

"Ah! Nicely done you two," Jeremy praises us, taking the phone away.

"What are you going to do now?" I hear my husband ask.

Jeremy screws up his face in mock consideration. "Hmmm... let's see... So many options ..."

"Cut the shit, you motherfucker!" Matthew yells from his end of the line.

Jeremy becomes serious again. "You know, Matthew, I'm not really sure how all this is going to end. But I can tell you what's going to happen in the next twenty-four hours. Your blushing bride and I are going to get reacquainted. Intimately reacquainted."

He's leering at me now and I can just imagine Matthew trying to sound calm as Jeremy baits him. He's probably going to punch a hole in the wall as soon as he gets off the phone.

"Jeremy, you may hate me. But please don't take it out on Julia. It's me you want to hurt, not her. There was a time when you cared for her..."

"Oh, please. She's just a stupid slut like the rest of them," Jeremy replies icily, unmoved by the plea. "Besides, don't you see it, Matthew? Sure, I could beat the shit out of you or torture you or some sadistic shit like that, but what fun would *that* be? No, my friend, I want you to suffer. I want you to think about all of the unspeakable things I'm going to do to Julia. All of the violent, disgusting ways I'm going to fuck her.

And fuck her and fuck her. Then, I'm going to beat the shit out of her. After that, I'll fuck her some more."

"Please don't kill her," comes Matthew's breathy reply.

Jeremy ignores him and prattles on, clearly enjoying the sound of his own voice. "And as the hours go by, you'll be imaging the worst. Only, for Julia, it won't be in her imagination, will it? No, it will be her reality. She'll suffer. And you will be helpless. You'll be responsible for her suffering, Matthew. You did this to her, just as surely as if you were raping her and beating her yourself. I want you to think about *that*, Matthew."

I feel my mouth go dry and slack at the same time. Oh, my God. The man standing in front of me is totally certifiable. I have the sudden, undeniable realization that there will be no reasoning with him. I'm going to have to think of something, and fast.

"I'm going to hang up now. I'm sure you'll want to call the police but we both know what a bad idea that would be, right? We both know she'll be dead at the first sign of a cop car. Do I make myself clear?"

"You do." Matthew's voice has become small and shaky.

"Oh, Matthew, I almost forgot, congratulations on the baby!"

Jeremy hangs up the phone before Matthew can reply. But Jeremy does *not* hang up the phone before the blaring foghorn of the P.-Jefferson Ferry filters into the kitchen, right on time.

Chapter 37

Matthew

I t's there, in an instant: the image of our kitchen, the view of the back yard and harbor. David, yelling *"Boat!"* Holy shit, Julia did this. She planned this. She must have. I turn to Brett, phone still in my hand. "I know where she is," I exclaim excitedly.

"What? How could you possibly?"

He heard the entire conversation on the speakerphone and didn't catch what was so glaringly, or, in this case, *blaringly* obvious to me.

"The foghorn. Right before he hung up? That was the Pt. Jefferson Ferry. We've been complaining about it for weeks now. You can hear it every night at the same time. The sound comes right up into our kitchen."

Brett is shaking his head, as if trying to shake out the cobwebs. "Wait, wait, wait... are you saying that you think Jeremy took Julia... home? To *your* home? On Long Island?"

"Exactly! She was stalling for time, so I'd be on long enough to hear the horn!" I practically burst. "That's my brilliant girl! Always thinking. She's going to come out on the other side of this. Jeremy, on the other hand, won't be so lucky. Not when I'm through with him.

"But why...?"

"Think about it, Brett, it's actually fucking brilliant! The house is isolated, it's quiet... and it's the last place we'd ever think to look for her!"

Suddenly the color seems to drain from his face. "What? What is it?" I ask, almost afraid to hear what he's thinking.

"Yeah, and it's the *first* place we sent my mother and David," he replies in a horrified whisper.

Oh, Christ, he's right. I look at my watch. "You've got to call her. Tell her to get off at the next stop and catch a train back to the city..."

But Brett is shaking his head at me. "No, man, I can't. She doesn't have a cell phone," he groans miserably.

"What? Who the hell on this planet doesn't have a cell phone?" I bark.

He shrugs. "Trudy."

I take a deep breath and close my eyes. Think. "Okay, let's go."

"Where?"

"We've got to try and beat them out there."

"Matthew... are you *sure* you don't want to involve the police?" I shake my head adamantly and he holds up his palms in surrender. "Your call. I'm just thinking they can get there before any of us can..."

I'm about to tell him to drop it, but he's just given me an idea. "They're not the only ones who can get there before we can."

* * *

"Holy fucking shit!" Tony yells so loudly that I have to pull the receiver from my ear. "Fucking cocksucker! I'll kill him! I'll *fucking* kill him if he hurts a hair on Julia's head!"

I think that may be the first time I've ever heard Tony use Julia's name. He's called her 'Red' since we were kids. I find it more than a little unsettling. "Tony, where are you? Can you get to her? We're just getting on the expressway..."

"Yeah, yeah, of course. I'll drop everything. You didn't call the police did you?"

"No," I assure him.

"Good. No telling what that fucker'll do if he feels backed into a corner. He'd kill her right in front of them just to stick it to you..." he stops, abruptly, realizing I might not want to hear this. "It'll be okay, Matt. I'm at my place in Lido Beach."

"Dammit," I murmur. "You're not much closer than we are..."

"No. Don't worry about that. I know all the shortcuts. I'll be out the door in less than five minutes, and I'll check in with you from the road."

"Alright," I say, the relief evident in my voice.

"Matt?"

"Yeah?"

"No matter what, you wait for me to get there. You hear me? No matter what, you do *not* go into that house without me."

"Why? That's crazy. If I get there first..."

"If you get there first, he'll kill her just so you can watch her die, Matthew."

Once he says it, there's no doubt in my mind that it's the truth.

Chapter 38

Julia

Jeremy is true to his word. When the phone call is done, he pulls a pocketknife out of his pants, squats down, and cuts the ties on my ankles. He looks up at me. "I'm going to cut your hands loose, but don't do anything that you'll regret, Jules. Because, believe me, you'll regret it."

I nod my understanding and he stands up, walks around behind me and liberates my sore and swollen wrists. I rub them, and my arms from shoulders to fingertips. He's watching, waiting for me to finish.

"Are you hungry?" I ask him.

"No knives, no boiling water, no stove."

"Okay. How about sandwiches? I have ham and cheese. There's some leftover potato salad in there, too. If you'd prefer, I can sit here while you pull it out. I don't need to go into the kitchen," I volunteer helpfully.

He nods and I direct him to all the ingredients. Once he's laid them out on the counter, I start to assemble his sandwich just the way I know he likes it. Heavy on the cheese, light on the mayo. I spoon a heap of the chilled salad onto the plate and push it towards him.

"There's beer in the refrigerator," I remind him. He nods and pulls one out for himself. "May I have a bottle of water while you're in there?" He grabs that as well, without comment.

"Thank you," I say as he sets it down in front of me and twists the cap off his Michelob. He takes a long swig from the bottle and a big bite from the sandwich, grunting his approval of both. "When was the last time you ate?" I prod, concentrating on my own sandwich.

"Breakfast," he mumbles through a mouthful of potato salad.

"You must be starving," I observe, looking up at him. "Do you want another one? There's plenty here." He's looking at me suspiciously. "Jeremy, I'm not an idiot either, okay? You don't think I know it's in my best interest to keep you in a good mood? Jesus! It's just a fucking sandwich," I huff with some irritation of my own.

"Yes, I'd like another fucking sandwich, please," he parrots me with an amused smile. Amused is good. I'll take amused at the moment.

I nod, take a bite out of my own sandwich, and start making his second. The kitchen is quiet, save for the whir of the appliances and the occasional gust of wind through the trees in the backyard. If Jeremy was concerned about the sound of the foghorn earlier, he hasn't mentioned it. Maybe that's because he hasn't made the connection. It hasn't occurred to him that Matthew will recognize the sound and know exactly where I am. That's what I'm counting on. Even so, it'll take time for Matthew to get here.

As I chew my sandwich, I'm making a mental inventory of the living room, dining room, music room and den. All of them are on this floor and all of them can be reached from one of two directions, giving me some options. But is there anything in any of those rooms that I can use as a weapon? There's a letter opener on my desk; a pair of scissors, too. In the den is a trophy with a heavy marble base. Matthew's office, the living room...

"May I use the bathroom, please?" I ask in my most non-threatening voice. "There's a powder room in the hallway. I don't need to go upstairs or anything."

"We'll see."

I raise an eyebrow at him. "Really? You're not even going to let me pee? Stand in there with me if you want. I'm sure you made use of the facilities while I was out cold."

"Jesus, just shut the fuck up already!" he grumbles between bites of sandwich. I continue to glare at him until he rolls his eyes. "Fine, go. You have one minute. If you lock yourself in, you're going to be so sorry. And don't even think about the front door—"

I cut him off before he can continue his laundry lists of threats. "I won't. I'll keep the bathroom door open if it'll make you feel better. And, I know—you're faster than me. You're stronger. I get it. I was a fool, certainly. But I'm not stupid."

"You've just wasted fifteen seconds of your minute with that little speech," he informs me, making a point of looking at his watch.

I nod and turn to leave the kitchen slowly, carefully. I go into the bathroom and turn on the faucet so the sound of the water will buy me a little time. I reach behind the mirror and feel for the small key taped to its back. Then, once I've stuck my head out into the hallway to be sure I'm still on my own, I move quickly and silently to the room directly across from me, Matthew's office. I steal over to the closet, noiselessly sliding the door open on its track.

Inside, I stand on my tiptoes and grab the lockbox from the high shelf where it sits. I bring it quickly back to the desk and, with shaking hands, I unlock it, thanking God that I knew where everything was. But, as it turns out, my thanks are a bit premature. The box is empty.

Empty?

Please, Jesus, don't tell me the one time he finally decides to listen to me and get rid of the damn knife is the one time I need it!

"Looking for that big bad knife you had in there?"

I jump at the sound of Jeremy's voice. He's leaning in the doorway watching me.

"Hey, great hiding place for the key, too. Behind the mirror in the bathroom. I never would have thought to look there. Oh, yeah, except, I did," he sneers and steps over the threshold and into the office with me before he continues.

"Did you really think I wouldn't have been through every square inch of this place before I brought you here? Not to mention your apartment? I had a lot of fun poking around your lingerie drawer by the way. Oh! And I like the little pink lacy number you've acquired since we were dating. I'll bet Matty Boy got lucky when you found it in bottom of your suitcase!"

Oh. My. God.

How could I not have seen it? Of course! It was *him* all along! He got into the house right before David was born, too. But after that, Matthew installed alarms and cameras and reinforced doors. He thought we would be safer here than anyplace else. Apparently he thought wrong. We both did.

"And, you can forget about the knives in the kitchen and that God awful marble statue in the living room, too. I managed to disengage your alarm system and the home phone line, so you can forget about whatever other little tricks you think you have up your sleeve," he says, watching me watching him.

I come around to the front of the desk. We're about twenty feet apart in this large room, but he's blocking the only way out. I don't have to look around me to know that there's nowhere left to go. He comes closer, but I stand my ground. This is *my* home.

"I'll be paying David a visit soon, you know," he informs me. I don't respond, just glare at him. "Oh, he's going to get to know me real well, Jules."

I take a deep breath and try to stop my body from convulsing with the trembling that is taking hold of it. I muster every bit of power I have and channel it into my tone as I address him.

"Jeremy Corrigan, I want you to hear me when I tell you that you will *never* touch my child. Because, if you do, I will kill you with my own bare hands. And, if you happen to get the better of me, if you get your way and I'm dead, then you had better start praying for salvation, Jeremy, because I will be there. Every bad thing that happens to you, that will be me. I will make your life a living hell from beyond the grave. I didn't believe in things like that until I had David. Now I know. Not even death will sever the relationship I have with my son," I hiss at him from across the room.

He gives me a condescending smile. "Don't you mean *our* son, Julia?" he croons, crossing over the threshold and moving slowly toward me.

I shake my head stubbornly. "No. He is not *our* son, Jeremy. He's mine. Mine and Matthew's," I insist, taking an involuntary step backwards to maintain the distance between us.

"Saying it doesn't make it true." Again, that galling smile. What I wouldn't give to smack it off of his smug face. I feel my fingers twitching with the possibility of it as he pushes me further into the corner. "You seem to be running out of floor," he observes.

I recognize the line from the first time we made love in my apartment.

"Maybe we should take this to the bedroom then?" he suggests.

"No," I snap.

"I'm sorry, what was that?" He clearly thinks he's misheard me.

"No."

"*No?*"

I glare at him now.

"You heard me. I said 'No.' No, I do not want to have sex with you. I do *not* give my consent. I want you to be crystal clear on this point, Jeremy. If you touch me, it will be by force. It'll be rape."

"Seriously?" he marvels with an incredulous smile. "Have you met me, Jules?" he laughs. "I mean, what the hell makes you think I care whether or not you consent?"

My expression doesn't change. My eyes never leave his. "We both know you're better than that, Jeremy. Rape is a little... common for you. isn't it?"

The question is a crapshoot. I'm hoping, once again, to appeal to his ego. "And what makes you so sure that you know me so well, Jules? Hmm?"

"I loved you. I shared a bed with you. As you've just pointed out, I had a child with you. Yeah, I think I do know you."

He shakes his head at me in disbelief. "And to think we used to call you The Mouse."

Before I can reply, he lurches forward, grabbing me by the shoulders and slamming me hard against the wall behind me. I gasp, trying to reclaim some of the breath that's been knocked out of me, but then, his big hands are around my neck as he leans in close to my ear to speak.

"Oh, Jules, always so naive. You have not even begun to scratch the surface of what I'm capable of. But David, he's going to know. He's going to get a real good idea of the kind of pain I can inflict."

"No," I gasp, shaking my head. "No!"

He smiles and nods. "I'm afraid so, Jules. Your boy will grow up without a mother," he murmurs in faux pity. "But you know what? At least he has a father. And I don't mean Matthew. I mean his *real* father, his biological father. Me."

"What are you talking about?" I manage to huff out.

"I mean, a simple DNA test will prove he's mine, and with you dead, well, Matthew won't have a legal leg to stand on."

"You don't want him!" I croak.

"You're right, I don't. But I don't want Matthew to have anything. Not you. Not that sea monkey you're carrying and not sweet little David. No, I'm going to take him away from the only father he's ever known—from the only home he's ever known."

"You can't!" I object. But it even sounds pathetic to my own ears.

"I can. And then you know what I'm going to do, Jules? I'm going to throw your son away like a piece of trash. I'm going to sell him to the most deviant fuck I can find. A pedophile with a sadistic streak who will keep little David alive as a toy to be shared with all his friends. To take pictures of. To torture. And I will make sure that whoever gets him tells David every single day of his life that his mother hated him. That she abandoned him. That he was never loved.

"He will live in a hell on earth, Jules. Your sweet little redheaded cherub will suffer every single day of his short life. Because, believe me, it will be short. Guys like that aren't interested in their toys once they get too big. And with no one to report him missing... well, even if his body is found, no one will ever know who he is or where he came from."

My blood has turned to ice in my veins, and I feel as if I'm going to pass out. I know this man well enough to know that he is not exaggerating. He's thought this out carefully. He probably already has a plan in place, someone in mind to take my baby.

"This, Jules, is *your* torture. Your punishment for everything you've done to me, you bitch. You're going to die knowing that you cannot save either of your children. Your last thoughts will be of your son's pain and Matthew's grief."

My breath is coming in quick pants now. There's nothing I can do. Or is there? I read once about a woman who lifted a car off of her child, trapped underneath it. She just grabbed it by the bumper and lifted it up. One woman, so fueled by love and fear and the protective instinct, that she was able to transcend the bonds of human limitations. Jeremy is the twisted wreckage of that car, bearing down on me and my family. I feel the danger to my child as surely as if he were pinned under ten tons of steel.

He's loosened his grip on my throat, allowing my feet to slip back to the floor as he chatters on about what he's going to do to my baby after he kills me. It's now or never, and I have nothing left to lose. I put my hands together, just like the teacher in my self-defense class taught us, finger to finger as if I'm in prayer.

"Do you really think God is going to help you, Julia?" Jeremy mocks me.

Even as he says it, I thrust my arms upward, using the connected hands as leverage. I'm just strong enough, and he's just surprised enough, that it breaks his hold around my neck. I only have a matter of seconds before he regains the power position. I reach up and grasp either side of his head with my hands, using the thumbs to dig straight into his eyes. He howls in pain as I push forward, away from the wall. Still with his head in my hands, I close my own eyes against the blow that I know is coming, and then I yank his head forward into my mine. Hard. Once, twice, three times. When I finally open my eyes, I see blood running down his face. I don't allow myself the luxury of feeling the pain myself. I just let go of my grip on his head and he falls backward onto the ground. I skirt around him and run out to the hallway and toward the back door.

"You fucking bitch!" he bellows from behind me. *"I'm going to fucking kill you!"*

I fly down the hall and back through the kitchen, toppling chairs and stools in his path as I go, praying that they will buy me just a few more seconds. When I get to the sliding glass door that opens onto the back-yard, I unlock the handle and pull, but it doesn't give.

Shit!

I look down and see the broom handle that Matthew put inside the track for added security. I reach down, grab it, and drop it again. I finally get the thing out of the way, and I try the handle again. This time the door gives. But, this time, I can see Jeremy's reflection in the glass. He's right behind me. I drop to the floor and fumble around for the wooden handle. At least it's some kind of a weapon. But I'm not fast enough. Or lucky enough.

Jeremy grabs my arm and yanks me to my feet, dragging me away from the back door. I thrash and scream and try to break things as we go. Finally, tired of fighting me, he simply picks me up and throws me over his shoulder, so that I'm hanging upside down against his back. I pound on him with my fists, screaming and clawing, but it doesn't seem to faze him as he carries me through the kitchen, the living room and then up the stairs to my bedroom.

When we get inside, he slams the door shut behind us with his foot, stomps over to the king-sized bed, and tosses me down onto it so hard that I bounce a full foot off of the innersprings. The fury is coming off of him in waves. I make one last attempt to get off the bed, but he drags me back by my hair.

"Don't you move!" he spits at me. "Don't you fucking move, Julia!"

I don't, until he pulls another pair of zip ties from his pocket. "No," I protest as I try to sit up. "No, not again..."

The punch comes so hard, and so fast, that it knocks me off the bed, onto the opposite side of the room. I'm amazed that I don't feel the pain at first, just the immense and uncomfortable pressure of his fist against my flesh. What I *do* feel is the thick slick wetness that's running down my face. Jeremy makes his way around to where I'm lying, dazed, on the floor. He looks like a giant as he stands over me. A very angry giant. Before I can even finish the idle thought, he delivers a quick, vicious kick to my ribs. I grunt in pain and curl up into a ball on the floor.

"Please," I cry into my hands. "Please..."

Jeremy bends over and grabs a fistful of my hair. I have no choice but to follow it upward and onto my unsteady legs. When I'm upright again, he takes my right wrist and uses it to pull me back onto the bed and all the way up to the headboard. At this point, I am in too much pain and too stunned to protest, as he uses one of the plastic fasteners to secure it to the wrought iron headboard. In a matter of seconds, the left wrist joins it. Then he is leaning over me, his face only a couple of inches from mine.

"Beg and plead all you want, you stupid cunt. All you're succeeding in doing is giving me a hard-on. I'd kick that fucking thing out of you right now, but I don't want to deal with all the blood while I'm screwing you."

He runs a hand over my rapidly swelling cheek and then holds it up so I can see the bloody smudge on his fingers.

"See that, Jules? If you think that's a sticky, painful mess, just wait until you feel your baby leaking out of you," he taunts softly with a smile that sickens me. "You know, I was going to wait until later, but I'm thinking maybe we should take advantage of this big old bed right now. What do you think?" He's patting the mattress next to me. "Hmmm? Still think rape is a little too common for me?"

I turn my face away from him and he straightens up with a chuckle.

"Uh-huh. That's what I thought. I'm going to get another drink, and while I'm gone, I want you to think about how badly I'm about to hurt you. Just wait and see what I can do when I really put my mind to it."

I still have my face turned away from him when he leaves the room, whistling a Mozart horn concerto as he moves into the hallway and down the stairs.

.

Chapter 39

Matthew

"For God's sake, Brett! Can't we go any faster? Jesus! Every second she's with him..."

"Matt, you need to stay calm," he says, putting a hand on my shoulder from the driver's seat of the car. "This is not the time to have a meltdown, man. Julia needs you to be calm and clearheaded."

I sigh and rub my temples. I have never felt so helpless in my entire life. Jeremy was exactly right. This is worse than anything anyone could possibly do to me physically. Julia is suffering. She's bleeding. He's probably got his hands all over her right now... No. I can't let my mind go there. Besides, I'm not the only one with something to lose here.

"What do you think will happen if your mom walks in on them?" I ask quietly.

He gives me a sideways glance from the driver's seat before he speaks again. And when he does speak, it's with an iciness that reminds me of the man Brett Corrigan used to be.

"If I know my brother—and I do—he'll be surprised. And then, he'll be happy."

"What?" I twist around in my seat to get a better look at him now. "What do you mean he'll be *happy?*"

"She's next on his hit list, I'm sure. She'll have saved him the trouble of tracking her down. And then, after her, it'll be me he's gunning for. Then Maggie, most likely. Jeremy is nothing, if not thorough."

I can't believe what I'm hearing. I mean, I always knew that Brett had an insight into his brother's mind that the rest of us didn't, but I never realized he could peer so deeply into the murky depths of Jeremy's soul. That is, if he had a soul.

"I'm sure I'd be up before you ..." I start, but Brett's mouth turns into a tight little smile that gives me the chills.

"Oh, no, Matthew. That would be too easy. He wants you to live on and suffer."

"You mean after he ... kills her?"

My question shakes Brett out of the dark place he's in and brings him back out into the light. "No," he asserts, shaking his head emphatically. "No, man. He's not going to kill her..."

I turn back and face forward, watching the scenery on the Long Island Expressway go by in a blur. No, he won't kill her, because I'm going to get there before that happens. But that doesn't mean she won't be begging him to kill her by then.

Chapter 40

Julia

There was a point in time when I wanted to know about my father. What had happened to him that day I was taken into state custody. Matthew had Tony dig up the police and CPS records for me and I spent a long, rainy afternoon sitting by myself, reading page after page of reports and statements and evaluations.

The snapshot of that day slowly began to come together as I put the pieces of the puzzle together. Rex had been arrested at the construction site where he worked. By the time he was processed at the county jail, he was complaining of police brutality. The arresting officers stated that they took him into custody like that, with a broken nose and some teeth missing.

While all of this was going on, I was three towns away at the hospital, having my chest x-rayed. They took pictures of every square inch of my tiny body. Every burn, every scar, every healed-over break and scab and scratch. Those pictures were in the files, too, and I looked over each one as if I was looking at a stranger.

I didn't recognize the painfully thin, malnourished little girl with the blank expression on her face. My eyes looked too big for my face and my hair hung around me, matted and tangled and dull. For the first time in my life, I looked back at the child I had been, and I saw what they saw.

I put everything back in that box and put it away inside the depths of my closet, where it still sits, untouched since that day. I refuse to throw it away, because it's a reminder of what I was, how far I've come, and just how much one small child can endure in her fight for survival. That little girl was my shame back then. She's my hero now, as I suffer blow after blow at the hands of the man I once loved.

Jeremy doesn't leave me tied to the bed for very long. Not once he realizes he can do a lot more damage by throwing me around the room. And, he was right, I had no idea you could experience this kind of pain and still be alive. After the first blow to my face, I was stunned. When he hit me again, the pain erupted in my head, literally causing an explosion of light behind my eyes. Right about then, my latent survival instincts kicked in, and I felt like an observer, outside of my own body.

The impact and the pressure of each punch was there, but they weren't accompanied by the blinding pain anymore. It was like the day David was born. The epidural blocked the pain of my body being torn apart. It would appear now, that I can manufacture that effect all on my own.

I'm flat on my stomach on the floor now, lying where the force of the last blow sent me sprawling. I try to make a quick mental inventory of my injuries, but it's hard to localize the pain at this point. I do know that one of my eyes is swollen completely shut, and my mouth is filled with the metallic taste of my own blood. He's avoided punching me in the stomach and ribs, thankfully. Of course, that's no guarantee that my baby is alright.

The worst of it is the disorientation. All of the trauma to my head has made me lose some of my sense of spatial awareness. I know I'm on the floor, but I can't quite place where in the room I am. I can hear every word he says, but I can't process them all immediately. I close my one good eye and let my mind pull away from my body. And then, I scream.

My attempt at dissociation is interrupted by the indescribable pain of my arm breaking under the weight of Jeremy's foot. It's the first noise I've made in nearly half an hour, save for the occasional grunt as he pushed, shoved, punched and slapped. Now he's pulling out the big guns.

"Awww, I'm sorry, Jules! Did that hurt? Well, you only use that arm for bowing," Jeremy taunts me from above. "But don't worry about it, you won't need it anymore anyway."

I'm breathing hard, panting really, as the few tears I have left bubble out of me and spill to the shiny oak planks below me. They mingle with the blood that has already dripped all over.

"I want Matthew to see your blood on every surface of this room," Jeremy explains, as if reading my thoughts.

I try to pull the broken limb to me, to protect it against further attack, but it's too painful to move even an inch. Jeremy takes care of that for me, though, when he grabs me by the foot and drags me toward the dresser. I let out a cry of pain as he lets go with an unceremonious thump. Maybe he's tired. Maybe he's going to take a break. Maybe...

My wishful thinking is disrupted by agony as he bends over and grabs ahold of me from under my armpits, hoisting me up high enough so I can see myself in the mirror. It's like looking at those old police photos all over again. My face is so swollen and distended, I actually wonder for a brief moment if there's something wrong with the mirror. Blood is smudged and drying all over my face. It stains my torn blouse, and cakes in my wild hair. My jaw doesn't look quite right, but that might just be the way it looks through my blurry vision.

"Lookie there, Jules! What a transformation, eh? I'll bet even your daddy didn't do *that* big of a number on you, did he? No, I'm guessing this is the worst you've ever felt. And you know what? I think it's time we commemorate the occasion, don't you?"

Before I can even form a reply in my fuzzy, agonized mind, he reaches into his pocket and pulls out my cell phone. The one that's been missing for weeks. The one I was so certain David had taken. Now, he holds it out in front of me, and uses it to snap a picture of my face like some perverse selfie.

"Perfect!" he quips. "Now, let's just send this to your husband..." He's holding me up with one arm and using the other to send the image to Matthew from my phone number.

It rings back in less than ten seconds. Jeremy puts it on speaker, but Matthew is yelling so loudly he needn't have bothered.

"Jeremy you motherfucker! I'm going to kill you with my bare hands, you fucking animal!"

I can't tell where Matthew is exactly, but I'm praying it's in a car, on his way here.

"Now, now, Matty Boy," Jeremy purrs. "Julia and I have just been having some fun! Too bad you're not here to join in."

"You're a dead man," I hear Matthew hiss from the other end of the line.

"Maybe, maybe not," Jeremy counters. "I think things are a little more decisive for sweet Julia, though. Say hello, Julia," he lilts, putting the phone to my bloody mouth.

"Matthew," I manage to whisper.

"Baby, you're going to be alright. It's all going to be okay," he echoes back to me the same words I used to comfort David in his crib. The room is starting to spin around me, and I'm afraid I will be sucked into its vortex before I can get the words out.

"Take David and go, Matthew! Jeremy wants to take him. Go, Matthew. Protect him..."

It doesn't take Jeremy more than a second to pull the phone away and give my broken arm a twist that makes me see stars as my body slides to the floor in slow motion.

"Don't bother trying to trace this phone," he is saying to Matthew. "The SIM card will be out of it as soon as I hang up. But don't worry, I'll find some other way to get you a picture of your wife's body. Just so you can have a little something to remember her by." He sneers and hangs up before my husband can respond.

He looks down at me and shaking his head with faux disappointment. "Oh, Jules, that was a very bad idea. You were supposed to stick to our script. Now, I'm really going to have to punish you," he sighs, leaning down.

I try to pull my broken body inward, curling into a ball to protect myself from his next kick or punch. When he realizes what I'm doing, he starts to laugh.

"You stupid bitch, I'm not going to kick you!"

He scoops me up in his arms and brings me back to the bed, like a groom carrying his bride on their wedding night. "No, no, no! I've got something much more fun planned for the two of us."

He smiles down at me as I turn my head away. It's quite clear to us both that I'm done fighting.

Chapter 41

Trudy

I don't know this house, but I know something doesn't feel quite right inside of it as I roll the baby's stroller through the front door. I stand there for a long moment, listening to the silence. Nothing. I'm letting my imagination get the better of me, I think, shaking my head as I unbuckle David and hoist him up onto my shoulder. The two of us make our way up the stairs to the nursery, and his crib. When I lower him down into it, he fusses for just a second before sighing contentedly, as if he knows he's home—where he's supposed to be.

I start at a loud thump coming from the other end of the hall, realizing instantly that my original instincts were right. We aren't alone in this house. And that's when it hits me, like a vision from the Lord Almighty, Himself. I slip my shoes off and take a deep breath before returning to the upstairs hallway and making my way to the closed door at the other end. I place my ear against the hollow panels and listen carefully to the muffled sounds within.

"Jules, if you fight me, you're going to get hurt. Just relax. It's not like we haven't done this before."

I'd know that voice anywhere on the face of this earth. A softer voice follows, but I can't make out what she's saying. He comes back at her, his mocking tone loud and clear through the door.

"I've already told you. It doesn't matter what you promise, or offer, or threaten. Once I'm through with you here, it's a couple of sharp blows to the gut and No. More. Baby."

More soft murmurs and some crying. He's laughing at her.

"Stop begging, you stupid cunt. You should know by now it's not going to help. Neither is the crying. So, unless you want me to gag you while I fuck you then I suggest you shut up right now."

"Go to hell!" I hear her spit. That's followed by the sound of a hard slap. I have to put a hand over my mouth to keep from crying out as I slowly, carefully, pull back from the door and retreat to the nursery.

Once I'm safely inside, I rummage around in the diaper bag until I find what I'm looking for—some baby allergy medicine. I fill the tiny spoon and poise myself over the crib. This has to be so quick that David doesn't fully wake up and cry. I count to three in my head and, with my left hand I pluck the pacifier from the little boy's mouth and then spoon the sticky, sweet liquid into his mouth and down his throat. The instant I see his face start to crumble, I pop the pacifier back in, lay him back down, rubbing his tummy until he drifts back to sleep. This stuff will keep him out for a while. I hope.

I hesitate for just an instant before I leave the nursery. "Oh, dear God in heaven," I whisper. "Lord, give me the strength to do what I have to do. Give me the words that I need to speak. Give me the light with which to follow your path through the darkness."

I step into the hallway once more, slowly closing the door behind me, and tiptoe back down the stairs, cringing with each little creak and groan of the wooden steps. I hold my breath until I am safely on the first floor again, and out of sight of the upstairs.

Calling the police is not an option. I've learned that lesson the hard way over the years. My son can talk his way out of anything. He could be holding a bloody knife, standing over a dead body and still find a way to divert the blame to someone else.

No, I'm going to have to handle this myself.

Once and for all.

After one last deep breath to try and calm my racing heart, I start my preparations, praying all the while that Julia can hold on just a little longer. I consider where I saw the garage from the outside of the house then push the stroller in that direction, opening doors as I go.

A closet, a guest room a playroom and finally, there it is. One stop down and I am surrounded by the smell of oil and gasoline. This is the smell of my sweet husband. I close my eyes for just a moment and breathe in deep. He is here with me, just as he said he would be in his letter.

Yes. I can do this.

I feel along the wall for the light switch and flip on the bright florescence overhead. Once I've moved the stroller out of sight, I stop and survey the shelves around me. Tools hang from hooks on pegboard. There's a hammer. That might do. If I can find the car keys I might find a tire iron in the trunk.

I scan the big cardboard boxes on the shelves labeled CHRISTMAS and MATERNITY CLOTHES. Then I spot something on the other side of the car. It's a baseball. Well, where there's a baseball, surely there must be... And there it is. I stretch to reach the wooden bat and pull it to me. I let it fall into the palm of my hand a few times. It's got good weight to it. Yes, this will do quite nicely. I can almost hear Danny's voice in my ear.

"Time to play ball, Trudy, my love."

Yes it is. And I'm ready.

Chapter 42

Julia

I can just make out the glow of the alarm clock on the other side of the bed. Matthew's side of the bed. Though, right now, it's Jeremy who's occupying it. His breathing is soft and even as he sleeps. I'm not so lucky. The respite of sleep is impossible right now.

My face, my gut, my arm, my jaw are all sending out wave upon wave of pain. Everything else is just one dull, amorphous ache. And then there's the rest of it... I try not to think about it. I don't have the luxury of feeling sorry for myself. I have to figure out how to get out of this situation.

From beside me, Jeremy sighs in his sleep and rolls so that he's facing the other direction. I'm looking at his strong back. I used to love to run my hands along the taut muscles there. Now I can only think about how I'd love to drive a knife right between his shoulder blades. I can't stand to look at him for another second. I turn away from him, inch by agonizing inch.

Good. This is good. Anger is good. It will keep me motivated to push through the pain rather than just curl up and die. I will *not* leave my child without a mother. I swallow a sob as I think of the tiny life inside of me. I can only pray for a miracle. Jeremy has been so brutal already that I can't be sure... Now I can feel the anger filling me up. It brings a harsh, metallic taste to my mouth and it makes me breathe heavily through my nose.

If my calculations are right, Matthew could be here in the next forty-five minutes, but more likely an hour or so. I'm not sure how long I can hang on. In fact, right now there is only one thing of which I can be absolutely certain. One of us is going to be dead by morning. And, as of right now, the odds are most definitely not in my favor.

I jump when I feel his hands on me. He's turned on his side to face me and is positioning himself close behind me, as if we were lovers again, spooning in my bed in the city.

"How you feeling there, Jules?" he murmurs in my ear. "Did that bring back any memories?" I don't respond. "Oh, come on now. You used to love it when I fucked you. You used to beg me for it. Has your pussy husband turned you off of sex? Is that what it is? I mean, I know we tried a couple of new things, but I thought maybe you should open your horizons a little. You know what I mean?"

When I remain silent, he keeps going. "No? Ah, well. I enjoyed myself anyway and that's the most important thing." He grabs me around the waist, pulling me closer to him and I let out a low, involuntary moan from the pain. "That's what I like to hear," he chuckles. "A good moan makes me good and hard. I think maybe I'm ready to go another round. How about you?"

We both know he's not asking. Suddenly, he pulls away, and I'm flat on my back, looking up at him. I think I might vomit, but I force back the bile as it rises in my throat. It would only make him angry. Over the course of the last hellish hour, I've discovered that if I just do what he wants without a fuss, he's much less likely to go out of his way to cause me pain. Unfortunately, I had to figure it out the hard way.

"I think one more time for old times' sake and then we'll tend to our baby business, shall we? I mean it's entirely possible we've already dispatched that little blob of cells, but I want to be sure."

I close my eyes tight and brace for his latest humiliation. But he doesn't move an inch. I wait another few seconds and then open my one good eye. But he's not looking at me. He's staring at the bedroom door. It takes me a few seconds to understand why. From outside of the bedroom, I catch the telltale creak of the third step from the top. Someone is either coming up or going down the stairs.

"Jeremy?"

We stop breathing in unison, both of us startled by the sound of a woman's voice coming from downstairs. He slams a hand over my mouth before I can scream for help.

"Jeremy, I know you're up there. Come out and talk to me."

"What. The. *Fuck?!*" he hisses.

He looks down at me and I can see he's trying to decide whether or not he should leave me here alone to go and investigate. But at this point I'm so bloodied and bruised, it's clear to both of us that I'm not going very far.

"Stay here. Don't you fucking move. Do you understand?"

I nod and he pulls away from me, getting to his feet and going out into the hall to investigate, slipping into his jeans along the way. As soon as the door shuts behind him, I hear voices. Jeremy and a woman, but I can't tell who it is. Jesus, who *could* it be? My head is so foggy that I can't tell. Right now, his words are clearer than hers, closer.

I take a deep breath and steel myself for the pain that I know is coming as I drape myself over the edge of the bed with tremendous effort. I allow myself to roll and drop slowly onto the floor, stuffing my good arm into my mouth to keep from screaming when my broken one gets caught under me.

It feels like hours before I can try to move again, and when I do, I'm like a giant inchworm, wriggling my way across the room, little by little. Every part of my body throbs with the effort. I stop to take a breath, ignoring the hot tears that are streaming down my face. The door may as well be a mile away for the little progress I'm making. I no sooner have the thought than the door flies open.

Shit!

I cringe, expecting him to deliver another brutal kick or drop down onto the floor to strangle me. But, surprisingly, Jeremy doesn't even comment on my slow-motion escape attempt.

"Come on," he mutters, grabbing my forearm roughly and literally dragging my bloodied, naked body across the floor and out into the hallway with him. "There's someone here who wants to see you."

It looks like Trudy Corrigan. Could it be? I can't tell if it's really her, or if my mind is playing tricks on me. God, my head feels as if it's going to explode.

"See, Mom?" he crows, pulling my unbroken arm up as if I'm some trophy. "I told you, she's just fine."

I'm not imagining this. That's Trudy.

"She doesn't look so fine to me, Jeremy," I hear her say from below.

"No? Huh. Well, let me see what I can do about that." He seems to consider for a second before letting go of me so that I fall abruptly to the floor. Then he delivers a quick and brutal kick to my back. My mouth twists into a scream that I can't seem to get past my swollen lips. I can see Trudy through the spindles of the railing that runs across the upstairs landing. Her eyes move from me on the floor, up to her son towering above me. And she looks pissed.

"*Stop it, right this instant, Jeremy!*" she demands in as harsh a voice as I've ever heard.

But Jeremy isn't put off by her tone in the least. He moves closer to the head of the stairs so he can look down at her.

"Why don't you come up and make me, Mom?" he suggests, holding out a hand toward her.

"No, thank you, Jeremy. I'll stay right where I am," she snaps back at him.

"Are you really foolish enough to think you're safer down there?" She doesn't respond. "You're not safe *anywhere*, Mom. Do you know that while Dad was gasping his last pathetic breath, I told him not to worry, that you wouldn't be far behind him? That man died in a state of fear and dread, believing that I was going to murder you and he wasn't going to be around to help you. That was my little parting gift to him."

She doesn't reply. Eventually Jeremy gets tired of waiting for a response and continues.

"My little parting gift to you will be that tidbit, plus the knowledge that after I kill you, I'm going to kill Maggie and frame Brett for it. I've already started gathering what I need to put that little plan in motion. I'll take his life and his love, then I'll take the money you left him and use it to start over again on some nice tropical beach somewhere."

"Well," I hear her say. "That's quite a plan."

"I know! Right? I'm nothing if not an exceptional planner."

"So, what's next in this plan, then?"

He pretends to ponder. "Oh, hmmm, good question. Well, there's the decision about who to kill first, you or Julia here. But see, Julia's a little more complicated. Part of my punishment for her is to help her lose that little bundle of joy swimming around inside of her. But you know, she's a kind of out of it right now... and she's not going anywhere, so I guess she can wait. Maybe you and I should have a little mother-son bonding time."

"Whatever you think is best, Jeremy. But you'll have to excuse me for a moment, I was just going to call the police," Trudy starts to turn toward the kitchen.

"Yeah, I wouldn't do that, Mom."

She stops and looks up at him as if she is surprised that he wouldn't want her to make the call. "No? Why not?"

"Because if you do, I'll strangle you before they even pick up."

There is something nagging at me. Something right there, on the fringe of my cloudy mind. I know it's important, but I can't quite grasp it.

It's okay, I'm going to be okay. I can do this.

I close my eyes and I breathe in and out slowly, trying to block out the pain, allowing my subconscious to show me the way. I see Matthew's face, strong and loving. And then there is my sweet little boy with his rosy cheeks and sparkling eyes. I can almost hear his laugh. I think about the tiny life inside of me, not yet strong enough to protect itself.

And then, it comes to me.

"Sometimes, the best decision you can make for your child is to leave them behind."

I hear Trudy's words so clearly that, for a split second, I'm certain she's said them aloud. But she hasn't, she's too busy absorbing her son's taunts. No, this is a message from my subconscious, and it tells me exactly what I need to do.

Jeremy isn't paying any attention to what I'm doing as he berates his mother, so he doesn't notice as I roll over and—drawing upon every molecule in my body—rise up onto my feet. I back up against the wall and slide along it, inch by inch until I'm nearly behind him. That's when he turns around.

No!

It doesn't help my plan, but it doesn't really hurt it either.

Please, please, please.

"Oh, ho! Look who's up and about! What's the matter Jules? Did I spoil your surprise? Were you thinking you were going to push me down the stairs?" he mocks me with his hideous smirk. "Good luck with that! You don't have that kind of strength on your best day, let alone now."

While he chatters on, I catch Trudy's eye as she stands twenty feet below us. I give her a nod that is barely perceptible, but when she returns it, I know she understands.

"Jeremy!"

She yells his name so loudly that she actually startles him, and he turns his attention from me to her.

And there it is. A window of opportunity so small, I'll lose it if I even pause to blink. With every ounce of strength I have, in every cell of my body, I propel myself forward. Jeremy is turning back in my direction, but it's too late. He's too late—I'm already in motion. As I hurl myself forward, I wrap my arms around him tightly. He tries, but he cannot right us against the momentum I've generated. We tip. We fall. We tumble. We roll.

With a blind reach, I somehow manage to grab hold of one of the spindles in the railing on the way down. This stops me from falling, along with Jeremy to the base of the stairs. I'm too weak to hold on for more than a few seconds, but by extricating myself from Jeremy's weight and pull, my descent is more of a bumpy slide on my back than a brutal somersault onto my head.

Not that it matters. I'm unconscious before my feet hit the first floor.

Chapter 43

Trudy

There's a principle in physics called the *'Tipping Point.'* It's the point at which an object is no longer balanced and adding a small amount of weight can cause it to topple. There's a more philosophical definition of the principle, which is the point in a situation at which a minor development precipitates a crisis. Both of these principles are in play at this very moment, as I stand at the bottom of the stairs watching, helplessly.

It started when I screamed Jeremy's name to divert his attention away from Julia. That action caused him to reflexively turn his head toward me, twisting his body slightly as he did. And, although he didn't realize it, with that single movement, he sealed his fate. In this instance Jeremy is the object, and he is no longer balanced. It would only take a small amount of weight to topple him, e.g. Julia. But, this is where I am inclined to switch to the secondary definition. The minor development of Julia pushing herself into Jeremy's arms, precipitates the crisis of the two of them tumbling violently down the stairs.

For a brief time, they appear to be intertwined—so enmeshed that I cannot tell where one begins and the other ends. But then, by the grace of God, I see Julia's frail, bruised arm snake out and grab hold of a wooden spindle on her way down the stairs. It's enough to stop her violent descent and peel Jeremy's weight from hers. Gravity is not on

Jeremy's side as it draws him down the stairs with increasing velocity to his inevitable collision with the immovable flagstone floor.

I gasp as Julia loses her grip a few seconds later and continues to slide down the staircase until she, too, is a heap at my feet. She is to my left, he is to my right and they are both perfectly still. I fall to my knees next to Julia, my fingers searching for a pulse in her neck. Yes, she's alive—though just barely.

Her face is so swollen that I'm not sure I'd have recognized her had I not known already. One of her arms is bent back at an unnatural angle and here's a large gash in her forehead that I think she may have gotten on the way down, judging from the freshness of the blood there versus the dried and caked smears around her nose and mouth.

I continue my downward inventory and redness and swelling from her ribcage to her toes. My eyes pass quickly over her thighs, which are wet and slick with red warmth. I allow myself the small luxury of not speculating on what else my son has done to her.

Getting to my feet, I run quickly from room to room, looking for something to cover her. Finally, I find a large, soft throw and bring it back to where Julia is lying so I can drape the blanket over her naked, battered body and lift her head just enough to slip the pillow under her neck for support. I don't have much time, so I turn my attention to Jeremy.

He is in considerably better condition, with no blood to speak of. Though, he could easily have internal injuries that I can't see. His left leg is clearly broken. I feel for his pulse and find it to be strong.

Of course it is.

It takes more than a fall down the stairs to kill Satan.

Chapter 44

Julia

Trudy has a bat. A baseball bat. And she is saying something to Jeremy, who is lying a few feet away from me on the flagstone entryway at the foot of the staircase. I can't seem to speak or move, but I can just see the two of them in my line of sight. I notice that his leg is twisted at an unnatural angle. He is awake and looking at her as she speaks, but I am floating in and out of consciousness, only catching bits and pieces of the conversation.

"Matthew thought this was the safest place for David to be. Of course, no one had any idea that this is where you'd taken her..."

Is that why Trudy is here? Matthew had her bring David here? Oh, God. Please don't let my baby see me like this. I don't want him to remember me like this, sprawled out dead on the floor of his home.

"Please, Mom, please. It hurts so much. Help me, Mom..." Jeremy begs quietly.

Even in my haze, I'm struck by how different he sounds—almost human. Somehow, I know that I should try to stay awake—that the longer I lapse into the abyss, the less likely I am to ever wake up, so I force myself to focus on what is happening around me. Trudy is kneeling down beside Jeremy now, brushing the hair back from his forehead.

"What a disappointment you've been to us all. Your Grandma Ruth saw it when you were just a boy, but I didn't want to believe it. Eventually though, there came a time when even I could not deny that fact that evil itself was living under my very own roof."

I can hear his breathing as it becomes more labored. Or is that my own breathing I'm hearing? I can't even tell anymore. Blackness again, I'm not sure for how long this time. When my eyes open, she's standing again, now with the bat in her hand.

"Please, Mom, don't..." he rasps.

"I'm sorry, Jeremy, but I stopped being your mother a long time ago. The only parent you have now is Satan," Trudy laments. "Well, I don't have the time to wait for you to die on your own. I've already called the ambulance for Julia and I need to get in touch with Matthew. And, well, for all we know, the doctors may still be able to save your life. I can't have that.

She sighs. "We tried to tell you all those years ago," she recalls wistfully. *"'They that sow the wind shall reap the whirlwind.'* I'm the one who brought you into this world, so now it is my job to deliver you to the whirlwind."

Trudy Corrigan raises the bat high over her head. I close my eyes so I won't see, but, unfortunately, I cannot close my ears. "You have a good trip to hell, Son," she hisses.

Jeremy and I are engulfed in blackness at exactly the same moment.

Chapter 45

Tony

When I throw the door open, my gun is drawn and I'm prepared to shoot at the first sign of the sick bastard, Jeremy. As it turns out, he's the first thing I see when I open the door, but there's no need to shoot him because he's already dead. Good and dead. A pool of blood is spreading from underneath his head, which appears to have been crushed by a blunt object. Like the bloody baseball bat lying on the ground next to him. A few feet away is Julia.

Holy Mother of God.

Departed or not, looking at what he's done to her, I feel like emptying a round into his skull anyway. I return my Glock to its holster so I won't be tempted. And, it's a good thing I do, because the woman who walks in from the hallway startles me so badly that I could have easily shot her on instinct alone. She's carrying a bottle of bleach and roll of paper towels, and she stops suddenly, just as shocked to see me as I am to see her.

"Are you...Trudy?" I ask slowly, quietly, so as not to spook her. She nods. I hold up my hands to show her I'm not carrying the weapon I would have been had she come in twenty seconds sooner. "My name is Tony Ruggiero. I'm a friend of Matthew's. He and your son are on their way here, but I was closer..."

"Are you a police officer, Mr. Ruggiero?" she asks flatly.

I shake my head. "No, Ma'am. I'm a private investigator, but not any kind of law enforcement."

She looks at me quizzically, as if trying to decide if she should trust me or not. "Mr. Ruggiero, did you come here to kill Jeremy?"

"I... I—I," I start and stutter. "Yes," I affirm finally. "Yes, I was prepared to do that."

She nods. "Well, clearly, that's not necessary at this point," she informs me, nodding her chin in the direction of her dead son.

"Clearly," I repeat, looking at the bloody bat again, and then at the bottle of bleach in her hands. "Because you did it already..." I murmur, more to myself, than to her.

"Yes."

"And...Julia?"

"I didn't hurt her, if that's what you're asking," she replies with some irritation.

I shake my head quickly. "No, no, Ma'am. I just wasn't sure... how all of this transpired."

"She wasn't strong enough to push him down the stairs, so she hurled herself at him and they both came down."

"And he was dead when he hit the ground?" I ask, hopefully.

Her eyebrows go up. "What do you think, Mr. Ruggiero?"

Again, I look at her, at him, and at the bat. "I think you could use some help here, because when you call an ambulance for her, the police won't be far behind."

"Exactly," she agrees. "Now, what do you know about destroying evidence, Mr. Ruggiero?"

As it turns out, quite a bit.

Chapter 46

Matthew

We're less than a half hour away when Brett's phone rings, breaking the silence that has filled the car in the last hour. He looks at the screen. "Who the hell is this now?" he mutters and puts the phone to his ear. "Hello?" He listens for a long moment, his brows drawing together. "Where are you?"

Another long pause.

"What?" I ask impatiently. "What is it?"

He holds up one of the fingers on the hand that's steering the car telling me to wait. "Yes, of course." Pause. "Yes, I understand."

With a quick tap, the caller is gone, and Brett is looking at me. He flips on the turn signal and pulls into a deserted supermarket parking lot.

"What? Why are we stopping?"

"That was Tony..." he begins.

"Tony? Why was he calling you? Why didn't he call me..."

The answer to my own question knocks the wind from my lungs. There's only one reason he would want to talk to Brett first. I frantically fumble with the lock on my door and manage to get it open just in time to hang my head out of the car and vomit onto the asphalt.

"Matthew! Matthew, she's not dead," he's explaining, but I can hardly hear him above my own retching. "Matthew," he tries again when

I've dragged myself back into the car. "Listen to me. I need you to show me how to get to St. Francis Hospital. That's where Julia will be."

"Oh, God. Is she... is she alright?"

"Matthew, I can't lie to you, I don't know. All he'd say is that she's in pretty bad shape and that I should get you to the hospital. Maggie's on her way out to your house on the train. As soon as she gets there, he'll come right to the hospital to tell you everything. He doesn't want to leave my mother there alone with the police."

"The police?" I think I'm going to be sick again. Then I realize, there's someone not accounted for. "What about..."

I don't finish the sentence, but he knows what I'm asking.

"Dead," he says simply. "My brother is dead." Brett looks away from me and out the car window. "I'll stay with you at the hospital until Tony comes, then I'll go back to the house, too. The three of us will take care of things there and look after David until... well, until we know what's going on with Julia."

"I think... I think that's a good plan, Brett," I say.

It's clear that he's feeling conflicted. For, as much as Jeremy is—was—a monster, he was still Brett's flesh and blood. This is still a loss for him, and his mother.

"I'm sorry," I murmur so softly, that I'm not even certain he has heard me. But then, he turns to face me again.

"I'm not."

Chapter 47

Maggie

They don't tell you about the mess. That's the thing about a crime scene, or a suicide, or any other violent act that happens to take place in your home. After the police have gathered their evidence and taken their photos, after the coroner has carted off the body and the last detective has left the scene, you are left alone. With the mess. No fairies come to clean the brain matter from the walls. No special cleaning unit arrives to mop up the pool of blood in your kitchen. They don't even take the yards of yellow tape with them when they leave. I know this, because I've seen it too many times in my line of work. And because I see it now as I walk from room to room of Julia and Matthew's beautiful home. We—Brett and Trudy and I—will be the last ones to see the house like this. I'm going to make damn sure of that.

Trudy is resting upstairs in the nursery with David and I've sent Brett to the hospital with coffee and bagels for Matthew and Tony. I have a big job ahead of me, and not a lot of time to do it. The clock on the wall of the kitchen tells me it's nearly six in the morning as I start gathering cleaning supplies in the kitchen.

"Alright then, let's get down to it, shall we?" I mutter to myself, grabbing rolls of paper towels, trash bags, bleach, a mop, broom and sponges.

I take my time as I walk down the hall to the front corridor. When I get to the flagstone floor I stop. I haven't really allowed myself to take this in, but I have to now. I'm the only who can do this. It's bad enough, the memories that will be tied to this house for Julia. I'm not going to let Matthew walk into his childhood home and see it like this. Nor am I going to allow Brett or Trudy to mop up Jeremy's blood. Or his victim's, for that matter.

I start at the bottom of the stairs, where they landed, using the mountains of paper towels to soak up the blood on the floor. Once that's done, I mop it all with a bleach solution until the water turns a rust color. Then, I work my way up the steps, scouring each riser for drips and drops and smears, until they, too are clear of all biological material. When I get to the top of the stairs, I see a long trail of blood, presumably where Julia used the wall to support herself as she made her way toward Jeremy.

There are also some droplets on the hardwood floor. A little spray bleach and a sponge take care of these, too. And that just leaves me with the master bedroom, its door slightly ajar, looming at the end of the hallway. I walk toward it slowly, and give the door a reluctant push with my index finger. It swings the rest of the way open, silently revealing to me the gruesome scene within.

I know that she was beaten, but I hadn't expected there'd be this much blood. Not without a stab wound or a gunshot. There is smeared blood on every wall and areas of the bed sheets are soaked with it. There are small puddles and drops all over the floor, some intact, others smudged by foot- and handprints. I shake my head. Surely she has miscarried. With the amount of blood in the bedroom, the hallway, the stairs ... At this point, I'm not even sure if she's alive. Or brain dead or...

"Come, we'll do the bed together."

I jump at the sound of Trudy's voice right behind me. She's taking in the room from over my shoulder. I start to object, but she pushes past me and waits till I join her. Without speaking, we pull it apart in layers. Pillows and cases, sheets, blanket and mattress pad. No blood has seeped through to the mattress, thankfully.

"Alright, you go ahead and bring these downstairs, and put them in the washer to soak in hot water with bleach."

I nod and start to gather the sheets when I feel her hand on my shoulder. When I look up at her, she is staring intently at me. "The hottest water you can run, Maggie. And a lot of bleach."

I do as she asks. By the time I return, she has somehow managed to scrub every last drip and drop, splatter and stain from every surface. There are crisp, clean sheets on the neatly made bed, and she's opened the windows so the brisk, early morning air can displace some of the stench left behind from the events of the last twelve hours. She stands, silently, with her back to me, looking out through the sheer panels as the first light of dawn begins to crawls across the sky.

And so, it is done. We can all breathe a tremendous sigh of relief that Jeremy Corrigan has, at long last, left this world. The pity of it is, of course, that he could have had it all based solely on his talent. But something deep within him wouldn't give him the satisfaction of wining anything on merit alone.

For Jeremy, it wasn't worth having if it wasn't worth taking. Part of me feels guilty—it's not quite right to celebrate the death of another human being—no matter how evil he was. And yet, I know that I won't be the only one sleeping easier tonight. Or at least I would be if I were going to sleep at all.

Chapter 48

Matthew

My wife is almost unrecognizable as I hold her limp hand in mine. It reminds me of a night, not so long ago, when I sat by the side of her hospital bed. The night we found out she was carrying Jeremy's baby. Now, she is unconscious. There are tubes and monitors everywhere. It is nearly five in the morning when, from somewhere in my dozing brain, I sense that she's awake. I sit up, startled to find her watching me through the eye that isn't swollen shut.

"Oh, thank Christ," I murmur, pulling her hand to my face so I can feel it against my cheek. "I've been so, so scared, Julia. You've been unconscious for hours. They didn't know if..." my voice breaks off and I start to cry.

"David?" she whispers.

I look up and wipe the tears from my face. I need to get myself together. This is not the time to fall apart. "He's fine, Julia. He's at home, asleep in his own bed. Trudy is there with him. She insisted on staying on the couch in the nursery."

I see her battered face loosen with relief. She mouths the next word, "Nat?"

I nod. "She's going to be fine. She feels incredibly guilty, but she's okay," I assure her.

Julia closes the one eye and frowns for a moment, gathering the strength to ask the next question. I squeeze her hand.

"The baby is fine, Julia." She looks at me again, a look of total bewilderment crossing her battered face. "She has a strong heartbeat."

"She?" Julia croaks.

I nod and she tries to smile, but stops, wincing with the pain of the effort.

"Yes, our daughter is going to be fine. They don't know how, but she's fine. I told the doctors that she's obviously a fighter, just like her mother."

I give her a moment to let this miracle soak in before I tell her the rest.

"Jeremy is dead, Julia," I say at last. If she's surprised by this news, she doesn't show it. "He smashed his head in when the two of you fell down the stairs. Thank God Trudy came in when she did, or you would have died there, too."

It's clear that the IV drugs are kicking in again as Julia fights to keep her focus on me and what I'm telling her.

"He was begging her to help him," she mumbles.

"Who? Trudy? No, baby. You were unconscious. Jeremy was already dead when Trudy got to the house with David. She called the police."

Julia is shaking her head as if she doesn't agree with this version of events.

"Sweetheart, you had been beaten so badly by the time you went down the stairs, I doubt you ever regained consciousness once you hit the floor."

"How bad am I?"

"The doctors say you have a fractured skull, a broken jaw and nose. You also have three broken ribs and one broken arm in case you hadn't noticed."

I guess she hadn't noticed, because she seems surprised to find a cast on her right arm.

"I won't lie to you," I explain softly, "you're looking a little rough right now. You're going to need some plastic surgery down the road. And the broken bones are going to be a challenge, especially with you being pregnant. They have to be careful about the heavy-duty pain meds."

Her one good eye wells with tears. "I tried, but he was just too strong …"

"I know, Julia. I know. You didn't do anything wrong. You convinced him to not to take David, didn't you?" She looks away. "Julia, look at me, Julia," I command more sternly than I intend to, but I know she needs to hear this.

She turns her disfigured face toward me once again, and I lean in close so she won't miss a single word I'm about to say.

"I know what you did. I know that you threw yourself at him so that he would fall down the stairs. You knew that he would take you down with him. You didn't know if you would survive the fall. And, if you did survive, you didn't know if you'd lose the baby."

I use my thumb to gently wipe the tears from her cheeks. "I know you, Julia. Through the haze of the pain and the fear, you realized the only way to protect David once and for all, was to make sure Jeremy was dead. And when the opportunity presented itself, you decided it was more important for Jeremy to die than it was for you to live."

Even as I utter the words, the tears are slipping down my face again. I take her hand, already in mine, and press it to my damp cheek, holding it there against my face as I speak again. "You were willing to give your life for our son. And now, thanks to you, this nightmare is over. Jeremy Corrigan will never hurt us—or anyone else —ever again."

From underneath her bruised and swollen flesh I see the faintest flicker of the woman I have loved nearly every day of my life. It's going to be a long, rough road back, but, in my heart, I know that we are going to be just fine.

* * *

Julia is sedated and resting comfortably when Tony pops his head into the room. He gives me a look that asks if she's okay. I nod and smile, then get to my feet and follow him out into the hallway.

"You told her everything?" he asks.

"I did. But, she's in pain and in shock. She's got some processing to do when her head's a little clearer."

He nods thoughtfully. "Oh!" he says, suddenly remembering he's holding a cup of coffee in his hand. "I almost forgot. This is for you. Hospital coffee sucks."

"Thanks, man. How are things at the house?" It suddenly occurring to me that I have no clue what kind of a three-ringed circus is unfolding in my living room.

"The coroner took him away hours ago. The police stayed on for another hour taking pictures and asking a bunch of questions. It's relatively quiet now, though you've got a houseful. Maggie came out from the city so she and Brett could be with Trudy and David."

"How is Trudy?"

It's not a question I've wanted to ponder, but I know I should. She has, after all, just lost a son. He may have been an evil fuck, but he was her child.

"She's a rock, Matthew. She was serving coffee to the cops with one hand and shooing them off your oriental carpet with the other. David slept through everything. That kid is something else."

That makes me smile. He's always been a heavy sleeper, thankfully. "Well, man, I can't thank you enough..." I start to wrap-up our chat so I can get back inside to Julia. But there's something else on Tony's mind. I can see it in his expression. "What? What is it?"

"I don't quite know how to say this. It's just that..."

"What, Tony? Please, just tell me," I grumble, feeling the anxiety creep back into the pit of my stomach.

He looks down at his feet uncomfortably, then back up at me. "Matthew, I'm not going to give you too many details here, because the less you know, the better. But, there is something you really do need to be aware of." I realize I'm holding my breath as I wait for him to drop the other shoe. "It's Jeremy," he continues slowly, softly. "It's the way he died..."

"Wait, didn't he fall down the stairs? With Julia?"

"Oh, he definitely fell down the stairs."

"Then what, Tony? You're not making any sense."

His eyes dart around the hallway to make certain there is no one close enough to overhear us. "Okay, so, when I got to the house, Jeremy was at the bottom of the stairs. And he was dead."

"And...?" I coax, trying not to be irritated by this long, drawn out complication, whatever the fuck it is.

"But he wasn't dead when he hit the bottom of the stairs."

"I don't understand."

"I think he would have survived the fall. I think he *did* survive the fall, but Trudy... *helped* him along. To the other side... if you know what I mean." I don't. I just stare at him, perplexed, so he continues. "She wanted to make sure Jeremy was *good and dead* before she called the police. She wanted to make sure there was no way he was going to get put back together by the doctors like some fucking Humpty Dumpty."

I hear Julia's hoarse whisper in my head.

"He was begging her to help him."

The light bulb in my head finally goes on.

"Wait, wait, wait, you think that his own mother just...let him die?" He looks down at the floor again and I can see that's *not* what he thinks. Which can only mean... "Holy shit. You think...you think Trudy *killed* him?" I whisper, incredulously.

He leans in even closer to me and drops his voice. "Let's just say, the baseball bat you had in your garage? It's now a pile of ashes in a drumfire that I lit on the other side of town. After I scrubbed it down with steel wool and pickled it in bleach, that is." I can only stare at him. "She didn't tell me what she did," he continues, "and I didn't ask. But there it was on the floor when I got there. All bloody. I got rid of it for her."

"Jesus..." I murmur to myself. "So...what does that mean?"

He shrugs. "I don't think it means anything for you guys. My best guess is Trudy had some unfinished business with her son... and she settled it tonight."

I think about that for a second. Even Jeremy's own mother knew that he had to die, or there would never be peace for any of us. Just as Julia sacrificed herself for her son, Trudy Corrigan sacrificed her son for the rest of us. Given the same set of circumstances, I don't know that I would have—that I could have done either of those things.

What an extraordinary pair of women.

Epilogue

Julia

By the time their dark blue SUV crunches to a halt on our bluestone driveway, I've been standing nervously in front of the window for nearly a half hour. One by one they climb out, the two passengers and the driver.

"They're here," I call out to Matthew, who's in the kitchen with David.

He joins me, holding our boy in his arms, as we go to the front door together. When it swings open, there is Kelly Randall. My mother. Her emerald eyes, identical to my own, move down to the little boy squirming in his father's arms and I see the tears flood them and she puts a hand to her mouth.

Standing a little behind her are a teenaged girl with long dark hair and a tall, lean man with a salt-and-pepper beard and glasses. I recognize the girl as Corinne, my half-sister. She's looking down at her feet, fidgeting nervously with the bracelets that line her wrist.

"Julia, you remember, Corinne," Kelly says, and I offer the girl a reassuring smile.

"Of course," I murmur. "Hello, Corinne." I'm rewarded with a shy grin, shiny with purple-colored braces.

Kelly reaches behind her and the man steps forward. "And this—this is my husband, Drew Randall. He... he's the one who saved me, Julia. He got me off the streets..." her voice fades with the painful memory.

I consider the kind faced man in front of me and wonder what it was that he saw in her... what it was that gave him the courage to love a woman who was so deeply flawed.

"Drew..." I begin, but before I can do more than utter his name, he leans in and kisses my cheek. He looks as if he's about to cry, too.

"Julia," he breathes, "I've waited so very long to meet you."

For a split second I want to point out that he *could* have met me decades ago, had the two of them taken me out of the North Fork Children's Home. But I stop myself. That was then. This is now. And now, I understand.

I give my stepfather a shy smile of my own as I place a hand on Matthew's shoulder. "And this is my husband...my Matthew."

Matthew shakes Drew's hand and opts for a polite nod to the women. I'm stunned that throughout this entire exchange, David has sat perfectly still in his father's arms, his intense, hazel eyes moving curiously from face to face. But now, all eyes are on him.

"David," Matthew coaxes, "can you say hello to..." he stops suddenly, and I realize with growing horror that this is the one thing we have not discussed. What will David call this woman and her family? They're all staring at me now, waiting for the answer.

"Grammy," I reply after a thoughtful pause. "Sweetheart, this is your *Grammy.*"

Kelly opens her arms and moves forward. I step aside, assuming she's headed for her grandson...but she isn't, she's headed for me. Before I can react, she pulls me into her arms and smothers my face with kisses—the salty dampness of her tears mixing with mine.

I don't know how long we stand there, holding one another like that and crying, but when we finally separate, we are alone on the front porch. At some point, the others have gone inside to give us our privacy. And for that I'm grateful.

Kelly reaches out to put a hand on my immense belly, but stops short, looking to me for permission. I give it with a nod.

"How are you?" she asks, her eyes filled with concern as she rubs my baby bump gently.

"Better. Still tired, but much, much better," I assure her.

It's taken months, but the bruises have finally faded away, the fractures have healed, and the cast has come off. Still, as much as I may look like my old self, I'm not yet feeling like myself. There are still nights when I wake up drenched in sweat, gasping...sometimes screaming. The doctors tell me that it's PTSD and that, hopefully, with time and lots of therapy it, too, will fade.

With the baby due in another month, Matthew was terrified that I would be overwhelmed and has insisted on getting some live-in help to supplement Nat's role. I resisted at first until he cautiously suggested that we might ask Trudy to come and stay with us for a while. I realized at once that it would be more than having another nanny, it would be an opportunity for her and David to get to know one another.

And then, of course, there's my own mother, so anxious to be of assistance, to make up for lost time and memories.

"Any decisions on a name?" she asks me now.

"Carol. Carol Samantha Ayers."

"Oh, Julia, that's beautiful! How did you choose it?"

"I wanted a musical name and Carol was the only one that Matthew and I could agree on."

"And Samantha?"

"For an amazing man. A..." I consider whether to say this to her, but I do. "A father to me all of those years I was in the Children's Home... and after. Dr. Sam. You'll meet him soon, I'm sure."

She smiles at the idea that I'm including her in my future, that there is a place for her in my life. And she's right. There is a place for her because I have made one.

That night on the stairs, Trudy's words came to me. They gave me the courage to do what I did. Almost as importantly, they gave me a unique insight into my mother's mind. Standing there, facing Jeremy, I could only think about my perfect little boy. The helpless little creature with whom I am so wholly and completely in love.

It was just as Trudy had said it would be. I knew that Jeremy had to die to ensure my son's safety. And if that meant I had to die in the process, then so be it. Nothing else mattered in that one perfect second of illumination—not that David would grow up without a mother, or how hard it would be for Matthew to go on without me. The difficulty of their lives was less important than the fact that they would *be* alive.

And it was there, on those stairs that night, that I had a flash of insight into the mind of Kelly Randall. I understood, suddenly, that she had made the best decision she could at the time she left me. She hadn't thrown me out like a piece of trash. She'd left me with my father and his wicked temper in favor of taking me with her into the dark underbelly of the horrific world she was entering. A world where she might have, in a moment of sheer, drug-induced desperation, traded her five-year-old for her next fix.

My childhood was tragic, no doubt. But now I can make the distinction between tragedy and hell. And I'll take the former over the latter every time. Though, God willing, that's not a choice I'll ever need to make while I walk this earth.

From somewhere in the house, I can hear David squealing with delight, while Matthew, Corinne and Drew laugh.

"Let's go... Mom," I whisper, taking her hand in mine. "They're waiting for us."

She clutches my hand tightly as we step across the threshold and into my home. Once we're safely inside, I shut the front door behind us against the chill and the dark.

Epilogue

Trudy

Satan is not a cartoon devil with horns and a pointy tale. He is a soulless menace that takes human form so that he may walk among us—wreaking havoc and destroying lives—virtually undetected.

The first time I came face to face with pure evil was when I saw it in my father's eyes. He was cruel and abusive, taking delight in every moment of pain and anguish that he caused his wife and four children. Perpetually bored, he created increasingly more devastating ways to torture us.

Oh, he could play the role of devoted husband and father when he wanted to. No one noticed the desperation so clearly etched on our little faces or the haunted, vacant expression worn by my mother. No one questioned why rarely a month went by without one of the Purdy children ending up in the emergency room. At least, I like to think that no one noticed. Because, to consider the alternative—that people knew and did nothing to rescue us from the hell that we were mired in—is just too unbearable to contemplate.

Watching my father die wasn't as difficult as I'd thought it would be. Once he fell through that rickety wooden step leading down to the basement—and his liquor—it was a twenty-foot drop straight down to the concrete floor below. Later, I learned that he'd broken his pelvis and his left leg. He cracked open his head and bled into his cranium. It was a miracle he didn't break his neck and, had someone actually bothered to call for an ambulance, he would have lived on to torment us for years to come. But no one made that call.

My father lay unconscious for the first hour. After that, there was some moaning. Within a few hours he was lucid, in horrific pain, and furious. We ate dinner at the kitchen table in silence, his seat empty as he screamed obscenities at us from the ground below. My mother sent my brother and sisters to bed while I sat up with her. She could have turned on the television set or the radio, but she chose to sit on the couch and knit our winter scarves. My father raged on, although, with less verve as he bled into his brain.

"Will we go to hell, Mama?" I asked, breaking the silence of our vigil.

She considered me for a long moment before speaking. "Trudy," she began, looking at me as her hands continued their work unwatched. "In the Book of Genesis, God tells us that He will hold us accountable for the reckoning of a man who sheds the blood of another man. You see, God made us in His own image. We are, in a sense, a part of God. So when one person attacks another, he is attacking God. And the Lord Almighty is quite clear on the subject when He says 'Whoever sheds the blood of man, by man shall his blood be shed, for God made man in His own image.'"

She paused for a moment, trying to gauge whether or not I was grasping what she was telling me. "You and I and your brother and sisters are devout children of God," she continued after a moment, "and when your father attacks us, he is attacking God. That is unacceptable in the eyes of our Lord, and in my eyes as well. So, no, my love, I do not believe we will go to hell... though I do believe your father will be there before the first morning light."

And she was right. My father died in the early hours of the morning. She called the sheriff just after dawn and reported that her husband had fallen through a rotten stair tread in the middle of the night, and she'd found him when she woke up to make breakfast.

My father had sown the wind and he reaped the whirlwind ... with a little help from me and a handsaw. It was God's will and I was his instrument.

Now, all of these years later, I sit in a rocking chair, holding that man's great-grandson. The sweet little redheaded boy rests his head against my chest, one hand clutching a button on my sweater while he sucks on the thumb of the other. He tries, unsuccessfully, to fend off the sleep that is tugging at his eyelids.

I've decided to take Julia and Matthew up on their offer, and I will relocate here to Long Island to help them with the new baby and to get to know David. It will be difficult to leave the home I shared with Danny, but for now at least, the most important thing is to stay close to this child. I will nurture him and teach him and love him, as any grandmother would. But, then again, I am not just any grandmother. Every time I gaze into those hazel eyes of his, I will be watching closely and looking deeply. Because I know only too well what evil looks like.

I know how to spot the heart of the devil within the eyes of an angel.

Dear Heavenly Father,

When You called upon me to be Your instrument against the evil within my father, I obeyed, and saw to it that trip down to the cellar would be his last.

When You called upon me to be Your instrument against the evil within my son, I obeyed once more, seeing to it that he would never get up off that floor to harm another human being.

Lord, I pray that this little lamb is an innocent, untouched by the sins of his father and great-grandfather. But, should this not be the case, I pray that You will call upon me once again to be Your instrument against evil. I pray that you will, once more, give me the strength to do what needs to be done. And I will forever be Your willing servant.

Amen.

Acknowledgments

I'm a lucky girl to be loved and supported by so many amazing people. Thank you!

Tom ... You are always at the top of my list. And, while I know you'll never read this, I like the idea of knowing that it's here ... just in case you do. Someday. Maybe. I love you.

Vanessa ... My late night cheerleader and lifelong best friend. God has blessed me with you and Frankie and my sweetest Frankie Jr. and Ursie. In each other, we still have Mom.

Janet ... You're my 'other' mother. And, just like mother and daughter, we don't always agree. But, just like mother and daughter, our differences could never touch the depth of my love for you.

Kwaku ... Thank you for being there at so many important moments of my life. I love you so much.

David... You are the brother I never had. But that's not quite right, is it? Because you always were my brother, even though you aren't. I love you so very much and I'm incredibly proud of the man you've become. Even just the thought of you and beautiful, brilliant Kim and your amazing kids bring me so much joy.

Karen ... You wave away my fears and indecision and give me a million reasons why I *can*. Thank you to you and Michael, Jessica and Cheryl who bring me so much joy and love.

Cathy... you're more like my sister than my sister-in-law. I love you so much.

Elizabeth...my newly rediscovered cousin and fellow author. What a joy to have reconnected with you. I look forward to many more years sharing love and friendship.

Rita ... who's always at the ready with a boost for my confidence and a shoulder to lean on.

Julie...Good lord! You helped me take this one apart and put it back together again. Thank you for wading around in the muck with me until I got it all sorted. I adore you!

Pattie, Jannet and Victoria ... my dear friends and fellow-believers on this 'Secret' journey. You helped me to believe it would come true. And it did. *Your* turn!

Terez...your love of music and dance and your gift with words all inspire me to be better. What a joy to have you in my life!

Jennifer Mishler...editor, friend, champion. 'Thank You' seems so inadequate to express the gratitude and appreciation I feel for you.

Kelly...I could list you as a member of my 'tech' team, but that doesn't feel right anymore. You've become such a dear, treasured and trusted friend. How is it possible to love someone you've never laid eyes on? I'm not sure, but I do love you, my dear Miss Kelly.

I am the luckiest writer in the world to have my very own 'think tank!' My love and thanks to Sue, Kathy, Mary Beth, Laura, Lauren, Pam, Kathy, Gaby, Nicole, and Rosalie for reading my words, egging me on and holding my hand.

Thanks to Ernie who, somehow, manages to keep me just on the right side of 'sane.'

And thanks be to God for the gift of my words.

About the Author

Lauren Rico has earned a reputation as one of the top Classical music broadcasters in the country—introducing listeners to the stories of the great composers. But there came the point when she wanted to start writing some stories of her own, and in less than a decade, she's turned a hobby into several award-winning romance novels. By expanding into the world of Women's Fiction, Lauren hopes to create relatable characters and compelling storylines that will keep readers up all night turning pages. When she's not talking on the radio or tethered to her laptop, Lauren enjoys a quiet but crazy life in a lovely but messy home on Long Island with her husband and rescue pup, Sandy.

Lauren is represented by Jill Marsal of Marsal Lyon Literary Agency.

Dear Reader...

Thank you so much for taking the time to read Requiem!

If you enjoyed it, I hope you'll leave a review on GoodReads and wherever you purchased this book. I'm so grateful for your support—you have no idea how much an endorsement from you impacts the authors whose books you read every day.

I hope you'll check out of my other titles on the next page as well the free sneak-peek of another music-themed romance, Counterpoint *at the end of this book. And be sure to sign up for my newsletter at LaurenRico.com so you never miss a giveaway or the latest news.*

With all my very best wishes,

Lauren

Other titles by Lauren that you might enjoy...

This is the final book in the Reverie Trilogy but be sure to scroll down for a sneak-peek of _Counterpoint_!

The Whiskey Sisters series (Written as L.E. Rico)

If you're a fan of Hallmark Channel movies, then you'll love the sweet and sassy O'Halloran girls of Mayhem, Minnesota! These PG romcoms are funny and quirky—but don't let the humor fool you! There's a lot of depth to these characters, and a lot of love for family and friends up there on the Iron Range.

<u>Reading order:</u>

Blame it on the Bet

Mischief and Mayhem

Mistletoe in Mayhem (double novella)

Mismatched in Mayhem

<u>The Symphony Hall series</u>

Looking for something that's fun and flirty—but also has some dramatic teeth? Don't want to get invested in an ongoing storyline or cliffhangers? Check out these one-and-done New Adult romances featuring characters you won't soon forget and set in the world of Classical music.

Solo

Graduate conducting student Kate Brenner has been on her own for a very long time. Daughter of the most detested senator in America, the press won't leave her alone and her classmates won't give her the time of day. It's hard and it's lonely but she just has to hang on until spring when she graduates. _If_ she graduates. Because there's one professor who seems hell-bent on seeing Kate fail.

Drew Markham knows he hasn't treated Kate fairly, but he just can't seem to stop himself because Kate Brenner is a dead ringer for the woman who left him a broken, angry shell of the man he used to be.

Now, trapped together for the foreseeable future, Drew has to set aside his painful memories of the past while Kate has to relinquish some of her fierce independence. Torn between desire and duty, loss and loyalty, the notes they play may change the course of their lives forever.

Counterpoint

Brilliant young pianist Alexandria was poised for classical music superstardom... until the night she unraveled in front of thousands at her Carnegie Hall debut.

Brilliant young pianist Nate was poised for classical music superstardom...until the night a horrific accident took away everything—and everyone he loved.

Now fate—and a wily cowboy pianist named Wyatt—have brought them both to Texas for a summer of intensive study and healing. And, while neither is happy to share the spotlight with the other, it soon becomes clear that, together, Alex and Nate possess a dazzling chemistry that eclipses anything they might have done alone.

As Nate wrestles with the gut-wrenching guilt of his past, Alex is forced to confront the grim prospects for her future. Each must decide if there is enough power in their music and enough courage in their hearts to breach the chasm between them.

Enjoy this free sneak-peek at Counterpoint...

Counterpoint

Sneak-Peek

Chapter 1

Alexandria

I'm wearing *the* dress. The perfect black dress with the lacy hem that swishes around my ankles as I glide across the well-worn planks of the stage. The rich fabric is dusted with tiny little crystals that catch the overhead lights at every angle, making me shimmer and twinkle like the night sky. The effect is dazzling. I know this because my mother has told me a dozen times, trying to convince me that this really was a better choice than the deep crimson gown I had my heart set on. But that dress wasn't perfect. And anything short of perfection simply will not be tolerated tonight. The night of my Carnegie Hall debut.

I register a swell of applause as the audience greets me. Just as we've rehearsed, I turn my head slightly and acknowledge their welcome with my best smile. My *perfect* smile. It's the smile I've been working on in the mirror for months...not big and cheesy, not small and tight. It's a warm and welcoming smile that conveys confidence, friendliness and professionalism. The smile that goes perfectly with the perfect dress.

I shake hands with the concertmaster, a kindly gentleman old enough to be my grandfather. His hand is warm and soft in mine and he gives it an extra squeeze as he winks at me. An "Atta girl!" from someone who has seen countless others like me come and go over the decades. It's the perfect sentiment, meant to put me at ease. Unfortunately, it doesn't

When I've reached the Steinway concert grand, I turn to face the house, my left hand resting gently on the smooth black enameled lid of the instrument and I bow. One Mississippi. Two Mississippi. Three Mississippi. There. The perfect amount of time to stay in the downward position before straightening up again. I don't allow my eyes to sharpen focus on the people who fill the rows in front of me. My parents' reputations have ensured that this is a sold-out show. But if I can trick my mind into seeing them as a faceless blob, then I can pretend they're not real. That this is just another no-pressure rehearsal. Unfortunately, it's not.

Once the applause subsides, I slip onto the black tufted bench and face forward. There is no music in front of me because a perfect performance is one that is memorized—unmarred by the presence of a pesky page-turner to distract from my presence. I glance at the podium, where Maestro Bello is facing the orchestra, his head tilted just far enough to the side so that he will see the signal when I give it.

Well, here goes nothing...

I take a deep breath and give the slightest of nods. His hands go up briefly as his glance shifts from me to the timpanist poised to play in the back row of the orchestra. Satisfied that the time is right, the Maestro drops his strong hands into the pattern that sets Edward Grieg's *Piano Concerto* into motion.

The sound of the timpani roll is a whisper so soft and subtle that it seems to emerge out of thin air. It builds to an impossibly intense peak in an impossibly brief time, reaching its zenith at the same moment that the piano makes its grand entrance.

My two hands, separated by half an octave, move in tandem as a single, solid unit. They slam down, forming a powerful chord that rings out across the concert hall. It's as if it just hangs there for a second, teetering on the edge of some invisible precipice. And then it tips, tumbling into a cascade of chunky chords, each one as fiery as the first. It is dramatic in its presentation but by no means showy—because this isn't about flourishes and fripperies. Nor will this be one of those concertos where the piano and the orchestra have a genteel dialogue. This is the piano staking its claim right off the bat, controlling the melody and taking the lead. Once I've hit the bottom of the keyboard it's as if the two "unified" hands shatter apart and split up into ten distinct fingers. They start the mad rush, scurrying back up the intervals to the top.

Now, the thing about a downward spiral is that there are a couple of ways it can happen. The first is very, very slowly over a substantial period of time. In this scenario, your divergence from the plan is so subtle as to be nearly undetectable. Little by little you drift off course, totally unaware of the seconds ticking by as they bring you closer and closer to imminent distress. This kind of spiral is survivable, depending on your ability to identify and correct the problem before it's too late.

There's a lot less wiggle room in the second scenario. What often transpires in this instance is that a relatively minor event occurs. Under any other circumstances you would simply recognize the problem, take corrective action and resume without further difficulties. But these aren't just any circumstances. This "minor" event is only one in a chain of minor events that, when threaded together, become a major meltdown. Before you realize it, you've pitched forward at a terrifying angle, picking up speed with each passing moment. It is so violent and so unexpected that all you can do is hang on for dear life, frantically trying to figure out how things could've gone so wrong so fast as alerts shriek around you and the earth rushes up to meet you head-on. This kind of spiral almost always ensures a terminal outcome.

My spiral starts off as a single little bobble. One of my fingers misses a key on the rippling intervals that run back upward. That, in and of itself, isn't an insurmountable error. I can still adjust and correct course making the error nothing but a little hint of turbulence in an otherwise perfect journey. The problem is that perfection, by its very definition must be devoid of any errors—no matter how miniscule they may be. So in that respect, I am already doomed.

As an entire cluster of wrong notes unfurls from my fingers, I will myself to make it to the orchestra's entrance. It's only a few more bars away. If I can just hang on, I can take a deep breath and reset. But I can't. It's too late. I've already slipped, headlong, into the spiral, banking too far to pull up out of the nosedive.

The orchestra peters out as the Maestro brings them all to a halt. He's looking at me with clear disgust and barely-contained rage. I hear a quiet buzz humming throughout the house and flash upon an image of my father in his suit, hands gripping the armrests until his knuckles turn white and his face warms to a deep crimson color.

"Shall we begin again?" I hear the conductor whisper loudly from the podium, breaking me free of the picture in my head.

I force a smile at him and nod, knowing full well that I'm not ready to go again.

Maybe if I'd requested a few minutes backstage and a glass of water. Maybe if I'd taken a few deep breaths. But the déjà vus of the rising timpani roll tells me that it's already too

late for either of the above.

I repeat the same phrases as earlier—with a bit more trepidation— only this time I don't even get to the bass range of the piano before my traitorous hands falter and fumble. By the time I'm moving upward again, my wayward fingers are doing whatever the hell they please. I try to continue, but there's just no way. I can see the ground rushing up to meet me as I hurtle towards it, head-on. The orchestra stops again and this time the buzz in the audience is more like the excited murmurings and horrified gasps of people who have just witnessed a terrible tragedy. Probably because they have.

Before the conductor can even turn in my direction I've pushed back from the piano and am bolting for the safety of the stage left wings. Though, right now, safety is a relative term. I barely blow past a flummoxed stage manager when I run headlong into my father, nearly sending us both tumbling to the floor. Somehow, he manages to grab me by the forearms and stabilize us. And then I'm looking up into the hardest, steeliest gray eyes I've ever seen. It occurs to me that he must have left his seat to come back here before I even made the second attempt at the Grieg. He was waiting for me.

I hear a horrible raspy wheezing sound and it takes me a few seconds to realize it's coming from me.

"Alexandria? Baby? Are you okay?" my mother asks, pushing her way around my father and extricating me from his grip. She puts her hands on my slumped shoulders.

My chest feels unbearably heavy.

Oh my God, I'm suffocating. I'm going to die right here, backstage at Carnegie Hall.

"Jesus Christ!" my father hisses, interrupting my macabre reverie. "All that work. All that time. All that goddamned money and we're exactly where we were a year ago!"

"Hugh, stop it!" my mother demands in an uncharacteristically sharp tone. "Can't you see she's in trouble here?"

"Oh, she's in trouble all right…" my father mutters viciously.

"Can't you see that our daughter is suffering from—"

Before my mother can even finish her sentence, my father has redirected his scorching fury to her.

"You," he spits, the single word an accusation and threat rolled into one. "You did this, Madeleine! You and your incessant coddling."

She replies, but I can't pay attention to either of them for a moment longer. I'm too busy concentrating on getting oxygen into my lungs.

"Alexandria…" My mother is hovering too close to me. I wave her away even as I plant my palms on my thighs and hunch over.

"They're calling for an early intermission," I hear the stage manager say.

Oh, Jesus—are my parents and I going to be on the hook for lost ticket revenue if people walk out now and demand refunds? Suddenly I'm on the floor, diving for a trash can.

"Alexandria, sweetheart…" I feel my mother's hands pulling my hair back and away from my face as I retch.

"Ohhhhhhh…" I groan.

"I think maybe we should call an ambulance," the stage manager suggests.

"No. Ambulance." my father hisses at the suggestion. "In fact, let's get her out of here before someone else wanders backstage. I don't want anyone to see her like this or, God forbid, get a picture of her in this…this *state*."

I get to my feet slowly, noting the swaths of dust that now decorate my dress. The perfect dress.

"Come on, baby,' my mother whispers as she takes my arm and guides me down the back hallway and into my dressing room.

My father stomps along behind us. Once we're inside, he slams and locks the door so we won't be disturbed. I go right to the long couch and get myself horizontal before the urge to hurl can return. Mom sits down, gently pulling my feet into her lap. She removes my shoes and rubs my stockinged feet.

"It's all right, Alexandria," she soothes. "It's going to be all right."

I so want to believe her, but I can't. The way my father is glaring at me right now tells me, without a doubt, that it is most certainly *not* going to be all right.

"I'm so sorry, Daddy," I whisper. My vision blurs from the tears brimming just under my eyelids. "I'm so, so, sorry."

Hugh Fitch, violinist, Tchaikovsky Competition gold medalist, Grammy award-winning recording artist and one half of the renowned Mickelson-Fitch Piano and Violin Duo, regards my apology with clear disdain and open hostility. I'm in some serious trouble here. Not even my mother—the ultimate diplomat—is going to be able to assuage the kind of ire that's rolling off of him in waves. He paces for a few very long moments before nodding to himself and informing us of his plans.

"All right. Here's what we're going to do. We'll say that Alexandria was overcome by food poisoning and couldn't continue the concert. Then we're going to reschedule a recital for the fall."

"Daddy, I don't think I can do this again..." I protest weakly and am met with a withering stare and punishing tone.

"Don't you dare even *think* about saying no to me, Alexandria! You have embarrassed us for the last time. I will not let your childish insecurities impact my career."

"Hugh!" His name is a strangled gasp on my mother's lips. "Stop this right now!"

He continues outlining my new future as if she hasn't spoken.

"No more apartment, young lady. You will pack up and move home for the summer. You will practice six hours a day at a minimum. Your mother and I will give up our vacation so we can oversee every aspect of your preparation..."

I can hardly believe what I'm hearing. This is a nightmare—moving back home? My parents supervising my practicing? No, no, no...

"And I think we can safely say that the therapist isn't worth the paper her degree is written on. No, I think we're done with the airy-fairy, kumbaya approach here. You'll see my physician, Dr. Steadman. He can prescribe you a beta-blocker and perhaps a sedative..."

With great effort, I manage to sit upright, nearly kicking my mother off the couch as I do. By the time I'm right-side-up again, I'm already shaking my head.

"No. I'm not going to take any medications, Daddy. I won't do it," I say as fiercely as I can muster. He greets my exclamation with a snide, thin-lipped smile as he takes a few steps towards me, not stopping until we're face to face, barely a foot apart.

"Oh, you will, Alexandria. You'll do exactly as I tell you to do and you'll do it without question."

I gulp reflexively Having been in this position before, I know it doesn't end well for me. And he knows that I know it.

"Do we understand one another, Alexandria?" he presses.

I take a long shaky breath, my eyes never leaving his. There's nothing I can do. There's never anything I can do.

"Yes," I say in barely a whisper, my two-second mutiny squashed just like that.

"I can't hear you," he says, the smile turning to a sneer now.

"Yes, Daddy, I understand," I say louder this time.

He harrumphs and turns his back on me, walking to the dressing room door.

"Don't you so much as stick your head out of this room until I tell you," he instructs me, not even bothering to turn back around.

Once he's slipped out into the hallway, I turn to my mother, who's still sitting on the couch, her face damp with tear tracks.

"It'll be okay, sweetheart," she assures me once again.

Perfect.

Chapter 2

Nate

The day I didn't die was bright and sunny. A Tuesday in mid-October. I wasn't thinking about dying—or not dying, for that matter. Not that I was thinking about baseball or videogames or any of the other things that a normal twelve-year-old thinks about. But then, I was never a "normal" kid.

My mother used to say that I crawled onto the piano bench at the age of two and never got off. I was reading music before I could spell my own name, playing Chopin before I could "See Spot run." The pediatrician called me precocious. My neighborhood piano teacher next door called me a wunderkind. Several people seemed to think I was some kind of a circus freak. And who could blame them? I looked ridiculous in my micro-tux, playing chords that my hands weren't wide enough to span while working pedals that my legs weren't long enough to reach. It was insane. But it didn't stop me. By the time I was seven, I was performing with some of the top orchestras in the country. At eight, I went on my first European tour. At nine, I was scouted by the Juilliard School—an offer which my mother staunchly refused, saying it would leach the last ounces of childhood from my life.

So, there I was at last, after years and years of lessons; hours and hours of practicing. Countless recitals and endless guest performances around the globe before I was even in the double digits had finally culminated in a high point that ninety-nine-percent of professional pianists will never know. I was the first American in nearly two decades to take gold at the Rossi International Piano Competition—the Olympics of piano. I beat out competitors from a dozen different countries, not one of them under the age of seventeen.

The airline bumped my parents, my younger sister, Annika, and me up to First Class and announced my victory to the plane full of cheering passengers en route from Munich to New York City. I was even permitted to sip a little celebratory champagne once we'd reached our cruising altitude. And yet, when I think back to that time and its life-changing implications, it's not that heavy, gold medal in my carry-on bag that had the biggest impact on my future—it was the fact that the first class lavatory was occupied at the exact same moment I really had to pee. Talk about a twist of fucking fate.

* * *

When Wyatt finally picks up his cell—after nearly three hours of being relegated to his voicemail—he sounds as if he's running a marathon. In the rain.

"Wyatt...where the hell are you?"

"I'm out, Nate," he manages to rasp between heavy breaths. "Why? What's wrong?"

"I wanted to ask you something... Hey, is that...rain? Are you out in the *rain?*"

Considering the fact that I'm standing in Austin—where it hasn't rained for nearly three months—I'm guessing he's no longer in the great state of Texas.

"Nate, just tell me what you need."

"Where are you? When will you be back?" I ask, feeling more agitated by the second.

"You realize I don't need to report to you, right? I'm the teacher. You're the student. I'm thinking maybe you don't quite appreciate that dynamic."

"You're my teacher because I allow you to be," I point out with a sense of entitlement that I don't possess.

"No, actually, Nate, you're my student because *I* allow *you* to be.

Now, if you're done debating the semantics of our relationship, I'm a little busy at the moment."

"Doing what?" I press, trying my best not to sound quite as needy as I know I am.

"Trying to help someone."

"Who?"

"Hanging up now, Nate."

"Wait, Wyatt..."

"Nate—"

"I'm sorry. I just... Something happened and I got a little freaked."

There's a long pause, filled only by the sound of the rain in whatever state he's in. Finally, he takes a deep breath and softens his tone considerably.

"Okay. Tell me about it. What's going on?"

"I was practicing tonight. And I thought... No, I was certain someone was there, in the concert hall, watching me play. Listening to me."

"Okay. And was there? Someone there, I mean—listening to you?"

"No."

"You looked."

My turn to pause. It takes a full five seconds for me to fess-up, finally. "Yeah. I couldn't keep playing until I'd walked through every row of seats in the house and the balcony. And checked backstage. And in the audio booth. And the coat closet. But there wasn't anyone."

"No one knows you're in Texas. Unless of course you told someone..."

"I didn't," I confirm quickly. "I didn't tell a soul." I leave out the part about how there's really no one *to* tell.

My parents have been gone for nearly a decade-and-a-half. In that period of time, it was my mother's sister, my Aunt Jennie, who kept watch over me. She ensured I had everything I needed. She safeguarded my health, protected my privacy and saw to it that I had all the physical and emotional support a kid could ever require. She did an exceptional job of keeping me as close to happy as someone like me is cable of being —quite a feat, all things considered. But, in yet another cruel twist of fate, breast cancer claimed her before she turned fifty. And then, I was alone.

"Nate?" I've missed whatever it was that Wyatt just said.

"Sorry, what was that?"

He can't conceal the sigh of irritation from his end of the line.

"I said, you know I would never tell anyone, right?"

When I hesitate just a second too long, he reiterates the question.

"Nate, you know that, don't you?"

Do I?

"Yes," I say softly into the phone.

He sighs heavily.

"If I know you, you haven't been anywhere but the music building and your apartment. Am I right?"

I see where he's going with this and he's not wrong.

"Yes," I mutter grudgingly.

"Right. So, unless someone recognized you waiting in the drive-through line at Jack-in-the-Box, it's not likely anyone is sneaking into the concert hall to secretly videotape you practicing. Make sense?"

"I suppose. But, do you think it's possible that—"

"No."

"You don't even know what I was about to say!" I protest.

"No, Nate. I don't. I'm really sorry, but there's something I have to do right now. I want you to go back to your apartment and watch something stupid on TV. Have a beer. Try to get a little sleep. Just get the hell away from the piano for a few hours. You need a break."

"I don't."

"You do," he replies flatly, all empathy evaporating with his annoyance. Clearly, I've pressed my luck a little too far. "And I don't give a rat's ass what you think you know. You came to me because of what *I* know. So, either you trust me to help you, or you don't. It's that simple. And if you don't trust me, then maybe you'd better pack up your things and go back home to Minnesota."

I want to tell him to piss off, that what I do is my own business. But then I remember that he's right. The simple fact is that I didn't come looking for Wyatt McFadden, he came looking for me. At a time when the only people interested in me were nosy journalists and ghoulish Lookie-loos—he was genuinely concerned about my wellbeing. And genuinely interested in seeing me play the piano again. He made a point of stopping by anytime he was anywhere in the Midwest and, to my amazement, Aunt Jennie took a liking to the blond-haired, blue-eyed, boot-wearing, hat-tipping music professor from Texas. It might have been those rugged good looks...or it might have been the fact that he wanted nothing more than to help. Not to pry. Not to poke and prod.

We'd been doing this dance for several years when he showed up at my aunt's funeral. He even insisted on sticking around long enough to help me sort out her house so I could get it on the market. That's when I finally agreed to play for him. There, in the kitschy country living room, surrounded by needlepoint pillows and angel figurines, I poured myself into the music as he sat on the couch behind me, so quiet that I forgot he was there. I pounded my anger out in Beethoven, fretted about my future in Bach and, finally, threw every ounce of grief and sorrow I had into Chopin. By the time I slumped over the keyboard, my body convulsing with each anguished cry and sob, he was there, next to me on the bench. Wyatt held me, shushed me, soothed me and, finally, helped me stagger to my bed where I slipped into the blissful oblivion of sleep.

When I awoke many hours later, I found he'd gone—leaving behind a full fridge, a realtor's business card, and a note telling me that he'd be waiting for me in Austin as soon as I was ready to go. At first, I dismissed the idea. But then, as the house grew more silent and still with each passing day, I knew that I had to leave. And I knew that I had nowhere to go. No one to be with.

Except for Austin.

Except for Wyatt.

So, right now, I take a deep breath, close my eyes and somehow, manage to get my emotions under control.

"I...I'm sorry, Wyatt," I start in a whisper. "I just—you know how I get..."

"I do," he agrees, his tone noticeably softer now. "Nate, I'm a man of my word. I told you I can help you, and I will. But only if you let me. So, please, take the rest of tonight and tomorrow off. I promise we'll talk about this when I get back. Okay?"

"Yeah. Okay."

"Trust me, Nate," he urges me quietly from someplace far away.

Like it or not, it's my only choice. And my only chance at finding my way back.

. . .

Get the rest of Nate and Alexandria's story in Counterpoint by Lauren E. Rico!

255

www.ingramcontent.com/pod-product-compliance
Lightning Source LLC
Chambersburg PA
CBHW020625120726
47905CB00003B/938